MY PUCKING EX'S DAD

Leighton Grace

Visit the following link for a free book when you join my mailing list!

https://bit.ly/free_steamy

contents

ELLIE

*S*hoot me. Someone, please shoot me.

I sat near enough to the blazing bonfire to be warm yet stayed outside the ring of "friends". Huddling in my thick winter coat, I wished, most fervently, I hadn't agreed to come on this camping trip. In January. In the southern Vermont woods.

It wasn't just the arctic night that troubled me. Oh, no. It's the arctic freeze deep within my heart that chilled me through and through. You see, my friends——and I use that term loosely——ignore my misery, pretending they don't know the reason why. None of them want to get involved. It's sort of like that situation where a person is attacked on the street, but no one in the immediate vicinity will offer help, or even call the cops.

"He's a prick," a voice said.

I glanced up to discover my depression had been noticed and elicited a response. Jen, a casual friend from college and a member of my circle, sat on the dead log beside me. Taking the beer can from my hands, she pushed a mug of hot mulled wine from the pot close to the fire in its place.

"I'd dump him if I were you," she said.

"Yeah?" I sipped the spicy wine in appreciation and grati-tude. "Somehow I don't think I have much choice."

"Probably not. Those two will be performing the horizon-tal bop before too much longer."

That stung. I shifted uneasily on the log and took another warming drink. "Sure looks like it."

In silence, Jen and I watched my boyfriend, Colton Al-dine, smile, laugh, flirt, and sit so close together that their bodies almost melded with my friend, Lindy Parker. With-out shame, Lindy leaned against him, her expression ador-ing, her cheeks flushed, and shattered our friendship.

"They won't hide it, either" Jen continued as though my heart wasn't breaking. "It's a one room cabin. We'll be smothering one another with our sleeping bags tonight."

Ten of us, all college pals, had reconnected to spend the weekend in a remote cabin in Montpelier. A fun time, right? It started out that way. Colton had driven four of us down in his truck. We unloaded sleeping bags, coolers, and booze into the cabin along with Jen, Lindy, Tommy, John, and the others.

I'd gazed at the cabin empty of furniture with only a wood stove for heat, and thought we'd survive comfortably enough. Between the stove and body heat, we'd sleep cozily despite the rough and rustic setting.

Maybe I should have been clued in when we first arrived. Colton hardly spoke on the drive up, ignored my attempt to take his hand as we stood inside for the first time, laughing and joking about our survival skills in the wild woods. I should've known.

I drank another gulp of my cooling wine and nodded. "Not much room in there."

From the corner of my eye, I saw Jen watching my face.

"Are you okay, Ellie?"

"No." I took another drink before the heat vanished. "Can't say that I am."

"I guess that was a stupid question." Jen sighed. "I'm so sorry. We all thought he adored you. That you two would marry, have rug rats. That's probably not likely now, is it?"

"I've been getting the cold shoulder lately," I admitted. "I should have seen it coming. Maybe I felt it, even if I didn't quite see it. I was losing him and too dumb to recognize what was happening."

"But with Lindy?" Jen snorted. "Christ, you two were tight. Colton is an arrogant, mean-ass bastard to treat you like this. Lindy doesn't have the sense God gave a baby goat. Cute, bouncy, and no brains whatsoever."

Jen's analogy should have brought a chuckle, or at least a smile. But I hurt far too badly to find the humor in it. Nor could I defend Lindy. Jen's analysis was dead on target.

"Need more wine?" Jen asked.

"No, thanks. I'm good."

She rose to pace into the ring of laughter, talking friends close to the bonfire, and dipped the ladle into the pot. I shifted my gaze from her adding wine to her mug.

Engaged in a passionate, tongue down one another's throats kiss, Colton and Lindy earned shocked stares, and not just from me. I caught several glances shot over shoulders in my direction even as my stomach turned upside-down.

I can't take this anymore.

Leaving my comfy log and the fire's heat, my chest aching, I fled down the pitch-black path. My eyes blurred with tears I tried to hold back. Stumbling over rocks and dead tree limbs, I followed the burbling sound of a stream. At its bank, the moon gave enough light for me to see the water rushing over boulders, crashing around nearly sunken logs.

Shivering from the cold, holding my arms tightly around my chest to maintain body heat, I perched myself on a boulder. High above the pines and evergreens, the stars gleamed down like brilliant crystals. Had I not been so unhappy, I might have found pleasure in gazing up at them. Only when one got away from the city lights could stars be seen so clearly.

"Ellie?"

I stood up and spun around at the sound of his voice. *Colton.*

"What do you want?" I snapped.

"I saw you leave." He paced close to me, tall, broad shouldered, wickedly good looking.

In school, every girl wanted to sleep with him, and all the guys wanted to be him. The son of a pro hockey star, Colton had it all——the money, the looks, the future. I'd fallen head over heels the moment we met.

Blond, blue-eyed, a thick dick that satisfied me in bed, Colton was my everything. My world, my future, my heart. Even as he stood, silent, at my side, my soul cried out for him to love me. To never forsake me. To apologize for his drunken behavior and tell me he loved me.

That didn't happen.

"I guess it's over," he said at last. "I'm moving on."

Bitter cold sliced through my last hopes. A crushing pain hit my chest until I couldn't breathe. I struggled to inhale, to cry, to scream, to deny this was really happening. But I did nothing. I stood beside him, hurting, and gazed at the rushing water, splashing silver under the moonlight.

"Why?" I finally choked.

His coat rustled as he shrugged. "I fell out of love with you. A while ago."

"A while ago? How long is that?"

"I don't know. A few months."

My neck creaking audibly, I turned my head to stare into his face. "Months? And all that time you've been fucking me? Letting me believe you loved me?"

"Yeah, so call me a jerk. I don't really care. I suppose I should say I'm sorry for letting you down, but I don't care about that either."

A slow, burning rage built a fresh fire amid the hurt in my chest. I clenched my hands into fists, watching the shadows play over his face, turning him into a monster. A monster who brought me to the heights of orgasmic pleasure, using me until he found a new squeeze.

In Lindy. My friend.

"Have you been sleeping with Lindy behind my back?" I demanded, my voice almost unrecognizable to myself.

Colton's chin dipped in a nod. "Yeah."

"For *months*?"

"Pretty much. We hit it off at the party you and I went to last fall. She's good in bed. Well, so are you, but I was getting tired of the same old, same old."

The callousness, his dismissal of my feelings, his cold attitude combined to fuel my fury.

I stood beside the stream in both disbelief and believing every word he said. "You fucking bastard."

"Sorry and all. You're a nice girl, Ellie. You'll find another dude to fuck."

"You piece of shit!" I screamed, probably loud enough to be heard at the camp. "You goddamned asshole!"

Before I thought myself capable of it, I stepped a pace away from him.

Then I body slammed him as hard as I could.

Caught off guard, Colton stumbled, tripping over rocks, and fell into the stream with a yelp of surprise. I nearly went in with him, but kept my footing, and watched with satisfaction as he floundered in the icy water. Whether he got hurt on the rocks, I didn't care.

"You bitch!" he yelled as I turned to stride back up the path. "I could freeze to death."

"Eat shit and die!" I shrieked, and started to run.

Had I been less emotional and more practical, I might not have done what I did. I entered the camp as Lindy and several others stood up, gaping as I dashed past them, past the fire and the cabin, past the parked vehicles and into the night. I heard Colton's yells of fury, someone shouting at me to not go, to come back.

Naturally, I ignored them.

The dirt road leading from the cabin to the highway was wide and clear of obstructions. I saw fairly well by the moonlight, and slowed my pace to a fast walk. My running had warmed me considerably, but I kept my hands in my pockets as I walked the few miles to the highway. I wore no gloves, and in that cold, I might get frostbite.

"That was stupid," I muttered, my breath steaming in front of my face.

Still, I wouldn't go back. A part of me realized none of my "friends," not even Jen, had gotten into a car to come after me. I might die from exposure for all they cared. That hurt nearly as much as Colton's and Lindy's betrayal.

A few vehicles, headlights piercing the dark, passed me by as I walked along the verge. None stopped. The full and stark reality of what I'd done crept past my hurt, and stubborn pride. I truly *could* die of exposure. I walked in the bone-chillingly cold darkness, miles from the closest town. I had no money, no credit card, no means of paying for a room if I did make it to the small town up the road.

Sure, I had my cell. Yet, had no one to call for help. I had no family, and all my friends sat around the bonfire commiserating with Colton because I'd dumped him in the drink. Real fear sank into my bones. True, I had little to fear from any wildlife. There were no wolves out here, and bears slept the winter away.

But predators didn't always walk on four legs.

I trudged into the middle of nowhere, utterly alone.

Walking faster, I kept myself warm while hoping to reach my destination more quickly – did I have a destination? I wondered if a kind soul might let me sleep on their couch, then give me a ride home.

What home? I shared an apartment with that no good, cheating piece of shit Colton.

A car whizzed by, and its brake lights burned red in the darkness. My heart thudded heavily in my chest; my mouth dried of whatever spit I had left. Hitchhiking had grown so dangerous that only the bravest, or stupidest, chanced it. Serial killers roamed the highways in search of their next victim.

Everyone knew that.

The car stopped, then the white reverse lights came on. I thought of fleeing into the woods, hiding until the driver drove away. Instead, I stood, frozen in place and so cold I knew I'd never make it to the town up the road. Not outside a body bag, that was. The vehicle's engine growled like a beast from a nightmare as it backed toward me.

Run! Don't stand here like a deer waiting to get shot.

Terrified I'd soon stare into the barrel of a gun, here the gruff order for me to get into the car...I didn't dare move as the car pulled beside me. As though by not moving the driver wouldn't see me. I'd be as invisible as a rabbit under a thicket.

The car stopped.

The passenger window rolled down.

Grey

"H ey, do you need a——Ellie?"

My son's girlfriend——the purple streak in her long brown hair clear in my car's dash lights——stared at me in frozen terror. Her face, red from the bitter cold, was so stunned, I thought she'd faint on the spot. Huge blue eyes had grown nearly twice their normal size.

Alarmed, I put my car in park, and got out. "Ellie, girl, what are you doing way out here? On foot? Where's Colton?"

I put my hands on her arms, feeling her shiver even through the heavy winter coat she wore. She stared up into my face, her mouth opening and closing with a word emerging. Fearing something terrible had happened——an accident, my son injured, or dead——I opened the door for Ellie to get in.

"Get warm," I snapped, not intending to sound so harsh. "Tell me what happened."

Ellie obeyed, shaking like a leaf in a high wind, and sat in the passenger seat. As I walked around the car to get back in, I glanced back at the way she had come, looking for emergency vehicles. Except I'd just also come from that way and seen nothing.

Seated beside her, I took her incredibly cold hand in mine.

"Ellie," I said quietly, as scared as she was. "Is Colton all right?"

She nodded, her teeth chattering so hard I knew she couldn't talk until she got warm. Still, that nod sent relief rushing through my blood. If Colton was fine, enjoying his camping trip with his friends, where was he? Why was Ellie walking along the highway, alone, in below zero weather?

"H-he-he," she managed through her clenched teeth, "d-dumped m-me."

"Colton dumped you?" I stared through the windshield, anger gnawing at me. "I thought you were getting along just fine."

I turned as Ellie shook her head.

"Is he still camping?" I asked.

She gave a nod.

Grumbling under my breath, I let go of her hand to put my car into drive. "As long as he's okay and not dying somewhere, I guess we'll go on. Christ, what an asshole thing to do."

Ellie put her hands to the car's heater. "I-I know."

"What happened?"

"He c-c-cheated on me. W-with L-Lindy."

I glanced sidelong at her. "Who's Lindy?"

Ellie opened her coat to allow the heat to penetrate her body. Her skin gradually recovered its more normal peaches-and-cream hue as her shakes slowly lessened. I admired her from the moment Colton brought her home to meet me. A real beauty, Ellie was. She owned a perfectly oval face, long brown hair, and eyes that set my soul on fire.

Even when she belonged to my son, I was attracted to Ellie March.

"M-my friend." Ellie rubbed her hands together. "I wish I h-hadn't gone camping."

"So, you got mad and split?"

"Yeah."

Even though she could have easily died from such a foolish endeavor, I admired her guts for not putting up with Colton's shit. I scolded her anyway.

"Ellie, do you know how cold it is?" I glanced at the dash's temperature reading. "Minus ten. And dropping. You could have killed yourself."

Ellie shrugged. "No one gives a shit about me anyway."

"Colton knew you left, and didn't try to stop you?"

"No one else did, either." A crooked, self-hating smile creased her lovely lips. "So much for friendships."

"I should beat his stupid ass," I growled. "Yours, too. That was really stupid to leave shelter in this cold."

"I know. You can drop me off at the next town. But thanks for the ride."

"Do you have money on you? A credit card? Someone to call to pick you up?"

"No, on all counts."

"Then you're stuck with me. I'm not dropping you anywhere unless I know you're safe."

I caught her staring at me. "Why? Why would you care when no one else does?"

"Maybe I'm smarter than everyone else. You're worth caring about."

That silenced her. She shed her coat, the sweater she wore under it molded to her small breasts and flat stomach. I forced my gaze from her sexy, slim body, and focused on my driving.

I thought about what to do with her. *I'm already in trouble for missing the flight, I can't take her back to her apartment. I'm headed in the opposite direction.*

"Um," I said slowly. "I have to be in Boston. I don't suppose, since you no longer have plans, that you'd accompany me?"

Ellie sent me a wide-eyed look. "Boston?"

Feeling lame, I nodded. "I missed the team's commercial flight. As a result, I'm at the mercy of the powers that be."

"You were MVP two games in a row," Ellie protested.

I grinned. "You follow pro hockey?"

"Sort of. Colton bragged about you. And yeah, I've watched a few of your games."

"Even an MVP has rules to follow and bosses to answer to." I checked the mirrors for traffic and exited the two laned highway to merge onto the freeway going south. "Tomorrow, I have strategy meetings, and the game tomorrow night. I can get you a hotel room, and a VIP ticket, if you'd like."

"Sure," she replied, her enthusiasm rising. "That would be so dope."

"Even a jersey?"

Ellie glanced down at her sweater. "I don't have a change of clothes, a hairbrush or anything. Everything I brought camping is back at the cabin."

"I can help with that," I mused. "Springing for a toothbrush and a few clothes won't break the bank."

Ellie stared out her window into the deep blackness, silent, for a long moment. I saw her reflection in the glass but had no idea what she was thinking.

"Ellie?"

Offering me a wan smile, she said, "It's hard for me to accept it's all over between me and Colton. And here I am, spending the weekend in Boston with his old man."

I shrugged, helpless as to what to say to that.

"His loss," I finally commented. "He'll likely be pissed when he finds out, but I'm not gonna back out of my invitation. We can be friends, right?"

"Sure." She looked out the window again. "I need a friend right now."

"Count me in." I took her hand, resting it on the console between us. "He's an idiot if he doesn't care for you. He's too much like me when I was his age." I squeezed her fingers lightly. "I was dumb and arrogant at twenty-two. I learned the hard way that you reap what you sow. He'll wish he hadn't tossed you aside."

"I doubt it," Ellie said softly. "He fell out of love with me. Got bored. He'll do the same to Lindy."

"He might. And you know what? One day, he'll have his heart busted in all the wrong ways. Then he'll grow up, become a real man. Someday."

***

We reached the Boston metro area a few hours later after crossing from Vermont and into New Hampshire. Ellie had fallen asleep somewhere in western Massachusetts. Hungry, I stopped at a freeway truck stop, but didn't want to leave her alone while I ate a quick meal. I reluctantly woke her, watching as Ellie blearily gazed around, looking at the bright lights and rumbling semis.

"Hungry?" I asked. "Let's get a bite and maybe some coffee."

Nodding without speaking, Ellie donned her heavy coat, and stepped from the warm car and into the frigid night. Her hands shook as she zipped up the front, hunching her shoulders as she stuck them in her pockets.

I opened the diner's door for her, my hand on the small of her back. At that late hour, only a few truckers were at the tables drinking coffee. A tired looking waitress sat us in a booth, unconcerned about a big athletic guy like me being with a girl half my age. *Ellie may easily pass as my daughter.*

"Want breakfast?" I asked as the waitress poured us both coffees.

Ellie tried to hide a yawn behind her hands. "Yeah, sounds good."

She drank her coffee black, as I did, yet the caffeine failed to rouse her by much. Keeping her eyes down, she ate only half of what she'd ordered, and apologized.

"Sorry," she murmured. "I thought I was hungry."

"Look, you went through a hard time tonight. I get it. Don't worry. I'm not judging you."

She smiled faintly. "Thanks. That's the last thing I need, a judgement."

Taking my wallet from my jeans pocket, I took out a couple hundred in cash. I put the money in her hand before she could refuse.

"I'll get you a room to sleep," I murmured, not letting go of her fingers. "I have to get to my meetings, but you use this. Tomorrow, get a cab, get whatever you need.

Clothes, whatnot. Grab breakfast, or lunch. I should be back around four in the afternoon. Sound okay?"

Her face flushed pink, Ellie nodded, and stuffed the money into her coat. "Thanks, Mr. Aldine."

"Grey," I said automatically. "I don't go by Mr. anything. Got it?"

Smiling, Ellie looked at me over the rim of her cup. "Grey. That's an awesome name."

"Blame my mother." I picked up my own mug. "She picked it. Wouldn't let my dad change it."

"It's still dope. Unique. Like you."

I glanced away from the admiration in her bluer-than-blue eyes. Heat creeping from my neck to my face informed me I blushed.

Good Christ, you blush like a kid at her simple compliment.

"Thanks." I cleared my throat, finding anything to look at except her exquisite face. "You're a really nice girl, Ellie."

She set her mug down. "Nice doesn't get you anywhere. I discovered that the hard way tonight."

"Don't let what Colton did change you." I caressed the back of her hand. "You're sweet, kind, warm, exceptionally beautiful. Don't permit bitterness and anger to change your nature."

"I'll try," she murmured, staring down at my fingers. "You're not what I thought you were."

Surprised, I withdrew my hand. "You've met me before."

"And never spent more than five minutes in your company," she replied. "You used to scare me."

"I did?"

"Yeah. Your tattoos, your reputation as killer player, your size." Ellie flushed a deep red. "Your good looks."

"Oh."

"I've never met anyone like you before," she admitted. "So strong, you look like you'd crunch your opponents with one bite and spit out the bones."

I laughed. "That's for the other teams to think."

"And here you are, going out of your way for your kid's ex-girlfriend. Being kind, gentle, sweet." She lightly touched the back of my hand. "Giving. I can tell that you're a person who gives more than he takes."

"Stop it," I chuckled. "Someone might hear you say that, and my rep's burned."

"It's true. I can tell. Colton is in awe of you. He wants to be just like you."

"Nah. He only likes me because I'm a famous hockey player. My money. I love him, he's my kid. But he doesn't always feel the same way."

Ellie chose not to argue. "We'd better get going. You need sleep before tomorrow."

Now I chose not to argue.

I drove us into Boston's West End and found a decent hotel near TD Garden. I signed us both in, Ellie as my daughter, with separate rooms not far from one another. I had my small satchel, but Ellie carried nothing. She unlocked her room with her key card, then turned to me, holding the door open.

"Thank you," she said simply. "I mean it."

"I know."

Wishing I could take her into my arms, hold her, kiss her, make sweet love to her, I let her stand on tiptoe to kiss my cheek.

You're too old for her, dummy, I warned myself. *No good could come of sleeping with her. She's Colton's ex, for God's sake.*

Ellie smiled before she closed the door. "See you tomorrow."

"Yeah."

I stared at the shut door for too long before I slowly walked two rooms down the hall from hers. Letting myself in, I sat on the massive bed, and thought of Ellie. Her beauty, her smile, and most of all...her eyes.

Stop it. She's not for you.

ELLIE

olton's dad. Of all the heroes to come to my rescue, Grey Aldine had done it. Made of solid muscle, as hard as granite, tattooed better than any biker, Grey had the looks and more. His salt and pepper shaggy hair showed his age, yet his striking green eyes spoke of a much younger and, need I say it, *virile* man.

Exhausted from my excessive emotion from the night before, I slept until nearly noon the following day. Comfortable and warm in the big bed, I daydreamed of Grey. His raunchy grin, his brawny arms with the tats, his eyes that looked at me with appreciation.

And lust.

I rolled over, suddenly uneasy.

He's old enough to be my dad, I reminded myself. Just because I never had a father figure, doesn't mean I should make Grey into one. *No daddy issues, kiddo. Hands off Colton's old man. Not jumping from the son to the father, no way, nuh, uh, don't even go there.*

I showered with the hotel's shampoos and soaps, toweled off, and donned my clothes. Combing my fingers through my wet hair, removing the tangles, I stared thoughtfully into the mirror. The purple streak I'd put in for fun now looked silly and childish.

"Grey probably thinks it's stupid, too."

Who cares what he thinks? After this weekend, I'll probably never see him again.

Taking my key card, I shut my room, then took the elevator down to the main floor. The hotel had a decent restaurant, and I was famished. Using Grey's cash, I bought a Reuben sandwich and chips, washing it all down with a Coke. Who the hell cared about my figure? It'll be years before I trust my heart to anyone else again. If I ever do.

Later, again using Grey's cash, I caught a cab to a nearby mall, and shopped. I bought panties, thick socks, toiletries, a pair of jeans and a lavender blouse. With plenty of cash to spare, I wandered the mall, considering the idea of buying myself a new necklace to go with the blouse. After a bitter battle with my conscience, I declined the urge.

I was in the cab, returning to the hotel, when the thought hit me——*Check your phone.* I'd charged it up before getting into Colton's truck the previous morning, and hadn't looked at it since. Checking the screen, I found I had two missed calls.

One from Jen.

The other from Colton.

Clicking the message icon, I listened to Jen's voice.

Hey, Ellie, where are you? I didn't see you leave, but everyone said you took off like a bat out of hell. Come back, girl, it's not safe for you to be wandering around in the night. Call me, I'll come get you.

"Interesting," I muttered, erasing the message. "And too little, too late."

I glanced at the time her call came in. Long after Grey had picked me up. "Sure, Jen, you didn't see me leave. I'm not that stupid."

I listened to Colton's message.

"You bitch, I could have gotten frostbite. Get your ass back here, I'm not having your death on me. You'll freeze out there. Not that I care, but the cops will ask questions. I won't let you screw up my dad's career with your stupid ass frozen in the woods. Call me."

The cabbie glanced around at the sound of my bitter chuckle. "You okay, miss?"

"Yeah." I tucked my cell away. "Thanks for asking."

***

After growing worried enough that Colton may have sicced the cops on me, I sent him a text after I returned to my room. *I'm fine. Fuck off.* With a couple of hours to spare before Grey's arrival, I spent the time watching a movie on HBO. If Colton or Jen had called the cops to report me missing, surely they'd have stopped the search for my frozen corpse by now. Not that I cared. What I didn't need were police and rescue folks risking their lives in trying to find what wasn't there to find.

At 4:15, I jumped from the bed at the knock on the door.

Grey, in all his muscular splendor, smiled in appreciation as he eyed my new blouse. "That color looks good on you. Maybe you don't want this after all."

He held up a blue and silver Vermont Vipers NHL jersey, the hooded viper with its mouth gaping wide embroidered on the front. His name and number were written in black on the back.

I squealed in delight, grabbing it from him. "Damn right I do. Come in, I'll change."

He let the door swing shut as I dashed for the bathroom, tugging my blouse off as I did so. I didn't bother to close myself in the bathroom as I yanked the blouse off and donned the jersey. If he saw me change, he gave no indication he saw any part of me naked.

Not that I'd care if he had.

"Now that's what I'm talking about," Grey said excitedly.

He grinned as I twirled around him, showing off the jersey tucked into my jeans. "You look good enough to eat."

I laughed, giddy with excitement, inwardly stomping on my grief and anger over Colton's betrayal. I may have only this weekend with Grey, and I planned to have fun. Darkness and depression would have to wait until later.

"Grab your coat," he said.

I donned my jacket as Grey escorted me from the room, my change of clothes, toiletries, in a plastic carry bag. "Colton left me a message."

Grey cocked a brow as he looked down. "And?"

"He was worried I'd die and drag your name through the mud."

"That must have been before I left him a message," Grey commented, "informing him I found you along the road nearly dead, and that I'm ashamed of him."

"You said that?"

"I did. Because I am."

"That's so dope."

Grey took me into the TD Garden via the rear entrance. Security guards, recognizing him, nodded us inside. Hockey players from both teams strode in with us, yelling coarse insults at one another, laughing, swearing like dock workers, heading into the locker rooms.

"Wait here," Grey said, urging me against a wall. "I'll be right back."

I waited, nervous, catching unguarded looks of appreciation, heard snide comments, breathed in the odors of men, cologne, and sweat. I wished myself back in my safe hotel room, not liking the leers I received as I stood, waiting.

After what seemed like an eternity, Grey came back with a badge on a lanyard. He draped it over my neck, lifting my hair so the lanyard lay against my skin.

"This is your pass," he explained. "You still have money?"

I nodded.

"Okay, you won't need it except for a just in case. The game won't start for a few hours." He half-turned and beckoned a middle-aged man in a Vermont Vipers logoed shirt forward. "This is Jack. He'll take you to the VIP section."

I shook hands, smiling nervously at Jack. "Nice to meet you."

"I'll look after her, Grey," Jack said, "don't worry."

Grey winked. "See you soon."

"Okay."

Accompanied by Jack, I toured the tunnels, past the administrative offices beneath the stadium. Employees paid me no attention at all as they passed us, ID badges swinging from lanyards. Jack led the way up several flights of stairs to the rink side, and grinned as he gestured for me to sit in a glassed in box with armchairs rather than seats, tables, and potted plants.

"A waitress will be along to take your order," he said.

"A-a waitress?"

"Yep. Grey said to give you all the perks. Around here, his word is God's."

"What does it cost?" I tried not to panic as I thought of how much money I had left. Enough for a corndog and fries, but not much else.

Jack blinked. "For you, nothing. Unless you want to tip."

Stunned, I stared through the glass at the Zamboni cruising over the ice, the driver intent on his job. Fans began to fill the seats, eating food from the concession stand, drinking beer from plastic cups. A few VIP boxes slowly filled with high paying fans, yet others were still empty.

As the box was heated, I shed my coat and sat in glorious warmth. Music played over the speakers, the Zamboni's motor rumbled as it passed close by, security guards stood at all the entrances. I thought of Colton and Lindy freezing their asses off and chuckled to myself.

"Can I get you anything to drink?"

The smiling waitress handed me a menu——a menu! "Uh, is wine okay?"

"Of course. What would you like?"

"How about a chardonnay?"

"I'll be right back with it."

Tickled to my bones at this luxurious treatment, I watched as both teams skated onto the ice for warmup. The Vipers and their blue and silver uniforms contrasted with the Boston Bruins black and gold. His hair blown off his shoulders by the wind he created, Grey skated past my box, waving to me with a wide grin.

Fascinated by how the players seemed to float over the ice, the ease in which they turned, spun, whizzed down the rink at a speed that would leave a cheetah gasping,

I laughed in delight. The waitress brought my wine and reminded me to look at the menu.

How can I look at a menu when all that beefcake skated on full display?

The teams returned to their respective locker rooms. I finally chose a steak with butter squash, a baked potato with everything, and a side salad with bread.

I handed the menu back. "Thank you."

"Anytime."

As I dined on the delicious dinner, people entered the rink, and took their seats. I people watched, observing families, couples, most wearing Boston Bruins jerseys. I smiled to myself at the few who, like me, wore the colors of the Vipers.

How I managed to eat all that food baffled me. I'd just finished when the announcer's voice boomed over the speakers. Both teams skated in, and if Grey looked toward me, I couldn't tell. I stood when the national anthem played, the players at rigid attention facing the flag.

I stared, with bated breath, as Grey and the Bruins' captain faced off in center ice, their sticks ready for battle.

The ref dropped the puck.

Grey fought for it, won, and careened down the arena, charging headlong for the Bruins' goalie. Like a pack of wolves, both Vipers and Bruins raced after him, powdered ice thrown up from behind their blades. Two Bruins tried to steal the puck from Grey. A Viper sneaked up behind one and jammed his stick between the dude's ankles.

He fell, sprawling. Shockingly, the ref didn't call it.

The other Bruin aimed his stick at Grey's skates in a similar move, but Grey danced out of range, and sped up.

Grey aimed the puck at the goalie.

The goalie crouched ready to intercept.

Grey passed the puck to a fellow Viper at the last second.

Caught off guard, the Bruins' goalie failed to follow the puck's direction.

The Viper slammed the puck into the net.

I screamed, jumping up and down, as the buzzer sounded. Grey and his teammates skated in triumph, lifting their sticks over their heads. The Bruins also skated in circles, no doubt cursing Grey and his speed, agility, and power.

I saw the Bruin coming for him.

Scared, I shrieked, "Grey! Behind you!"

Grey, as though hearing me, half-turned, skating both sideways and backward. The Bruin body slammed Grey into the shield that protected the audience from catching a puck with their teeth.

In retaliation, Grey punched the Bruin once, twice, three times in the head.

The Bruin slipped and slid on the ice, bleeding from a massive gash over his eyes.

Grey

Most Valuable Player. Again.

After showering off the blood, the grit and some of the soreness that came with every game, I dressed under the vulgar jokes as to what the Bruins could do after their loss. A few of my teammates slapped me on the back, congratulated me on my latest title.

"Why don't you retire, old man?" joked Sammy. "Let us have a chance at MVP."

"Shit, Sammy," Dole protested. "We need Aldine until he wins us the Stanley Cup."

"Even then you won't get rid of me," I snapped, mock punching Sammy's nose. "I'll retire when I'm good and ready."

"Or he makes babies with that foxy chick outside," called Steve. "She's a hottie."

My anger at Steve's reference to Ellie tempted me to knock him on his naked ass. Still, punching him out would cost me the next game as punishment. Instead, I stared meaningfully at his paltry dick dangling from his crotch, forcing him to look down.

"What will you make with that?" I inquired. "Kittens?"

The locker room roared with laughter as Steve turned beet red. After cursing me out, which I ignored, Steve yanked his boxers on and hid the evidence of his limitations.

In the midst of the hoots and howls, Coach Brendan Hunt strolled into the locker room. He waited, patient, as the team saw him and shut up. I tossed my coat over my shoulder, ready to leave, but stayed to hear what he had to say.

"The weather has gotten bad," Hunt said. "Really bad. There's a blizzard warning all through New England, and our flight will likely be cancelled."

Mutters and swearing filled the fresh silence. I swore under my breath, unable to decide what to do. Stay or go. I had my car; I didn't need to wait on the flight home. But what about Ellie?

I'm responsible for her. I must keep her safe.

"I'm arranging for hotel rooms," Hunt went on. "We'll stay the night, head home when the weather clears. A bus is enroute to pick us up."

"How long before it gets really bad, Coach?" I asked.

He shrugged. "Reports say it won't really deteriorate for a few more hours. If you're thinking of driving in it, Aldine, don't."

"Fuck," I muttered.

Half listening to the talk of the bad weather, I fumed inwardly. Stay or go. If Coach was right, and this storm encompassed all of New England, there's no outrunning it. *Maybe we should stay the night. Play it safe.* Except in hockey, playing it safe didn't win games. Or MVP titles.

Leaving the locker room, I found Ellie frowning at her phone. She looked up as I walked to her, then back down at her cell.

"I can't reach Colton," she said, clicking letters on the screen as she texted.

"He's out of range," I explained. "Camping in the woods, you know?"

"No. The trip was supposed to end at noon, then they were going home. He should be at the apartment by now. Tomorrow's a workday."

A chill wormed its way through my gut. "You broke up. Maybe he doesn't want to talk to you."

Ellie sent me a look that clearly stated I was being stupid.

"Look. The radar?" She displayed the cell screen for me. "Deep purple all over southern Vermont. The storm's heart is right over them."

An image of Colton and his friends sliding off the road in the blizzard shot through my head.

I seized her arm. "All right, we're headed out."

"We can't help him if we're stuck in a ditch, too."

"Do you want to stay here then?"

"Well, no."

"Then come on."

The security guard held the door open for us. A thick blast of cold and snow struck us full in the face as we staggered out, leaning against the raging wind. I knew it was stupid to go on. Only an idiot would drive into a blizzard. I tucked Ellie under my arm and fought the snow and wind, my fears over Colton urging me to perform the impossible.

As only a few vehicles remained on the lot, finding my car wasn't difficult. I opened the door for Ellie, then quickly brushed the snow from the windshield, and got in behind the wheel.

"We shouldn't do this," I muttered, starting the engine. "It's lunacy."

"I still care about him," Ellie said softly. "I can't help it. I need to know he's okay."

"So do I." I drove the car through the snow-covered lot, the wipers barely able to keep up with the blowing snow. A headache developed behind my eyes as I squinted to see the road ahead. "Keep trying. If he answers before we get too far, we'll turn around."

"I have been," Ellie snapped. "Lindy, too. Jen. Tommy. None of them are answering their cells."

"Shit."

This was bad. If Colton and his friends were stuck at that cabin, would they be able to survive a blizzard? Would Ellie and I even be able to find it to help them? The drive under normal conditions took at least five hours. Double, even triple, that in a blizzard. I glanced at my watch.

"Nearly ten o'clock," I growled. "We won't get there until dawn."

"If we even make it."

I looked at her. "Should we stay?"

"I can't make that call," she retorted. "The towers might be down. There're perfectly reasonable explanations as to why I can't get through. If I say we go on and we get killed, what then?"

"My coach will kill me for dying before we win the Stanley Cup."

We stared at one another in the dash lights.

"Let's chance it," I said quietly. "If it gets really bad, we'll find a motel and stay the night."

Ellie studied her weather app's radar. "It looks like it's moving away from us. I think we'll be fine."

"Okay. We can do this."

Famous last words...

***

Whether the radar lied, or the storm shifted, the further we got from Boston while heading northwest, the thicker the snow became. Massive snowplows cleared the interstate to nearly bare asphalt, but seeing where I was going soon grew problematic. The front-wheel drive bit deep into the ice and kept us going.

Yet, I saw little beyond the car's headlights.

"I can't see the road," I muttered, my gut as tight as a coiled spring.

Ellie leaned forward as though that would help her to see through the sheet of white outside. "I think I see the edge of the road."

"As long as we don't go past it."

A few headlights, unseen until the last moment, blurred past my car. I knew this escapade was a bad idea. No way can we get back to Montpelier in this storm. Shit, we may get buried in a drift, and without supplies, we'll be dead before we're found.

"We have to get out of this," I said. "Does your cell have any signal?"

"Not much but yeah."

"Pull up the GPS, see if there's a motel somewhere close by."

Her tongue sticking out of the corner of her mouth, a sight that tempted me to take my eyes off the road far more than I should, Ellie clicked her phone. She peered at it, clicked again, then the fake female voice intoned, "Continue north on Interstate Ninety-Three for four miles."

"Four miles," I groaned. "We're gonna die."

"Don't say that," Ellie ordered. "We've come this far, haven't we?"

"Yeah, I guess."

"Aren't we close to the New Hampshire border?"

"Maybe."

As the road signs were either invisible in the whiteout or covered in snow, I saw none to inform me just where we were. The occasional yellow reflector at the highway's verge gleamed in my headlights. My car's digital direction said we were still headed northwest.

"At least the road is plowed," Ellie commented brightly. "That means it's open and we're not that far from civilization."

"We're screwed if the states close the highway."

"Try to be optimistic."

"I'm optimistic we're screwed."

The GPS voice counted down the miles. It suggested I exit the highway soon, but without seeing the sign, I might dump us in the ditch by accident. My headache intensified and my sore body grew sorer as tension kept my muscles tight.

"Exit in fifty feet," the voice intoned.

Bracing myself to drive into a ditch, I clenched my teeth and guessed when fifty feet arrived. I yanked the steering wheel a hard right.

No ditch opened up under the car's front end. Still, the plows hadn't been here in a while and my car almost bogged down in the deep snow.

"Your destination is on your right."

Rolling the window down, Ellie stuck her head into the whiteout. "I see the motel."

"Guide me."

I bounced the car over an unseen curb and caught sight of the motel's lights as we entered the lee side of the building. To my dismay, the parking lot appeared full as I drove around searching for a clear spot. Her hair white from the snow, Ellie was able to see a place to park.

Under her navigation, I pulled the car in and gratefully shut the engine off.

"Now let's hope we don't have to spend the night in the lobby," I muttered.

I grabbed my satchel, Ellie her plastic bag, and together we fought the wind and blinding snow to the entrance doors. Warmth struck my face, instantly melting the ice that crusted my hair and eyelashes. The motel was neither high end, nor a flea bag. At least it appeared clean, and the heat certainly worked.

The night clerk eyed us with disillusionment as we crossed the lobby to his desk.

"Two rooms?" I asked hopefully.

He typed on his computer. "I may not have anything available. The storm brought in travelers who can't stay on the road."

"Just like us," Ellie said.

He worked on his computer for several agonizing minutes, making me think the lobby would be our only option. If the clerk didn't toss us out, that was. My tension refused to dissipate despite being off the highway, out of the storm, and safe indoors. I shared a quick glance with Ellie, who timidly smiled.

"I have one room remaining," the clerk finally said.

Ellie jumped in before I could say anything. "We'll take it."

"Uh," I began.

The clerk didn't even look up. "Credit card and driver's license, please?"

I handed them over, thinking two beds might be safe enough. I made myself relax, smile at Ellie, and believe that nothing at all would happen. Nope, not with my son's ex-girlfriend. I was too old for her anyway. Once I got her home, we'd stay friends, maybe have coffee once in a while and laugh at our harrowing experience. But that was it.

"Sign here," the clerk instructed.

I signed as Ellie took the twin set of key cards.

"Take the elevator to the third floor," the clerk told us, marking the route on a map of the motel. "Go right, your room is three down."

"Thanks."

Ellie led the way to the elevator while I inwardly set my boundaries. *No seeing her naked, no sharing of the beds, this is an emergency situation. We sleep, we shower, we make a plan tomorrow. No sex, no intimacy, no touching.*

After running the key card through the lock, Ellie opened our room's door. The place was dark as housekeeping had left no lights on. She flicked on the nearest, illuminating the bathroom and little else. I stepped inside the room, letting the door wing shut as Ellie marched further in.

She hit the main switch.

I groaned.

A single bed.

ELLIE

"I'll sleep on the floor," Grey announced.

He set his case on the floor, his brows furrowed as he gazed at the single queen bed.

"No, you won't," I said.

I scuffed my shoe across the carpet. While clean, it appeared stained and worn thin. "This is too nasty to sleep on."

"I've slept on worse."

When he turned his eyes from me, I instantly read his mind. He feared that if we shared the bed, something may happen. I could tell he felt the same attraction I did. I eyed his muscular body as he took his coat off, his flat stomach, his lean hips, and felt a quiver of anticipation deep within my pussy.

"It's okay," I told him, shedding my coat. "We will make this work."

"Uh, huh." Grey toured the small room, examined the bathroom as though looking for the boogeyman, then switched the flat panel TV on. He scrolled through several movies before selecting one.

"Is this okay?" he asked.

"Sure."

Feeling cold despite the warmth, I took my bag and headed for the shower. I stripped, then stepped into the hot spray. As I felt my chill dissipate, I told myself – *he's off limits, no buts*. If I *slept* with him, there'd be hell to pay with Colton.

Why should I care what he thinks? I mused. *He dumped me, he cheated on me. Besides, how would he even know?*

But.... what if something *did* happen? Just as quickly, I pushed that fantasy away. He was too old for me. Old enough to be my dad. I was on the rebound, hurting emo- tionally. Needy. Not thinking straight. Once we got back, I'd return to work, Grey would practice with the other

Vipers, we might text a quick *Hi, how are you?* once in a while.

Donning my new panties, I put the Vipers jersey back on. I brushed my hair out, leaving it to fall in thick, damp waves over my shoulders and down my back. I brushed my teeth, and the long day finally caught up to me.

Yawning, I ambled into the main room, steam billowing from the shower, and thought of blissful sleep while the whiteout raged outside.

Grey looked me up and down, his expression tense, then away. His Adam's apple bobbed as he swallowed.

I glanced down at myself, seeing that the jersey covered me decently enough. *What's the deal?*

"What?" I asked.

His gaze steadfast on the TV screen, he replied, "Nothing."

I pulled the covers back on the side of the bed nearest the bathroom, and crawled beneath them. "Shut that off and come to bed."

"No."

"I'm tired."

He turned the volume down, and the lights off. I sat up, scowling as he continued to sit in the single chair, his body rigid, his eyes never leaving the TV.

"It's late, dammit," I said. "You're not sleeping on the floor."

"Wanna bet?"

"What are you afraid of?"

"Nothing."

"Liar."

Rising, the jersey flapping against my legs, I stomped around the bed. At this point, I figured, *what the hell? I mean, may we well make this messed up situation a little fun.*

Seizing the remote, I snapped the TV off. I grabbed Grey's hand and tugged. Of course, he outweighed me by more than a hundred pounds. I might have been tugging on a stubborn mule's lead rope.

Grey didn't budge.

"If you sleep on the floor, then so will I," I finally declared.

"The hell you will," he scoffed.

Grabbing the bed's comforter, I yanked it off, tossed a pillow beside it, then rolled myself into a ball. The thin carpet bit into my hip, but I planned to ignore the ache.

"The blanket's yours," I said.

"Dammit," Grey admonished.

Grey bent and picked me bodily off the floor. I yelped as he tossed me onto the bed, but I managed to seize his hand. Tangled in the cover, I could do little to hang onto him. He freed himself easily.

I reached out fast and snagged his jean's waistband. Grey pulled backward. I refused to let go. He tripped over the chair, swearing, and nearly fell on his ass. I, on the other hand, thumped back to the carpet, still tangled in the cover.

Grey scowled. "You little——"

Plucking me into his arms, he aimed to toss me onto the bed again. But I wrapped both of my arms around his neck, his face close enough to mine to kiss...

So I did.

Bent at the waist, my arms around his neck, my lips locked onto his, Grey had nowhere to go. My weight bent him further over the bed. He dropped me onto it, breaking our first kiss.

I expected him to retreat. He didn't.

I heard his zipper hiss, the rattle as he jerked his jeans off. Frantic I'd lose this opportunity, I escaped the cover, knelt on the bed to tear the jersey off over my head. It landed somewhere on the floor just as Grey's shirt flew from his torso. What he did with his underwear, if he wore any, I had no idea.

His bare chest pressed against mine, Grey grabbed the back of my head and pushed his tongue into my mouth. I inched closer, still on my knees, my panties soaked with arousal. Our bellies flattened together, I felt his long thick and very hard erection against my stomach.

I had to touch it.

Without losing his tongue, I slid my hand between us, and stroked up and down its length. It was wrong to compare him to Colton——but, damn! Colton had nothing on his pop. Grey's dick might not fit inside me. A tingle of fear melded with anticipation as I imagined the man sliding that monster into my pussy.

As though reading my mind, Grey muttered against my mouth, "I'll be gentle. Promise."

"I know," I whispered, and pulled back, falling onto the bed, and bringing him with me.

His hands yanked my panties off and they, too, vanished into the darkness.

Grey kept his weight on his elbows, his tongue colliding with mine, licking my teeth, arousing me until I thought I'd orgasm then and there. I clenched my thighs together to prevent my imminent explosion, but Grey's hand parted them easily.

"It's been too long," he muttered thickly. "I can't hold on."

"I need you," I gasped, wrapping my legs around his hips. "Do it."

He guided his dick into my pussy before lying fully on me. Frenching me with restrained passion, he slid slowly in, maybe an inch, then withdrew. I nearly screamed in frustration.

"I have to go slow," he whispered, his fingers tangled in my hair, his breath hot on my cheeks.

"Take me," I wailed.

He slid in a little deeper, withdrew, then pushed again.

My orgasm blasted through my core, spread outward until my fingers tingled. My pussy quaked and spasmed while I thrashed under him, pinned to the bed. In great rolling waves, my climax rolled me over and under until my breath came in rapid pants.

"Now you're ready," he growled.

Grey thrust in, hard, fast, to the hilt.

I cried out at the mixed pain and pleasure of his invasion, my pussy walls spreading, allowing him in. The pain vanished after three or four thrusts, and pure ecstasy filled me, my loins, all the blood in my body rushing south.

By his tenth thrust, a second orgasm built, climbing like a fiery trellis, higher and higher. I couldn't hold it back. No way.

Nor did I want to.

"I'm coming," I gasped, arching my breasts into his chest. "I can't stop it."

Grey offered a long, drawn-out groan as his body stiffened.

My climax exploded.

I saw stars behind my closed eyelids, my pussy on fire as he thrust deeper, slower, his tight-lipped groans in my ear.

My wild orgasm faded just as Grey, breathing harshly, collapsed atop me. I thought I'd never be able to bear his terrible weight, but with most of it on his elbows and knees, I felt comfortable. His cock still embedded inside me, I lay still and enjoyed the feeling of fullness, of the aftermath of great sex.

When Grey rolled off of me, the blast of cooler air on my hot, hot body made me shiver. "Dammit. I'm cold."

"Not to worry."

Grey struggled to get the blanket and bed cover in some sort of order, then crawled beneath them beside me. I snuggled against his broad chest, toying with the hairs between his nipples.

Languid and content, I caressed down his chest to his belly and back. "I said you weren't gonna sleep on the floor."

"You minx." His voice sounded as relaxed as I felt. "You planned this."

"No. Well, maybe. You're too sexy for my own good."

Grey kissed my brow. "It's the other way around."

"Whatever."

My head pillowed on his shoulder, I felt calm, warm, as loose as the proverbial goose. I started to drift. His heavy arm around my shoulders gave me the deep comfort of swaddling bands. Sleep tugged at me, pulled me into its embrace...

"I'm too old for you."

I jerked out of my early slumber. "Huh? What?"

"You know I am," he said. "I know it. This shouldn't have happened."

Muzzy, I ran my fingers up his chest and covered his mouth. "Don't care. Reason for everything."

"You're Colton's girlfriend."

I sighed. "Nope. Go to sleep."

Grey's chest vibrated as he groaned. "I can't let this go on. You're off limits. Or should be. Christ, I put us into a real mess."

Unwilling to wake up fully and argue with him, I muttered, "Not on you. Shut up."

Grey shifted under me. "I can't. This is eating at me. What will people think? What will Colton do? Shit, I don't even know if something happened to him."

"He's fine." I rolled onto my right side, facing the wall. "I'm going to sleep. You should too."

"Ellie, I'm sorry."

Like I had nothing to do with it, that I wasn't a willing participant. "Don't be."

The bed sagged as Grey also rolled over, his arm around me as he pulled me into the circle of his body. "We have to talk about this."

"There's plenty of time…just enjoy…now." I forced my rising annoyance down so that I might return to my previous lethargic state, hoping Grey would take the hint and go to sleep. I waited for him to start in again, forcing me to listen to his self-castigations. He didn't. He nuzzled his face into my hair, his massive arm tightening for a moment.

Growing sleepy again, I snuggled into his warmth, comforted by his strong presence, his weighty arm. I breathed in his masculine scent, the odor of the shampoo he washed his hair with after the game. All these dropped me into a deeper slumber.

I didn't dream at all.

***

I woke to dull sunlight streaming past the white curtains.

For a moment, I had no idea where I was or how I'd gotten there.

Rolling over, observing the motel room, the crumpled covers, I suddenly remembered. Grey, the whiteout, making love. My pussy ached at the memory of his massive erection buried deep within it.

"Grey?" I called out.

No answer.

I got out of bed and found my panties and my jersey on the floor beside the bed. Confused, I put them on, listening for sounds of Grey showering in the bathroom. But there was no telltale hiss of water. Cautious, as though expecting a serial killer behind the door, I slowly pushed it open.

"Grey?"

The bathroom was empty.

I was alone.

Nervous, I crossed my arms over my chest and paced the small room. I heard nothing, not even voices, TVs, or bathroom noises in the rooms to either side or above. As though I'd been dropped into an episode of the Twilight Zone. *Lonely Girl Abandoned in Ghostly Motel.*

The door swung open behind me.

I uttered a tiny shriek, spinning.

Grey, fully dressed, a tray of donuts and cups of coffee in his left hand, tossed the key card on the table with his right. "What's wrong?"

"I, er, nothing," I fumbled.

Trying to smile, I swiped my hair back from my face. "Coffee, yum."

He handed me a cup, not smiling. "The highway is shut down. We aren't going anywhere. Not for a while."

Grey

Looking sinfully sexy in that jersey, her tight butt undulating under the cloth, Ellie paced the small motel room. She frowned, her pink tongue protruding from between her lips, and clicked at her cell with her thumbs.

"He still hasn't replied to my texts," she finally said.

"Nor mine." I watched her walk, her long hair swinging, admiring her lithe body. I wanted her. Badly. Thinking a dunk in a cold shower might cool my ardor, I forced myself to try Colton's cell again.

Still, nothing.

"There's no way to know if the towers are down," I said.

"What about the news?" Ellie suggested.

I turned the TV on and scrolled until I found a national news cable program. Ellie stopped beside me as we listened to the talking head speak of politics, sports——the Vipers win last night, though I had vanished before the reporters got a quote from me——and finally the weather.

"Coach will be mad I didn't talk to them," I commented as we listened to every weather report except New England's.

"He'll get over it," Ellie muttered.

"It's part of my job. I have to talk to the press."

She eyed me. "I didn't see any reporters."

"I think they were on the upper level. They usually aren't allowed near the locker rooms. We snuck out the back."

Finally, the weather gal spoke of the tremendously dangerous blizzard that was currently hitting all of New England.

"Power is out for much of the population," she went on, gesturing toward her map, "and crews are working diligently to repair the lines. However, the whiteout conditions are hampering their efforts. Stay indoors at all costs, stay warm, and stay safe."

I clicked the channel to an HBO movie. "Nothing about cell towers."

"If power lines are down, so are towers." Ellie sat on the bed beside me, wriggling until she tucked herself under my arm. "What are we going to eat?"

I shrugged. "Vending machine crap. The clerk said any local restaurants are closed."

"I like junk food."

"That's not healthy."

"I doubt vending machines dispense salads."

"They should."

"I'm hungry."

"You just had two donuts."

"What's that got to do with it?"

I eyed her slender, bare legs. "Maybe we should grab enough stuff to keep us alive if the power goes out here, too."

Ellie bounced to her feet and seized the key cards. "Dope."

Alarmed, I rose from the bed. "Where the hell are you going?"

"To the vending machines."

"Put some damn pants on."

Grinning, Ellie donned her jeans but refused to put on her shoes. I growled as I looked at the icky carpet under her bare feet.

"That's nasty."

"I'll shower when we get back," Ellie said.

Only a handful of other guests prowled the hallways and main lobby. They wore the defeated, worried expressions of people trapped, unable to make their son's birthday party, their grandchild's Christening. None seemed eager to dine on junk food, and left the vending machines to Ellie.

"I think that's enough," I said, eyeing the wealth of candy bars, chocolate cakes, cookies, crackers, sodas, and bottles of water.

"Help me carry it back," she said triumphantly.

Hoping no one noticed, I stuffed candy in my jeans pockets, loaded my hands with cans and bottles. Ellie had her own hands full and pushed the elevator button with her toe. I hoped no one noticed that either.

"Get in the shower," I ordered, dumping my loot on the bed.

"Yeah, yeah."

She bathed, singing under the spray, as I sorted everything out. I put the sodas and water in the tiny fridge, but kept a bottle of water back to drink. Listening to her voice, I stared out the window toward the empty interstate.

The blizzard hadn't slowed at all, as far as I could tell. Only when the wind died a fraction could I see the local buildings, the cars buried in the lot below. Nothing moved out there, not even a snowplow.

"We're stuck here but good," I said.

"What's that?"

I turned. Ellie, garbed again in the team jersey, toweled her hair. My cock twitched at the thought of those bare legs wrapped around me.

In for a penny, in for a pound, a small voice teased me.

"I said we're stuck here." I draped my arm over her shoulders as she joined me at the window.

"Jeez," she murmured, her tone shocked. "It's worse than I thought."

I imagined us stuck in my car, buried, somewhere along the snow-bound Interstate. "We're lucky we got here."

Peering up at me, Ellie frowned, scared. "Colton is all right. Isn't he? Please say he is."

I folded my arms around her. "He's not dumb, honey. He's safe."

"I just want him to be okay."

I braced myself before asking the question that had been on my mind since yesterday. "Do you want him back?"

She shook her head. "No, never. He hurt me too badly. But I still care, you know? Maybe I always will, I don't know."

I squeezed her slender body. "He's an idiot. He never should've let you go. You're a real treasure, Ellie."

"I'm just me." Her arms snaked around my waist.

"You're special."

"Then why did he dump me?" Her face buried in my chest, she started to cry. "Why would he cheat on me with *her*? Why wasn't I good enough? Why?"

As she wet my shirt with her tears, I rested my cheek against the top of her head. I had no answers to those questions. True, Colton was young, stupid, arrogant. Thinking he had the world by the balls.

You don't, kid. Believe me, you don't.

***

Her bout of weeping over, her cheeks red and swollen, Ellie huddled in my arms as we both sat on the bed. Though a movie played on the TV, I don't think either of us comprehended anything about it. My thoughts continued to squirrel around and around inside my mind——what the hell was I doing? Why did I let myself make love to my son's ex? What the hell do I do now?

We should have the talk...

But I couldn't. Not yet. Ellie's vulnerability and susceptibility kept my mouth shut. Later, maybe once we hit the road again, I could remind her of our vast age difference. That it's unacceptable for us to be sleeping together. That I didn't love her.

I *couldn't* love her.

Except that wasn't exactly true.

Colton's mom walked out on us ten years ago. When she did, she broke both of us. I struggled to repair the damage she had done. And Colton? Well, I can't say he ever got past her loss. How she abandoned him as easily as she might abandon a kitten by the side of the road. Colton not only knew that, but blamed himself for her leaving us.

I wondered if that enabled him to treat Ellie the same way. Just...dump her. As though she had never meant anything to him.

"What are you thinking about?" her little voice asked.

I glanced down at Ellie's upturned face. "Colton."

"I'm sure he's all right."

Now she was repeating my own words back to me. "I know. I'm just thinking about my influence as a parent. Or the lack thereof."

Ellie caressed my chest. "I'm sure you're a great dad."

"How do you know? You've only really known me for three days. For all you know, I beat him regularly, and twice on Sundays."

Laughing, Ellie lightly slapped my stomach. "You're kidding, right? Colton wasn't abused, and you're not an abuser."

"What if you're wrong?"

She shook her head. "It's hard to explain. I just know you're a good person."

I wanted to protest, to explain that a true psychopath could conceal their real selves, but decided against it. I hugged her tightly instead. "I'm glad to have your vote of confidence."

Abruptly, the TV blinked out. The lights vanished. The heater ceased its hum.

Ellie clutched me, crying out, "Shit."

"There goes the power."

A niggle of unease crept into my belly.

Ellie got up from the bed and crossed the room to the window. "It's really bad out there."

"The storm won't last forever," I assured.

She turned, her expression in the now shadowy place haunted. "Will we be okay? Will we?"

"Sure." I beckoned her with my fingers. "These buildings are well insulated. We've got blankets, our coats, snuggling together we'll maintain body heat."

As jittery as a deer, Ellie returned to bed. I covered us both with the blanket and cover, holding her against my chest.

"Too bad we don't have a deck of cards," I joked, trying to lighten her worries.

"Let's hope this place doesn't become a second Donner Pass," she muttered.

I couldn't help it. I broke into wild laughter, trying to imagine the hotel guests, including Ellie and I, eating one another. "Good lord, what a thought. Where'd that come from?"

"The blizzard," she replied, her tone dark. "Trapped by it, no food, water. We can't even make a fire."

I wiped my eyes, still chuckling. "The blizzard will be over by morning. The plows will open the highway, and we can leave, power or no power. If we can't leave right away, the power will still come back on eventually."

"It might be out for weeks," she said, stubbornly. "It's happened before. Lines down, people without heat for weeks at a time."

"Your imagination is running wild," I commented. "That's true. But folks come together to help one another, not become cannibals. We'll be fine, I promise. How about a Snickers Bar?"

"I'm not hungry."

"I'm getting us each a candy bar and a soda. Just so you know we're not going to eat each other." Before I stood up, however, I lifted the blankets and studied the region where her slim legs joined. "Though I might have to eat you."

Ellie yanked the covers back, scowling. "Yeah, yeah."

Grinning, I fetched us both a candy bar and a soda, then joined her on the bed to dine. Ellie recovered her sweet good humor, joking about eating a fellow human being if they happen to be tasty enough.

"Too bad we don't have a barbeque grill," she said, taking a swig of her soda.

"We'll start a fire in the lobby and set a grill over that," I replied.

Ellie snickered. "Invite all the neighbors."

"To eat or be eaten."

Laughing like kids, we ate and drank our sweet dinner. Ellie never mentioned it, but the room slowly grew decidedly colder.

How cold might it get in here? Low fifties?

Outside the window, the whiteout continued, the wind howling past the building as darkness dropped with an almost alarming suddenness.

Ellie's giggles were cut off instantly when I rose from the bed. "Where are you going?"

"Just gathering our coats to put over us. An added layer."

"Isn't there an extra blanket on that shelf?"

Sure enough, a nice woolly blanket sat neatly folded on the shelf above the open closet where guests might hang clothes. I put that over the bed, then added the coats. I slid under the mass beside her, appreciating the new heavy weight over us.

"No freezing to death now," I said.

"Grey!"

I chuckled, nuzzling under her chin to kiss her creamy throat. "Let's play caveman and cavewoman. Pretend we're lying by the hearth fire, buried under a mammoth hide."

"Sounds stinky, not romantic."

I slid my hand over her breasts, one after the other. "Caveman does what comes naturally."

Ellie gasped as I pulled the covers back, and her shirt up, enough to lick and suck each nipple, my fingers trailing down her belly to play with her clit.

"Oh, my," she breathed.

"Caveman is hungry," I rumbled, sliding down her body, buried under the blankets.

As I promised, I parted her thighs had my way with her.

ELLIE

G rey certainly knew how to please me. His hands kept my hips still as I thrashed, moaning, his talented tongue teasing me until I knew I'd go crazy with need. I bucked my hips upward, into his tongue, my pussy gushing my arousal into his mouth. I nearly orgasmed, unable to hold back the heat that surged with every lick of his tongue.

Only his taking his mouth away prevented my climax.

I groaned, panting, needing him, needing more, and he refused to give it to me. Gliding up to lie beside me, Grey fumbled with removing his clothes. Under the weight of the blankets and coats, it became a crazy, goofy game of whether we could strip naked or not. At least I got my lower half bare, which was good enough for me.

"I'm on top," I panted.

Grey chuckled breathlessly. "Caveman don't care."

For this to work, the covers had to go. I pushed them back, baring Grey's magnificent body. With barely enough light to see by, I stared down at his massive chest, his bulging biceps. I straddled his hips, my juices dripping down my thighs to wet his hips.

I took a long, savory moment to caress his skin, his iron hard muscles, and bent over to kiss him. He opened his mouth under my pressure, our tongues dancing the tango, licking each other's tonsils.

Tonsil hockey. The thought brought a swift giggle against his mouth.

"What?" he demanded.

"We're playing tonsil hockey."

"I'm the world champ at tonsil hockey."

"Now kiss me."

Grinning, Grey obeyed, his grip behind my head made sure I couldn't break our kiss. My arousal grew as he inserted his fingers into my honeypot, teasing me, bringing me closer to orgasm. I held it back, soft moans escaping my lips. Despite my efforts, my climax burst through me like a bomb, shattering all my willpower.

I cried out, throwing my head back as the exquisite pleasure rocked my core. Thunderous, it rolled across my stomach and centered in my loins. Hissing through my locked teeth, I rode the waves of the sweet and addictive pleasure, never wanting it to end.

"Ride me, baby," Grey commanded.

Before my orgasm fully abandoned me, I lowered myself onto his monster prick. It slid in as though going home, spreading me wide, its passage eased by my slick tunnel. The head of his cock knocked against my G-spot, and nearly set off another explosive orgasm.

Rising slightly, I rode Grey, then slid down, working my hips back and forth, and up and down. He bucked his hips upward in an erotic rhythm that hampered my ability to hold back my second climax. Gritting my teeth helped for a short while, but not nearly long enough.

"I'm coming," Grey moaned through his clenched jaws. "I can't stop it."

I couldn't either.

His jizz exploded inside me at the same moment my orgasm spilled forth like a dam bursting. His cock spasmed, undulating, a tidal wave of sweet, delicious pleasure. The exquisite high stayed with me longer than it ever had before, then gradually faded into obscurity.

Breathing heavily, I slid off his cock, and lay beside him. My juices and his cum trickled to the sheet under us as Grey half rose to gather the blankets and coats over us once again.

"Caveman is happy," Grey rumbled, taking me into his brawny arms. "Is cavewoman?"

"Very."

I snuggled against his side, buried under the heap, my cheek resting against his arm. Lassitude swiftly carried me under, and I forgot to worry about freezing to death, forgot to think about the Donner Party. Warm, comfortable, and safe, I dropped into a deep sleep, listening to his slow, steady breathing.

***

Brilliant sunlight forced me to blink in pain. Lifting my head from Grey's shoulder, I saw my breath puff in the incredibly bitter air of the motel room. The power hadn't come back on, but at least the blizzard had moved away to trouble the Atlantic Ocean.

"What time is it?" Grey mumbled.

"No idea. Go back to sleep." I returned my cheek to his shoulder, our bodies well protected from the room's temperature.

I'd just started to drift off when Grey's movement startled me awake. "Now what?"

"We might be able to leave."

The chill hit his naked body. I giggled as he jumped around, rubbing his arms as he sought his clothes. He grabbed his coat from the bed, then went to the window. Looking past the curtain, he stared out for what seemed like a long time.

"What?" I asked again.

"It looks like the plows are running on the interstate," he said. "There's a truck plowing the parking lot."

"Are there any cars moving?"

"Yeah, a few."

"Then let's hit the road."

Shivering, I quickly dressed, ignoring the hunger that protested its lack of decent chow. After collecting our things, as well as the candy, chips, and sodas, Grey and I left the room. Glad to be out of there, I almost ran down the stairs to the lobby.

Grey slid the keys across the counter. "Bill me when you get power again."

"Yes, sir," the clerk said.

Outside, the icy air almost had me turning back. Snow reached my hips, the cars buried in the parking lot. Folks from the motel dug their cars out even as the plows opened the way to the town road, and to the interstate. Our breaths steaming, Grey and I warmed ourselves by digging his car free.

I was so eager to leave, I scarcely noticed the snow that clung to my hair, my coat, and soaked into my jeans. Only when I got into the car, felt its wonderful heat, did I realize how cold I was. Far worse than when I abandoned the camp and my so-called friends.

"Here we go." Smiling with good cheer, Grey drove us from the lot, and onto the snow packed interstate.

He drove us north, toward home, and hopefully to a region that had power. My hunger craved a hot breakfast with coffee and orange juice.

"Hand me a bag of chips, please?" he asked.

I handed him a small bag. "I'm so sick of candy and chips."

He chuckled. "Like that's a surprise."

"How long before we get to Montpelier?"

"I'll guess maybe five hours."

I gazed out the window at the white landscape, ignoring my hunger, and wondered what to do when I got home. What home? The apartment I shared with the guy who doesn't love me? Who kicked me to the curb just a few days ago? I didn't have the money to rent a hotel room.

My cell phone buzzed, jerking me from my thoughts. "Whoa."

"Is it Colton?"

I yanked it from my pocket and looked at the screen, then at Grey. "Yeah."

He breathed deeply. "Thank God."

I clicked the answer button. "So you're still alive."

"I guess you are, too," Colton's voice sounded in my ear. "You okay?"

Biting back the desired response——*What do you care?*——I simply said, "Yeah."

"Are you still with my dad?"

I glanced at Grey, wondering how much Colton might guess about what happened between his dad and me. "Yeah."

"Can I talk to him?"

"No, he's driving. The highway is icy. What happened to you? He's been worrying about your dumb ass."

"We left the cabin," Colton replied, his tone subdued, "and no one had a signal. We got stuck in some flea bag hotel for three days. We just got back and now we have service again. I'm heading home."

I held my breath, searching for the courage to say what I needed to say next. "Great. So, you should pack your things. My name's on the lease. You have places to go, but I don't."

Silence filled my cell's speaker. I felt Grey's eyes on me, shifting from the highway to me then back.

At long last, just when I thought Colton would hang up on me, he said, "All right. I guess that's fair."

"Did you bring my stuff back?" I wanted to know.

"Yeah, it's all here. Your purse, everything."

"Where will you go?"

I heard Colton's shrug down the line. "Maybe move back in with my dad for a while. If he'll let me. I'll be gone by the time you get back."

"Good."

"Look, Ellie, I need to say this: I was an asshole. I'm so, so sorry I treated you like shit."

My bitter anger and grief all but drowned me. "Yeah, sure you are. You've got Lindy to fuck now."

Colton chuckled which sounded almost like a sob. "She kicked me to the curb. Said I'd just do to her what I did to you."

I raised my eyebrows in surprise. "She has more brains than I gave her credit for."

"I didn't love her. Not the way I love you."

Shaking with rage, with humiliation, with an extreme emotion I couldn't name, I shouted, "You *don't* love me. You never did. You're an immature boy who plays with hearts like they're Legos."

"You're right. I need to grow up. I'm trying to acknowledge the harm I've done. Can you give me that much?"

"No. I'm glad you're okay, so is your father, but don't be there when I come back. I never want to see you again."

I hung up on him, fuming, furious, wanting to cry, to scream, to run away from this entire situation. Escape my problems and the heartbreak that came with them. I wanted the impossible: that this agonizing pain hadn't happened at all.

"Feel better?" Grey asked gently.

I glanced at him through my tears. "No."

He took my hand, resting both mine and his on the console between us. "I'm sorry."

"Don't be."

"He'll leave the apartment?"

I wiped my tears with my free hand. "Yeah. He wants to move in with you."

Grey clicked his tongue. "I might let him. I might not. If I do, he pays his share of the mortgage."

I sucked in a deep breath, willing my tears to be gone. "That's fair."

"What about you?"

"What about me?"

"You can afford to live alone?"

"I have to." I stared out the window at the snow again. "I have no choice."

***

Grey walked me to my apartment door.

Colton had, courteously, left it unlocked since my keys were in my purse. I strode in, half expecting to see him. But he'd taken a few of his clothes, some of his books, and a picture of him with his mother when he was a kid. That was all. Everything else was the same as when we walked out last Friday.

"Are you gonna be okay?" Grey's green eyes gazed at me with undisguised concern.

I smiled and gripped his hands within mine. "Yeah."

"If not, I'm only a phone call away." He made a phone symbol with his thumb and pinkie sticking from his fist and held it to his ear. "Call me."

"I will."

"I mean it."

"I know you do. And thanks. For a really good time."

Grey chuckled, then planted a quick kiss to my lips. "I had a good time, too. Except for the worrying about my kid part. And the part where we thought we'd end up like the Donner Party."

I laughed. "Go home. Go back to your life."

Grey started to turn, then swung back, his smile gone. "I mean it, Ellie. Call me. If you need anything, including rent money."

"I promise I will."

I hated to see him go. My soul cried out, *don't leave me! Please stay, hold me, love me.*

I couldn't. Grey couldn't stay. He was my ex-boyfriend's father. He'd told me he was too old for me, and I reluctantly agreed. There wasn't a future for us. Not with the eighteen-year age difference there wasn't. Even without Colton in the picture, hanging over us like a dark spectre, we had to think about his career.

The press would love to write about him and his twenty-two-year-old lover. His son's ex-girlfriend.

"Take care," he said at last, leaving my apartment.

"You, too."

He paused and looked me in the eyes. "Bye."

"Bye."

I closed the door behind him and began to cry.

Grey

I missed her.

"Aldine, you stupid fuck, what the hell are you doing?" Coach skated toward me; his expression dark red with fury.

Embarrassed by the easy shot I missed because I wasn't focused on my job, I lowered my eyes.

"Sorry, Coach," I said, my tone low. "Too much on my mind, I guess."

"Get it off your mind, Aldine. We're in the fucking playoffs. I need everyone paying attention, got it? Including you. You don't get a free pass here, dumb fuck. Now let's get with the program."

He skated off, taking a moment to yell at Steve for some minor infraction, then signaled for practice to start again.

I forced Ellie from my thoughts.

Focusing, planning three moves ahead, I skated circles around my teammates, stole the puck from Jerry, passed it to Steve, who passed it back, and sliced the thing into the goal net. Our goalie, Eddie, wasn't quite fast enough to stop me.

He whooped and raised his stick in triumph. "Aldine, you piece of shit! Try that again."

I did.

My speed, my ability to keep the puck no matter what, had always made my team a winner. Outracing a Viper half my age, I stole the puck, spun, charged down rink. Eddie waited, watching, concentrating, and skated out to meet me.

I spun around him like a dancer, my stick propelling the puck, and slammed it into the net.

Eddie took his helmet off, grinning. "Man, how do you do that?"

"Just lucky."

"Lucky my ass. You do that against Toronto, and we're headed for the Cup."

He smacked my butt in team camaraderie as I collected the puck and skated past him. Others yelled affectionate insults, made as though to slam me into the guard, but slapped my ass or shoulders instead. Coach nodded in grim satisfaction and offered me a salute.

After the showers, we gathered in the team conference room, watching the videos of our session. Here, we learned what we did wrong, how to fix the problems. Watching myself spin like a figure skater around Eddie, I had to admit it was a dope move.

Dope.

That's what Ellie would've said. My body ached to have her in my arms again. I needed to see her smile, that goofy purple streak in her hair. It has been a week since I took her back to her apartment. A week of meetings, practice, working out on exercise machines. Of running on the treadmill for eight miles at a stretch.

A very long and lonely week.

"All right, that's it," Coach announced. "Get your beauty sleep, ladies, because tomorrow, I'll work your tits off."

Eddie slung his arm over my shoulders as we left the conference room. "You okay, bro? You're all down in the mouth again."

I raised a small smile. "I'm dope."

He laughed. "You sure are, man. Keep the faith, brother."

He veered left while I went right, striding from the rink and across the parking lot. The night air was cold enough to burn my throat as I breathed. I remembered that night in the motel room with Ellie when the power went out. How she freaked at first, then cuddled against me, soft and warm, after our second session of love making.

I wanted her again. Not as a fuck toy. I craved her company outside of sex...then sex, then more of her company. Since my divorce, none of my few lady "friends" made me crave their time outside of bed.

Ellie was different.

Morose, I drove home, wondering if I should call her. I wanted to give her space. Was she doing the same for me? She never called, didn't text. Did she not like me enough to call? Did she find another guy? The latter thought had me grinding my teeth.

I parked my car in my garage, clicked the automatic door to slide down, then grabbed my gym bag. From the garage, I stepped into the kitchen. I paused.

Colton sat at the kitchen island, eating a sandwich. He glanced up from the book he read and offered a smile with his mouth full.

After swallowing, he said, "Dad, hi. How was practice?"

I almost said *dope*. "It was good. Coach thinks we're headed for the Cup, maybe."

"That'd be awesome."

Since Ellie kicked him out, Colton had come to stay with me. I guess I didn't mind, he was my son. Thus far, a whole week, he'd performed his share of the household chores, did his own laundry, and worked at his job five days out of seven. I couldn't complain about his presence.

Colton and I screwed the same girl. Is that messed up or what?

At the cabinet, I took down a glass. "Want some wine?"

"No, thanks."

I poured chardonnay into the glass, put the bottle back, then sat opposite Colton. He'd set his book aside and pushed his plate away. By his slightly tense expression, he had something on his mind he wanted to talk about.

"Dad," he began slowly.

"Yeah?"

"I know I've been an asshole. To Ellie."

"I'd say you have."

He flushed. "Yeah, you know. I want to make it up to her."

"Why?"

"Why?" Colton blinked. "Isn't that the right thing to do?"

I shrugged. "From what I heard that day, she wants nothing to do with you."

"She doesn't." Colton sucked in a deep breath. "She won't return my calls, or texts."

"You dumped her for her friend, son," I said quietly. "You embarrassed her, shamed her in front of her friends. You told her you didn't care if you treated her badly."

His flush deepened. "She told you?"

"Yeah. And you think she wants to make kissy face with you again?"

Shunting his face to the side, his mouth turned down in a self-castigating frown. "No. I know she doesn't want to. I want her back. You know that old saying, 'You don't know what you've got till it's gone'?"

I dared not look at him. "I've heard that a time or two."

I wanted to see Ellie perhaps as much as Colton does. Was I falling in love with her? Or was it my dick who wanted her in bed again? My confused emotions didn't help any.

We both want the same girl. Talk about messed up.

"That's me," Colton went on, his tone as morose as I felt. "I didn't realize how much she really meant to me until——"

"You got your dumb ass kicked to the curb."

He met my gaze. "Pretty much. I think I'd have realized it even if Lindy hadn't dumped me."

"So, you'd have thrown Lindy to the wolves just as you did Ellie, then demanded Ellie come crawling back?" I didn't bother to hide my disgust. "When will you learn you don't treat people that way?"

"Since I learned it from you, I guess I never will."

"What the hell are you talking about?" I met his sullen and defiant blue gaze. "I don't treat people like shit."

"It's your fault Mom left us," Colton snapped. "*Yours*. You were never home; your career came first. Remember? I do. She was always alone, and you didn't give a rat's ass for either of us."

I gripped my glass so tightly I felt it begin to crack under the pressure. Swallowing the wine down, I carefully set it on the table and maintained enough self-control not to throw it at him.

"Your mom wanted my success as much as I did," I said slowly, my voice a growl. "She wanted the money, the fame of being married to a hockey star. I broke my leg. Rumors started that I'd never play again. Your mom, in all her loving and supportive nature, chose to leave us both. I heard, years ago, she'd snagged an NFL quarterback."

"That's not what I remember."

"You were a fucking *kid*, Colton," I grated. "Your memories are distorted because you weren't old enough to understand a damn thing."

"So why didn't you tell me that's why she left?" Colton demanded.

"Would it have helped?" I glowered as I stood to get more wine. I spoke over my shoulder as I poured. "Would you think differently of her if you knew she was in it for fame and glory? Maybe I thought it might be better for you to believe I neglected her. Direct your anger at me instead of thinking she left because of you."

Colton flushed. "I admit I did think that for a long time."

"I know you did. When you got older, you blamed me. I let you. I could handle it, and I *did* handle it."

He stared at the table. "So, now I'm behaving just like she did. Dumping Ellie for my own selfish, stupid reasons."

"It's not too late to change," I murmured, my guilt at screwing Ellie when Colton still loved her wrenching my conscience into twists. "You can grow up, be a real man. Own up to your mistakes and make amends."

"That's hard when Ellie won't talk to me."

"It's her choice. Maybe you should respect it. Move on."

Colton shook his head. "I should, but I can't. I want her back so bad. I'm gonna keep trying to win her back."

My gut twisted into pretzel knots, churning the wine until I thought I'd hurl it into the kitchen sink. I had no idea what to say.

Good luck? I'm sure she'll love you again once you apologize? I didn't want him to succeed in winning Ellie back. Yet, how could I vie for her affections in competition with my own son? Christ, what a fucking mess.

"What will you do?" I finally asked.

Colton shrugged. "Get her to talk to me. Somehow."

I stared down at my wine. "Yeah."

"I still have a key to the apartment," Colton went on. "I could go over there, make her listen."

"That's breaking and entering," I said dryly. "You might get tossed in the slammer if Ellie decides to call the cops."

"Both of our names are on the lease," he replied, stubborn. "I've a right to be there."

"Nope, you don't. Not after you walked out."

"Ellie won't call the cops," he said. "All I want to do is talk."

"And hope she doesn't think you're there to slap her around."

He glared, indignant. "I'd never hurt her."

"You already have."

"Shit, Dad, you don't have a very high opinion of me, do you?"

"At the moment, no."

He ran his hands through the blond hair he'd inherited from his mom. "That's on me, I guess. It's time for me to do better."

I said nothing. What could I say? "*Do better and win Ellie's heart*"? I suddenly realized that would be best. I'm too old for Ellie. She's too young for me. I should stand back, let Colton earn her trust. Watch them grow in their love, have kids, and be happy for them.

After all, Ellie didn't need an old man like me in her life.

Walk away, dude. Leave it. Find a lady closer to your age, maybe find love for yourself one day.

"Where are you going?" Colton's confused voice trailed after me as I walked from the kitchen.

"Nowhere special."

Striding down the stairs and into my basement, I flicked on the overhead lights. My myriad of exercise equipment gleamed under the fluorescent lighting. Maybe if I ran ten miles on the treadmill, I might forget the feel of Ellie in my arms, sweating away the image of her sweet smile.

I changed into the sweatpants and shirt I kept down there.

And began to run.

ELLIE

I missed him.

I missed him far more than I ever thought I'd miss anyone. Including Colton. While I still grieved for the loss of my relationship, my thoughts constantly roamed to Grey and his powerful arms around me, soothing my fears. Colton never did that. He failed to make me feel safe. Loved, yes, for the most part. He made me laugh, but then he made me cry.

Grey would never make me cry.

I sighed, forcing my attention to the job at hand. If I didn't work, I didn't get paid. Freelance, remote workers like me had few safety nets when it came to money and payments. As a social media manager for three companies, I needed to work more than eight hours a day, every day, to make rent.

Especially since I now had no one to share the cost with.

Pushing thoughts of Grey and Colton from my mind, I researched my article topic, and made some notes. My work soothed me, helped me to heal, to not think about Colton and Lindy and their betrayal. I hummed as I worked, fresh contentment seeping into my soul.

What will come, will come.

A hard rap came to my apartment's door.

Annoyed at the interruption, my first thought was to ignore the visitor. Most likely a neighbor wanting to borrow a cup of sugar and stay for an hour, talking. I shook my head and returned to work.

The knock came again, harder this time.

"Go away," I muttered. "Can't you see I'm busy?"

The idea that Grey had come to see me entered my head, but I dismissed it. He'd be too busy to just drop by, and if he wanted to see me, he'd call or text first. Not that he would. He's too old for me——we both knew it. My thoughts and daydreams regarding him were just that——dreams. I needed to move on from *both* father and son.

My apartment door's lock clicked.

Alarmed, I shot to my feet, fearing an intruder and casting about for a potential weapon. Why didn't I have a baseball bat handy? I live alone now! Outside the room I used as an office, footsteps brushed against the carpet. The front door closed.

What the hell? I reached for my phone in my pocket.

Tiptoeing to the doorway, I peered around the corner just as Colton called, "Ellie?"

My held breath rushed from my lungs in a sharp gust.

I paced into his view, my fear replacing my fury. "What are you doing here? Did you forget something?"

Garbed in a business suit, his tie loosened, Colton appeared as sinfully attractive as his old man. He stuffed his hands into his trouser pockets, a faint, little boy smile creasing his lips. He'd always used that smile as a weapon against me, forcing me to forgive him for his infractions in an instant.

My heart wanted to melt, gush in a torrent down to my stomach. I wanted to kiss him, to hug him, to smell his cologne. I craved his naked body in bed——

Until I remembered his sensual lips locked on Lindy's.

"I wanted to talk to you," he replied. "Is this a bad time?"

"It's always a bad time," I snapped, wishing for that baseball bat. "You don't live here anymore. You can't just walk in any time you please."

"My name's on the lease too."

"So?" I folded my arms over my chest despite the obvious body language telling him I was on the defensive. Maybe because I *was* on the defensive. "Leave the key and get out. I have to work."

Instead of obeying me, Colton ambled toward me, his easy smile widening. "You're so cute when you're mad."

"Oh, please," I snorted.

He lifted his hand to my face, toying with a tendril of my hair. "Please listen to me, Ellie."

"No."

"I still love you."

Gaping, I backed away, putting distance between us. "Sucks to be you, huh? You dumped me for that bitch Lindy, and now you get to live with that."

"Come on, Ellie," Colton said, his tone impatient. "Can't you give me a second chance? I made a huge mistake, I know that. Let me make amends, earn your trust again. I'm so sorry I hurt you. It'll never happen again."

His voice put me on edge. As though he believed that all he had to do was show me contrition, and I'd curl up and die for him. That all the hurt, the grief, the humiliation he put me through didn't truly matter since he apologized. That the sight of him beside the fire with Lindy, his coldness when he said he fell out of love with me, was no longer relevant, or important.

"No," I said softly, "it won't happen again."

"So, you'll take me back? Let me move back in?"

Colton smiled, pacing the few steps between us. I put my hand up, my palm out, and stopped him.

"You've done too much damage," I said. "No, you're not moving back in. What's done is done, and I'm not risking more hurt."

Reaching for my hand, Colton's sorrowful expression deepened, as though I'd just cut him. I jerked my hand out of his reach and put air between us again.

His mouth suddenly tightened. "Why can't you believe me, Ellie? I want you back, I love you."

"Your control freak is showing," I said. "Might want to cover it back up."

"I'm not trying to control you."

"No?" I laughed bitterly. "You think I'm an easy lay, that I'd swoon into your arms. You come over, break into my home, say the magic words and I'm your girl again. Easy peasy. Much easier than moving on and find a new squeeze since Lindy saw you for what you are: a predator."

Colton blinked. "A what? Is that what you think I am?"

"Yep."

Turning, he strode into my living room as though he belonged there, staring out the picture window. I wanted him out, and suspected the only way to evict him was to call the cops. But I didn't need the damn drama. So, I waited.

At last, Colton turned. His better-than-good-looking face had morphed into something akin to a haggard expression. As though my comment hit him where it hurt.

"I guess I need to be a better person," he said. "A better man."

I very nearly let myself get suckered into feeling bad for him, to start thinking of us as a couple again. To apologize, and hug him, kiss him. I opened my mouth to say…What? That I have faith that he'll become a star at self-improvement?

I pointed to the door. "Do it somewhere else."

"You've really become a cold bitch, Ellie."

"Now that's the pot calling the kettle black," I replied, smiling. "You obviously forgot, most conveniently I'm sure, how you informed me with all the warmth of an Arctic blizzard that you fell *out* of love with me. Months ago, wasn't it? Even as you were sticking your dick into me, you were sticking it into Lindy too. But *I'm* the cold bitch?"

Colton cheeks turned a deep, dark red as I spoke. "No, I didn't forget. I treated you badly and now I'm saying I was wrong. I'm sorry."

"You *are* sorry, Colt," I said with a harsh bark of laughter. "You're one sorry son of a bitch. Now leave before I call the cops. And leave the key. I don't have the cash to change the lock."

"Ellie——"

I reached for my cell. Colton lifted his hands in a gesture of surrender and walked slowly past me to the entrance. Taking his housekey, he dropped it on the table.

Opening my door, he hesitated long enough to give me a long, searching look. "I won't give up on you."

"Don't come back," I said lightly. "Be a good boy and find someone else to hassle."

He left, quietly closing the door behind him.

I crossed the apartment quickly, locked the door before he had a chance to change his mind. Listening, I heard his footsteps treading the hallway outside as he made his way down it. Breathing deeply, quelling the rioting in my stomach, I pocketed the key.

"Damn him," I muttered, leaning against the door. "Damn him, damn him. Just...why the *fuck* does he think he can sashay back into my life?"

My anger, my grief and pain, forced me into pacing. No way could I work now. I had the attention span of a gnat. I doubted I could sit still for even five minutes. Cursing Colton helped a little. Calling him every vile name in the book eased some of my stress.

Heading into the kitchen, I brewed chamomile tea, thinking the herbal remedy might calm me enough so I could once again focus on my project. As it steeped, I leaned against the counter, wishing for Grey's solid strength beside me more than ever.

"No, I won't call him," I murmured. *"He doesn't need me whining to him about his kid. He might even take Colton's side."*

Thankfully, the tea did indeed calm my shattered nerves. Sitting once again at my computer, I resumed my research for the article. After a second cup, I hummed as I worked, feeling quite proud of how I handled Colton.

That idiot won't be back, he's not that stupid.

By early evening, I finished my task, and e-mailed it to my client. Hunger stirred vaguely, and I thought of a quick dinner break before starting my next project.

Just gotta check my inbox quick, see if I have any offers of more work...

My client's company e-mail popped up at the top of my unread pile.

"That was quick," I said, clicking on it.

As I read the short note, my blood grew cold. Like ice crystals in my veins, clogging them until nothing short of Drain-O might uncork my pulse. My breath halted abruptly, nor did it return for what seemed like an hour. I clenched my fists so hard my fingernails made deep, crescent shapes in my flesh.

Dear Ellie, I regret to inform you we will no longer need your services. Unfortunately, we cannot currently pay our outstanding invoice for work in progress. Good luck in the future.

"Oh my God."

I sagged into my chair. These people owed me thousands. *Thousands.* I'd received their comptroller's assurance I'd be paid promptly. I counted on that money to pay my rent. My bills. And put aside the extra for a rainy day.

"Oh my God, how can they *do* this?"

Because they can. Because they've likely done it before. Not just to freelancers like me, but to anyone small enough and unable to hire an attorney and sue them.

I pondered taking them to small claims court where attorneys didn't matter. I might win in that event. I have their signed contract, their comptroller's promise of payment in a written e-mail. I also looked at my calendar. I had five days before the rent was due. Groaning, I covered my face with my hands.

My apartment's management company did not accept late payments. If I didn't pay on time, they'd start eviction proceedings. Greedy, inhumane, and soulless bastards that they were.

"I'm in so much shit."

Desperate enough to think of Colton and his need to have me back, I almost called him. Let him pay the rent, deal with him until I didn't need him anymore, then give him the boot.

I can't do that, it's fucking wrong.

I had no family. Thanks to Colton, I no longer had any friends, either. No one I could turn to for help. Staring at my cell in panic, I dared recall what Grey said to me the day he dropped me off. *Call me. If you need anything, including rent money.*

I had to.

Biting my lip, I found Grey's number in my contacts, then clicked it. Breathless, sweating, hating myself, hating the world...I listened to the line ring.

Grey

Hi, Grey, it's me. It's Ellie. I, um, remember when you said to call if I needed anything? Even rent? Because I, uh, well I'm in trouble and I need rent money. I'm sorry to have to ask——but do you mind? It's a loan, I'll pay you back. Promise.

I listened to her voice in both delight and alarm. Ellie sounded so scared, as though terrified I'd refuse to help her. Like I would. Immediately, I clicked her number. Instead of the line ringing though, I received a harsh *wah-wah-wah* sound in my ear. Puzzled, I glanced at my screen. I had signal, all right, but that call wasn't going through.

No matter. I knew where Ellie lived. I grinned to myself as I grabbed my coat, then headed for the garage. I had a very handy excuse to knock on her door and say hello.

Hey, sweetie, here's your rent money, take your time in paying it back, it's all good. Let's get some dinner.

With these pleasant thoughts running through my head, I stopped at my bank's ATM to withdraw a couple thousand dollars. The bitter Vermont air frosted my breath as I stuffed the cash into my coat pocket. Crusted snow from the blizzard covered the streets and yards where the plows failed to reach.

There it'll stay until spring, I thought.

I parked in Ellie's building's lot, then trotted up the stairs to her floor. Music drifted from behind closed doors as I walked down the hallway. Finding her apartment, I knocked.

Listening, I heard Ellie shriek, as though a poltergeist goosed her with her own hairbrush. I listened to her hard tread as she stalked toward the door.

"Fucker, I told you to never come back——"

Violently, Ellie swung her door open.

Her jaw dropped as she stared at me. I read the signs of her stress, her wide blue eyes sparking anger and fear, her hair falling in tangles over her chest. The redness over her cheeks spoke of her fits of weeping. Gaping, her lush lips opened and closed without a word passing them.

I stepped in, forcing her back, and closed the door. I said nothing as I swept her into my arms, feeling her slender body tremble as she wept against my coat. Caressing her tangled hair, I murmured something stupid about me being there, it'll be all right, shit of that nature.

At length, I urged her further into her apartment, and sat her on the couch. Shedding my coat, I sat beside her, then pulled her against me. Ellie melted into me, hiccupping, and sniffling the last of her tears away. I simply held her, letting her take her time.

"I thought...I thought, you were blowing me off." Ellie tried to smile, but it looked crooked and strange.

"Never, honey," I murmured. "I tried to call, but it wouldn't go through. So, I just came over."

"Oh."

Grabbing my coat, I fetched the cash from the pocket. "Don't worry about paying me back. At least not right now. Pay your rent. Get yourself together. Okay?"

Ellie nodded, clutching the money as though she seized a life preserver. "M-my client refused to pay me. Just like that. And I can't sue because it'll cost too much."

"Bastards."

I'd heard of predatory companies who made extra profits at the expense of their small-time employees and vendors. Owing workers tens of thousands, then dumping them like bad trash. Few if any had the means to pursue a legal route.

"There are ways to get your money, Ellie," I said.

"Small claims court?"

I nodded. "That's a good option. Look, I've an idea."

"What?"

I tapped her nose, smiling. "Wash your face. Brush your hair. I'm taking you to dinner."

Ellie's smile rivaled the sun. "That's so dope."

"You know it."

***

After making sure Ellie deposited the cash safely into her bank's ATM, I drove her to one of my favorite restaurants——McDougal's Pub. A steak and seafood place, it catered to the slightly higher end of the pay grade. Yet it was also casual, jeans and T-shirts accepted without question.

The host escorted us to a quaint, somewhat secluded table. Ellie gazed around the place in awe. As though she'd never eaten at a restaurant that cost more than Wendy's. Perhaps she hadn't. There was so much more to Ellie I wanted to learn.

"So, who was it you expected when I knocked on your door?" I asked. "You sounded pretty angry."

She glanced away with a small scowl. "Colton."

"Oh. I see."

"He said he wants me back," she went on, her tone low. "He apologized. Said he wants to be a better person."

I needed to ask the question but feared to raise it. Such a question might open doors best left closed.

Folding my hands in front of my face, I asked anyway. "Do you want him back?"

"No," she snarled under her breath. "Not just no, but *hell* no. He treated me like shit, then pretended to be all remorseful. He thinks he's all that."

A smiling waiter took our orders for wine, left us with menus. During the distraction, I had time to think of what to say. Or to *not* say, as the case may be. After he left, I rested my arms on the table.

"Ellie," I said softly. "Maybe he means it."

She snorted. "Please. I know he's your kid, but jeez, man, I'm not a toy he can throw away and regret later. Do you remember how he humiliated me? Why I ran away to start with?"

"I remember."

"He never came to look for me, did he? *None* of them did. If you hadn't come along, I know I'd have died that night."

Ellie paused, licked her lips, and stared at the table. "I was stupid to run, I know that. At the time, I *did* want to die. They didn't care, either. And I'm to forgive and forget all that? Like it never happened?"

"No. You're not."

Taking her napkin, Ellie tore it to shreds. "Colton behaved as though he was granting me a huge favor in asking me to come back. Can you believe that shit? I can't. I told him to get out and never come back."

"Sorry if that all sounds harsh-I know you two probably talk about me-but he sucks." She swiped her hair behind her neck, obviously flustered. "Why did you come? Tonight."

"You know why."

"No, you could have put a check in the mail. Instead, you came. Why?"

I leaned forward, meeting her defiant gaze. "You *know* why. Because I care. I wanted, *needed*, to see you. You offered me a prime excuse."

"Oh." Her napkin quickly turned into small puffs of white paper.

I put my hands over hers to stop her from shredding it even more. "I'm too old for you, Ellie. We talked about that. I can't help how I feel, but I still want to be there for you."

"Feel? As in...care?"

"Yeah. And no, not care like I care for you as if you were my daughter. It's not that kind."

Ellie smiled. It unnerved me, seeing that almost predatory grin, as though she'd successfully set the trap I'd blundered into. Or the lamb she led to the slaughter.

"So, you don't look at me like I'm a kid," she murmured, "*your* kid. That's good."

"Maybe," I replied, nervous. "Maybe it's wrong to feel that way."

"Age is just a number," she added primly.

"No, it's not. It's experience. It's many things. You agreed I'm too old for you. Remember?"

Ellie gripped my fingers, her smile fading until I wasn't sure if I'd truly seen it. "Yeah. But I can't help how I feel either. I like you, Grey. More than like. And I don't see you as a father figure. I don't have daddy issues."

"You never had a father, did you?"

"Foster dads who ignored my existence." Ellie ran her fingers through her thick hair with a deep breath. "Okay, maybe I *do* have daddy issues. But I don't look at you that way. If I had, I'd never have...you know."

She glanced around at the diners and waiters as though fearing they'd overhear and know she'd slept not just with an older man, but her ex-boyfriend's father. "Should I see a shrink?"

I chuckled. "No."

"Is being attracted to a dude old enough to be my parent a bad thing? You hear about it all the time; a twenty-something chick dates a celebrity in his eighties. Has his kid."

"Isn't that gold-digging?" I murmured.

"Am I gold-digger? I mean, I did just ask you for a loan.

I shook my head. "I don't believe so. My ex-wife was one, so I think I'd know the difference."

Ellie's fingers continued to shred the napkin's remains, and only stopped when the waiter returned to take our order. She'd barely glanced at the menu and asked for shrimp and a baked potato. I decided not to question her culinary decision and went with the same.

"Look," I said slowly after he'd departed, "what's going on between us is our business. No one else's."

"What about Colton?"

I winced inwardly. "If you decide you'd rather be with him, I'd understand."

"We went over that," Ellie snapped, taking a sip of her wine. "I ask because he could cause a stink. His old man and his girlfriend screwing each other."

"If he's not what you want, then it's not his business either," I replied. "I'm not worried about him."

"Maybe you should be." Ellie eyed me over the rim of her glass, her eyes older than her years. "He finds out, he might run to the tabloids, collect a fat check for exposing the forty-something hockey star who's sleeping with his girlfriend. Cannon fodder."

Would Colton do that? Oddly, I couldn't say yes or no to that. If he truly does love Ellie, and isn't bullshitting himself or her, he might be mad enough to sell me out to the papers. The internet chatter would go through the roof. Bloggers demanding my head on a pike, chat rooms picking apart my life as easily as Ellie shredded the napkin. Cancel culture at its best.

"I'm not going to walk on eggs around my kid," I said quietly.

"This could ruin your career," Ellie replied just as softly. "I think this should end here. Right now. Friends only."

***

So how did I wind up in bed with Ellie after her declaration?

I could say hormones. I could say the Devil made me do it. I could say Ellie was at fault——she threw herself at me. But that wasn't true at all.

We all know why I did, though.

My attraction to Ellie scrambled all my defense mechanisms. The threat of tabloid reporters and cancel culture, potentially losing my job, flew from my head the instant I walked her through her apartment door. In her darkened home, illuminated only by a small lamp in the kitchen, I seized her in my arms and kissed her.

Ellie didn't resist. Instead, she stuck her tongue in my mouth, her hands clutching my hair in fistfuls. The warmth of her apartment, our heavy coats, built up a heat between us neither of us bothered to deny. My cock grew hard, straining against my zipper, aching for release.

Seizing my coat, Ellie dragged me toward her bedroom. "This is a very bad idea."

My mouth on hers, stumbling over her feet, trying to shed my coat while she held it fast, I muttered thickly, "A *very* bad idea. This'll only lead to trouble."

"I know. We're doing it anyway."

ELLIE

We dropped our coats in the hallway. My sweater flew somewhere to vanish in the dark. Grey unzipped his jeans and pushed them down to his thighs, forcing him to duck walk into my bedroom while still licking my tonsils. I fell backward onto my bed, losing his luscious tongue, and tried to wiggle out of my jeans, panting with lust.

After losing contact, Grey quickly stripped. He tumbled to the bed beside me, discovered my struggles to get as naked as him. Laughing under his breath, he rose to his knees, lifted my jeans at my ankles, and yanked. I yelped as I went with my pants, my hips rising.

Free of my jeans, I fell back onto the bed. My pussy throbbed as Grey knelt over me, lifting my knees, and spreading them.

"What——" I began as he settled my legs over his shoulders.

"Hush."

I cried out as his tongue lapped at my rapidly swelling and highly sensitive clit. He sucked at my arousal, drinking it, teasing me, driving me insane with lust. Unable to writhe, to buck my hips with his strong hands holding them down, he forced me to endure the exquisite and torturous pleasure his mouth offered while unable to move.

"Oh, God," I groaned, my fingers tangled in his hair. "I'm gonna come!"

My orgasm built and climbed, growing, towering, before finally spilling over. Awash in sweet sensations, I cried out, moaning, my pussy quaking, on fire, burning, burning...I was helpless under its force, so I rolled along with it, tumbling out of control, its sweeping pleasure knocking me for a loop.

Grey lifted his face from my sopping pussy but didn't take my legs from his shoulders. Inching forward, he pushed his iron hard cock against my entrance and thrust in. Massive, like a hot steel rod, his shaft invaded, spreading me wide, splitting me open. In the weeks since our last love session, my pussy must have shrunk. A tingling pain accompanied his initial thrusting and almost had me yelling for him to stop.

Then the pleasure his cock offered sent the pain swirling away. My legs wide open, Grey driving forward at a sharp angle. He had little trouble reaching my G-spot. He struck it again and again, a fresh climax spiraling rapidly out of control. I bit my wrist to halt the wild scream that might alarm the neighbors, my head spinning under the sweeping and intense sensation.

Throbbing, my pussy undulated as my second orgasm clamped down on Grey's plunging shaft. Above me, he moaned through his clenched teeth, his cock swelling, slamming into me, his sweat dripping onto my bed, my breasts.

"I can't hold it," he gritted, burying himself into me so hard and so fast that my orgasm rolled on without stopping. Two climaxes combined into one it seemed. Seeing stars behind my closed eyes, I writhed under him, locking my cries in my throat.

Grey uttered a long, slow groan, his muscles granite hard, his entire body stiff as his cock spurted deep into me. His powerful thrusts slowed, gradually coming to a stop. Releasing my legs, panting, Grey laid atop me, his cock still deep inside.

In languid satisfaction, I slid my arms around his neck, holding his damp cheek against mine. I don't know how long we laid there, locked together in a tangle of arms, legs and cock, nor did I care. I could easily have gone to sleep with his heavy weight pinning me down, a man-sized blanket to keep me warm.

When he rolled off me, his dick slid from me in a wet plop, I nearly demanded he come back. Grey stood up from the bed and tugged the covers out from under me. I half sat up, wildly thinking he planned to cover me up, get dressed and leave.

"You're not going?" I asked.

Grey did cover me up, but then crawled under the blankets with me. "I should."

"I don't want you to."

Snuggling against his shoulder, throwing my leg over his, I idly played with his chest hair. Breathing in the scents of sweat and sex, I considered the consequences of us sleeping together yet again. We both agreed we asked for trouble by doing so. Not to mention that we have been less than careful and not given any thought to protection.

I could ruin everything for him. Screw up my own life more than it already is. Where's my good sense? My so-called intelligence?

"We can't do this again," Grey murmured.

"I know." I breathed in deeply. "I can't be responsible for ruining your life."

"I'm getting older. There are only a few years left where I can compete with the younger guys. After that, no one will care what I do or who I do it with."

"Are you suggesting we wait? Not see each other until after you retire?"

"I'm not suggesting anything," he replied. "I've grown too fond of you to not see you...but I'm still far too old for a young, virile girl who can take her pick of men."

I stroked his chest. "You make it sound easy. Pick a guy and live happily ever after. I wasn't born yesterday."

Grey chuckled. "Take my advice. Dump both me and Colton. Stay single for a few years, see the kind of dudes you'll attract. Go on normal dates. Live a good, decent life."

"And marry and have ankle biters." I sighed. "Become a suburban housewife, join the PTA, bake cakes for fundraisers. Is that the kind of woman I should be? Because that's not what I want."

His arms tightened around me as he kissed my brow. "Just promise me you'll find a guy closer to your age. That's all I want. For you to be happy."

I said nothing.

I laid awake for a long time, listening to his deep, steady breathing as Grey slept. What will make me happy? Grey would make me happy. The one man who I want to spend my life with, raise kids with, join a PTA for, was Grey.

The only man I can't have.

***

He woke before I did, and the sound of him in the shower forced me into stirring. I glanced at the clock——6:00

a.m. Groaning, I tried to shut my ears and go back to sleep. I never liked waking up before seven. A morning person I was *not*.

With the troubling conversation the previous night haunting me, returning to sleep became impossible. I knew what he'd suggested I do was not just the smartest idea, and the overall wisest move, I didn't want to take that route. Was I falling in love with Grey?

Maybe I was.

Maybe I was just infatuated, as his presence in my life, along with the great sex, had soothed me when I hurt the most. Grey offered a stabilizing influence just when I needed it. So, does that equate to love? If this was true, then would I cease to need Grey once my heart healed?

Tossing in my bed, my crazy thoughts whirling in my mind, I listened to the shower shut off, heard Grey first drying himself then dressing. I didn't fake sleep when he walked quietly back into my bedroom.

"Did I wake you up? I'm sorry," he said.

"No, it's okay."

He sat beside me and stroked my hair, his expression sorrowful. "I screwed up your life, didn't I?"

"No. I did it. I jumped from Colton to you without looking first. That's a burden you shouldn't have to carry."

"I'm strong." Grey smiled, his green eyes glinting with humor. "You're a special kind of someone, Ellie. I have to fight to not fall in love with you."

"Don't," I said. "That'll screw both of us up. It's best if we just both walk away. Right?"

He looked away from me, his smile gone. "Yeah. It'll hurt like hell, but you're right. If I were ten years younger."

"Or me ten years older. I'm not. Nor are you."

Bending, Grey kissed me tenderly, with love, with a promise he cannot keep. "I'm still here for you. Keep my number. You call, I'll answer."

"Thanks."

Grey stood, looking down at me without talking for a long time. I didn't know what his thoughts were, but I felt my insides ripping apart at the seams. I had to let him go.

For both of our sakes and sanities.

"I've got to go," he murmured. "Stay safe."

"You, too."

I knew I'd cry the moment he shut the door behind him. I tried not to, but the tears came anyway, hot and burning on my cheeks. Holding the pillow he used against my chest, I wept into it, needing him to come back, needing him to stay.

Forever.

***

Once burned, twice shy.

Is that how the saying went?

I worked with suspicion uppermost in my mind. Would other clients cheat me? Accept the work I performed and created for them, then refuse to pay me on the grounds there wasn't anything I could do about it?

Upon receiving an invitation to send samples of my work to a potential client, I looked the company up on the internet. In searching through reviews from past employees and vendors, I decided to take the risk.

I'm doing thorough research on everyone from now on.

With a grim glee, I posted my experience with the company who refused to pay me in as many places as I could think of. YELP, and Glassdoor, Facebook, Instagram as well as tweeted it. With hashtags galore.

"Payback's a bitch," I muttered.

My cell buzzed, making me jump. As though the company I'd just slammed found out and now called to say they planned to take me to court for slander. My hand trembled as I picked it up to look at the caller.

Not some unknown number who may or may not be a corporate lawyer.

Lindy.

Making my voice high pitched with a Southern drawl, I answered with a, "Oh, my heavens! Is this the slut who stole my boyfriend? Why, I'm so *pleased* you called, dearie."

Lindy said nothing for a few long seconds. "I guess I deserved that."

"Indeed, you did." I returned to my normal voice. "What do you want?"

"I wanted to talk to you, Ellie," she replied, her voice subdued. "I need to apologize."

"What for? You fucked Colton, fucked me over. I'm sure you thought you were doing right."

"At first, I didn't care if it was right or wrong," she said, her tone low. "I wanted Colton. You had him, I didn't. I got jealous, made him look at me. Well, he did. Then what he did to you, and...it hit me he'd do the same to me. One day."

"He would, sister. Did you know he's begging me to come back?"

"No. I didn't." She paused. "Will you take him back?"

"When hell freezes over, I might consider it."

"I wanted to go after you that night, before the snowstorm," Lindy said. "I told Colton we should, you could die in that cold. He didn't care. He said you'd be fine and realize it was stupid and come crawling back. You didn't though."

"I was willing to die before I'd crawl back to fake friends and a betraying boyfriend."

Shocked, Lindy gasped, "You can't mean that."

"I did, and I do. And if you think I'll forgive what you did, you can forget it. I was owed an apology; I'll accept. But no way in Hell will I trust you again. *None* of you. Not Colton, not Jen, not you. *Especially* you, dearie. Burned bridges, and all that."

"Just know I'm sorry," Lindy said stiffly. "I was wrong, and I know it now. I'll make it up to you by bettering myself in the future."

"Yeah, yeah. Lindy, you're so full of shit you squeak. Don't call me again."

I clicked to end the call and tossed my phone on my desk. I stared at my computer and thought about nothing except burned bridges.

Grey

Chased by furious Canadians, I zipped down the rink, the screams of the spectators a mere buzz in my ears. All my focus was on the puck I slid between strokes of my stick, my teammate Steve, and the opposing team's goalie. The rapid there-and-gone thought regarding the trick I'd pulled in practice swept across my mind's eye.

I may not be able to pull that off...

I whisked the puck to Steve.

He dodged a Toronto Maple Leaf spun, passed the puck to Devon, who then instantly passed it back to me.

The puck hit the net.

The buzzer ending the first period screamed across the rink.

The half Canadian, half American crowd stood in the bleachers, yelling praises or insults, depending on their nationality. Holding my stick high over my head, I skated in circles as my Vipers collided into me, slapping my ass, ruffling my hair as I removed my helmet, and yelling wordlessly in triumph.

"Lucky shot, Aldine," snapped as he skated past on his way to his team's lockers.

"Grow a pair, Felson," I replied. "Then you might get lucky, too."

My guys roared with laughter, slapping my shoulders as we headed for our own lockers. My insult hadn't passed the Maple Leafs by, no, not at all. I received many a dangerous glance from narrowed eyes as they flew past us. But, I hadn't skated my way to the top of the league by being thin skinned. Hockey wasn't for the faint of heart.

"Good job, Aldine," Coach Hunt declared as we sat on our benches, swallowing water, removing our mitts. "We beat them in this round, we're in the playoffs. Let's not get cocky, however. Let's go over the plays again. Aldine, you——"

During the halftime, we discussed the plays we had practiced over and over in the past week, but incorporated Toronto's strengths and weaknesses into them. Just as the Maple Leafs were discussing ours. With our three points over their none, I knew very well their coach busily instructed them to draw blood.

"They'll be after you, Aldine," Coach said, pointing his finger at me. "They take you out, they have a chance to score big. I want the rest of you to look out for him. Got it? You see them try to pull anything, you make 'em pay."

Murmurs and nodding heads met this proposal, many eyes on my face. The opposing team gunning for me was nothing new. Sucker punches, a stick slipped between my ankles, body slams to the ice or to the boards were all in a day's work for me.

Nor was I without my own wiles.

"Time," called a ref, sticking his head into the locker room.

"I mean it," Coach yelled as we stood, wobbling on our skates on the firm floor. "You watch Aldine's back. They're out for his blood."

So what else is new?

I smirked at the Maple Leafs' captain over the puck, curling my upper lip. He stared into my eyes, his fury glinting within his like twin burning chips of brimstone. I liked what I saw. An angry man seldom made smart choices, or acted with anything except his rage. Angry men made mistakes.

I counted on him to make one.

The ref dropped the puck.

The Maple Leaf hooked his stick around my right ankle, seeking to yank me off my skates and tip my ass onto the ice. With barely an effort, I slapped his stick to the side, stole the puck, and slammed my elbow into his nose as I zipped past him.

Skating with my team flowing around me, I fully expected to be called on my little escapade. Dimly, I heard the Toronto coach screaming at the refs, no doubt demanding I be called out for the foul strike.

I wasn't.

Not overly concerned, I ducked and dodged Maple Leafs, passed the puck, then swung wide around the opposing goalie and the net he guarded. A Maple Leaf followed me, certain I had something up my sleeve. As my team passed the puck around, hiding it, the Maple Leaf hung onto me like stink on shit.

I feinted to the right.

The Maple Leaf sought to block me.

Ducking to my left, I slid past him as if greased, collected the puck, then danced around the net. The goalie swung toward me, ready to protect his turf, his face behind his shield set and tight. No way was he going to let me shoot that puck past him for a fourth time.

I didn't.

Feinting again, my stick sliding the puck across the ice, I spun, then shot the puck toward Steve. On him fast, the Maple Leafs lost sight of the puck as I floated just outside the red pack. Steve, nimble and fast, broke free, returned the puck to me.

I sliced it past the goalie and into the net.

The crowd went nuts.

The buzzer sounded.

Vipers swept around me, protecting me from the Maple Leafs' vengeance. And we all knew how pissed the entire Toronto team was by now. Like a frenzied mob, they came for us, punching faces, body slamming my teammates to the ice.

"Fuckers," I yelled, blocking a blow to my head with my stick.

The crowd screaming in the background, we brawled across the ice, barbarians, bringing blood, punching, striking with sticks. Outside the bedlam, refs, coaches, assistant coaches, team members, all tried to halt the frenzied fighting.

Swept away from my teammates, I saw three Maple Leafs coming for me, sticks at the ready. I raised my own, relaxed, focused, no stranger to fighting for pride, for my team. I blocked a stick aimed at my head, ducked under the second, and hit the third Maple Leaf across the back of his knees.

He fell onto his back, bashing his head on the ice.

One down, two to go.

"You're dead," snarled Felson, and jabbed his stick toward my midsection.

I clashed my stick against his, blocking him from hitting me where it would hurt, and badly. My returning blow, my left fist, cracked him across the side of his head. My mitt absorbed much of the strike, yet he still stumbled back, his skates sliding out from under him.

Swinging back to the third Maple Leaf, I lifted my stick to block the swift attempt to knock me unconscious. I ducked. The stick flew over my head. Using the hardest bone in the human body, I sank my elbow deep into his solar plexus.

Jerking, he bent over, trying unsuccessfully to breathe, and dropped his weapon to the ice.

I never saw the Maple Leaf that hit me from behind.

Slammed into the boards face first, I saw stars swirling inside the blackness that overcame my sight.

His fist, without the heavy protective mitt, struck once, twice, three, then four times in rapid succession to my right ribcage.

Something cracked.

Pain, agonizing pain, flashed through my chest and back.

Just as four Vipers, a ref, and Coach Hunt dragged the Maple Leaf off me, I sagged to the ice, and collapsed.

***

"You can't play, Aldine," Coach snapped. "You're done. Forget it."

The team's doctor wrapped my cracked ribs in white strapping tape, hampering my breathing. The fire set in my chest and side hadn't subsided by much. Even so, pain didn't hurt unless you let it.

"Try to stop me," I grunted.

Coach rolled his eyes under the uneasy mutters of my teammates. "Planning your vengeance, are you?"

"You know it."

His hands on his hips, Coach Hunt stared at me with speculation. "It'll be the last thing they expect," he said. "Can you wait until the fourth quarter?"

I nodded, running my hand over my ribs.

"Let them think you're out of action," he went on, pacing. "We're four ahead. We play defense. Keep them away from our turf. We don't try to score until after the third ends. Are you sure you can, Aldine? This could put you in the hospital."

I smiled, and Coach Hunt recoiled slightly, blinking. "They'll wish they'd never started that fight."

The Maple Leaf who had busted my ribs was out of the game and may face financial and other penalties for his vicious assault. Felton and his gang were also out of the game, but as both teams fought like dogs, only the worst players were out. The videos clearly showed the Toronto players making the first attack, and Toronto faced harsh penalties for it.

Still, this game must go on.

I sat in the locker room, focusing on pushing my pain aside, practicing deep breathing, all but putting myself into a trance. I half listened to the crowd's roar as the third quarter continued, never hearing the buzzer that indicated a score from either team.

"Aldine, you're up," Coach called.

Time to pay the piper.

Rising, I headed for the rink, passing sympathetic team employees, many of whom slapped my shoulders in encouragement. My pain hadn't died as much as I'd hoped, yet once I started playing, my adrenaline rush would block the pain receptors.

A roar emerged as I skated onto the rink. Boos accompanied the cheers, and several Toronto players eyed me with both surprise and speculation as I took my position. My laser focus on the puck in the ref's hand sent my pain into the stratosphere.

The puck dropped.

I seized it a split second before Felson's replacement spun, and passed it to Devon. He in turn sent it flying past a Maple Leaf, only to have it stolen by another Canadian in a blue jersey. The stands went crazy, drumming the aluminum with their feet.

The Maple Leaf, protected by his teammates, skated fast toward our goalie. Zipping across the ice, I intercepted him, and our sticks clashed. Several Vipers joined the melee surrounding us, blocking the Maple Leafs who sought to push me aside.

Losing the puck, I chased the Maple Leaf. He blasted from the wildly milling group, the puck dancing between strokes of his stick. Edde crouched, ready to intercept it even as more Canadians raced to provide him cover.

The Maple Leaf shot the puck toward our net.

Eddie caught it.

Skating clear of the mob, I collected the puck the goalie sent me, then flew back across the rink. Steve joined me, protecting me as I set my aim on the opposing net. I didn't need to look over my shoulder to know the Maple Leafs pursued me with a red-hot vengeance.

"You got it, bro," Steve yelled.

The Toronto goalie skated to the edge of his turf, determined to stop me by whatever means necessary. I passed the puck to Steve, who feinted right. The goalie turned toward him.

Dodging left, Steve shot the puck in my direction.

Catching it, I fought to keep my possession of it as a Maple Leaf, knowing my current weakness, slammed his fist into my cracked ribs.

Agony exploded through my chest and back.

Coach Hunt screamed something unintelligible, loud enough that I heard him over the crowd's roar.

Steve body slammed the Maple Leaf away from me.

I staggered, fighting to stay upright on my skates and maintain possession of the puck. Ignoring the white-hot pain, the dizziness that came with it, I focused on the Toronto goalie and let my team deal with the opposition. It was just me and him now.

At the very edge of his territory, the goalie readied himself to move in any direction, to stop the puck from getting past him. Behind his protective mask, his eyes narrowed, his attention zeroed in on me, watching my every move.

I hadn't the strength for anything fancy. I needed speed. Rushing toward him at a breakneck pace, I slammed the puck toward the net.

The Maple Leaf goalie dropped to the ice in a dancer's split, stopping the puck with his skate.

The puck rebounded, sliding back toward me.

Retrieving it, I slid it past him with ease, the puck striking the net.

The buzzer sounded.

Someone hit me from behind. My forehead struck the net's frame. Despite my helmet, the impact was stunning.

Under the resounding roar, I went down, my vision blacking out. I hit the ice and unconsciousness pulled me under.

ELLIE

I held his hand.

He lay in a hospital bed that appeared too small for his big body, a bandage wrapped around his head. One of his teammates had told me he had a mild concussion and two bruised ribs, and that Grey would be fine in a day or two.

Seeing him lying there, sleeping, or unconscious, brought me nearly to tears. He looked so helpless despite his obvious strength. No number of assurances that he'd be fine were helpful. Several members of his team had looked in on him as I sat there, surely wondering what my relationship to Grey was.

His eyes blinked, unfocused, staring first straight ahead before he finally turned his head to see me.

"Hi," I hushed.

"Hi back."

I smiled, squeezing his fingers. "How do you feel?"

"Like I've been run over by a Mack truck."

Grey's green eyes suddenly narrowed, fixing on my face. "What are you doing here?"

"I saw the news. No way I wasn't coming to see you and make sure you're okay."

"Ah."

Taking a deep breath, he winced, taking his hand from mine to cradle his chest. "Word will start getting around."

"No one knows anything, except that we're friends."

"Yeah, maybe."

"That's what I tell your guys. You helped me out, we got to be friends."

Grey smiled slightly. "That could work."

"It *is* working. Stop worrying about it."

"Okay."

He fixed his gaze on me again. "I'm glad you're here."

"Me, too."

Of course, we looked at one another as though drinking in the sight of each other's faces, memorizing, as though this would be the last time we ever saw them. It may very well be the last time. If he hadn't been hurt in last night's game, I'd never have approached him. We agreed to walk away.

Still, I couldn't do that until I knew he'd be okay.

We might have continued to stare through the afternoon without speaking, if Colton hadn't walked in.

He glanced between Grey and I, as though he'd caught us doing something improper. As I was no longer holding Grey's hand, and sitting in the chair beside the bed, he couldn't have suspected there was more to our relationship than simple friendship. Grey rescued me. Colton knew it. He'd been told we were friends.

"I didn't expect to see you here, Ellie," he commented, setting the flower arrangement he'd brought on a table.

"Why not?" I glowered, refusing to give up my seat. "Grey saved my ass. I heard about what happened on the news."

Innocent stuff. No reason for Colton to be suspicious. Yet the sharp look he sent me told me he was.

Suspicious.

"She came by to see how I am," Grey added, rubbing his chest. "Thanks for the flowers."

"You bet." Colton perched his hip on the far edge of Grey's bed. "How you are doing, Dad?"

"Sore as hell. Did you leave work to come see me?"

As Colton wore his business suit with the tie yanked loose, I guessed he had.

"There was some stuff I had to deal with," Colton replied. "As soon as I could get away, I came here."

"Glad you did," Grey remarked. "We won last night. Now we're in the playoffs."

"So I heard. That's great, Dad. I also saw that Toronto is getting fined out the wazoo for their behavior. You know, trying to kill you and all."

Grey chuckled, wincing. "They won't learn. Nor will they ever forgive me for showing them up."

Colton grinned. "My dad, MVP yet again. Unbeatable."

"Maybe the powers that be will give me a raise."

"They should." Colton eyed me. "Is there something going on between you two?"

"Like what?" Grey asked, his tone bland.

"I don't know," Colton admitted. "You just seem...cozy with each other."

"He's my friend," I snapped. "He gave me a shoulder to cry on when you kicked my ass to the curb. He kept me safe in the blizzard. Of course I'm gonna be cozy with him."

"Your imagination is running wild," Grey added.

"I don't like you seeing each other," Colton said firmly "Even as friends."

"That's not your decision to make," Grey snapped, glowering. "I'll be friends with Ellie if I so choose."

"Dad, she's my girlfriend," Colton protested. "How's that gonna look to the Viper fans?"

"I'm *not* your girlfriend, dumbass," I growled. "Get over yourself already."

"I told you I'm not giving up on you. I love you."

"That's also not up to you," Grey said. "Ellie told you to kiss her ass, didn't she?"

Colton blinked. "She told you?"

"I *confided* in him, you piece of shit." I shook with the rage I suppressed, due to my being in a hospital room, and forced my voice to remain low. "My prerogative, and none of your fucking business. I'm never going back. Got it? Never."

Colton stood. "It looks like I'm outnumbered here. My dad and my girlfriend joining together to humiliate me."

"You know you did that to yourself," Grey commented dryly. "You think you can treat Ellie the way you did, then expect her to just forgive and forget? Son, you have a shitload of learning to do."

"Do I?" Colton stared first at him, then at me. "Maybe you need to learn, Dad, that Ellie is a treacherous bitch."

I gasped. "You fucker. You slept with Lindy for months while sleeping with me! So who's the treacherous one here?"

"You drove me to it, baby. I hated loving while you lay there like a frigid log."

I couldn't believe what I was hearing. How dare Colton twist everything to blame me for his actions. For an instant, a very brief instant, I knew the sort of rage that led to murder. The soul deep anger and hatred that had if I had a gun in my hand, Colton would be dead. Grey would lose his son, and I would jailed for life.

"Get out," a rough voice said, bringing me back.

Colton glanced at Grey. "What?"

"Get out of here, you victim blaming little shit." Grey had clenched his teeth and appeared ready to fling himself at Colton regardless of his bruised ribs and concussion. "I can't believe you are so *cowardly* that you'd blame Ellie for what you yourself did. Where are your balls? Where's your fucking spine? Get out of my sight, and don't come back."

His body rigid, Colton stared at Grey for a long moment. Without another word, or a backward glance, he stepped out of the room.

The door hissed closed behind him.

I looked down at my hands, shaking all over. Shutting my jaw failed to quell the rolling fury that consumed me. I couldn't think. I couldn't hear much over the roar of my heartbeat in my ears. Most of all, I couldn't look Grey in the eyes.

"I'm sorry," he said gently.

I stood. Through numb lips, I muttered, "I hope you get better soon."

"Ellie..."

If I didn't leave right then, I'd no idea what I might do. Scream, throw his vase of flowers against the wall, or perhaps both. Barely feeling my feet on the floor, I followed on Colton's heels.

"Ellie, wait!"

Ignoring Grey, I walked into the hallway, like Colton, without looking back. Hardly paying attention to where I was going, I strode past patients in hospital johnnies and nurses in colorful scrubs while a speaker overhead played classical music. I arrived at the end of the hall, made the only turn——a right——and discovered I faced a set of double doors that proclaimed in stark lettering, *No Admittance. Authorized Personnel Only.*

I had no idea where I was.

Reversing, I walked back, my head down, passing the nurses' station and nearly colliding with an elderly man pushing his oxygen tank ahead of him.

"'Scuse me." Ducking around him, I saw the sign that read "elevators" with an arrow pointing to the left. Amid doctors staring at charts, a pair of nurses discussing what they planned to do that evening, I looked at the floor while waiting for the elevator to arrive. Once inside, I stepped to the rear, my mind blank, my anger and hurt surging within me like a tsunami on steroids.

The gray afternoon had morphed into dark, windy, and threatening a storm. The bitter cold sliced through my coat with the ease of a hot knife into ice cream. My hair whipping across my eyes, the wind bringing stinging tears, I searched for my piece-of-shit car in the parking lot.

By the time I found it, I shivered from more than just my rage. I drove home on autopilot, hearing Colton's stone-cold voice in my head playing the same song.

You drove me to it, baby love. I hated loving while you lay there like a frigid log.

I couldn't rid my mind of him. Over and over, he spoke, condemning me, justifying his actions, blaming me, crushing my heart under his bootheel. Under the ever-thickening clouds and the heavy wind, I climbed the steps to the apartment I once shared with him, when I believed in fairy tales and was happy.

I didn't turn on the lights.

Still shivering uncontrollably, I changed from jeans and my blouse into a sweatshirt and matching pants. But I couldn't get warm. Opening the fridge, I seized a bottle of wine and took it to the couch. After wrapping myself in a blanket, I sat as the darkness grew, and snow tapped at my windows.

Drinking straight from the bottle, I sat, shivering, unable to think straight. More to the point, I barely thought at all. The wine went down smoothly, and, on my empty stomach, would enter my blood without much of a hindrance. I wanted that. The sweet oblivion of drunkenness, to let myself free fall for the first time in my life.

My cell buzzed from where I tossed it on the table by the door with my keys.

Of course, I ignored it. I had no one in the world. Who'd want to call me?

A few moments later, it beeped, informing me I had a voice message.

Who gives a flying fuck? This is the field where I have sown my fucks. It is barren. I have no more fucks to give.

Full darkness fell. The storm heightened in intensity, the wind screaming around the building. Though my furnace worked, blasting out heat, I still failed to get warm. My shivering eased slightly, but never went away. Watching the snow blow past the window didn't help much.

I have no more fucks to give...

My mind wandered back to that night in a storm not far removed from this one. The bitter cold and howling wind as I trudged into death. My thoughts of human predators who roamed the highways and byways of America. How that thought had scared me.

Not the notion I'd freeze to death.

I wanted to freeze. The slow advance of hypothermia, making me want to just lie down and sleep. To sleep. Sleep...and never wake up.

You just had to rescue me, didn't you? You should have just passed me by. If you had, I'd be blissfully dead. No longer hurting, no longer angry, the pain of this world gone as swiftly as a snowflake in the sun.

I drank the bottle dry. Then I went to the kitchen for another.

My blanket around me, the sweet darkness enfolding me, I longed for what Grey had stolen from me.

An escape from this cold and bitter hell.

Grey

S idelined, I sat in the penalty box watching the Vipers practice. The hospital released me only a few hours ago, and Coach Hunt had picked me up to bring me to the rink. As I'd never pass medical, I sat, fuming, furious, and utterly helpless.

Ellie didn't answer any of my five or six messages, pleading for her to call me. All I received, early this morning, was a brief text.

I'm fine, leave me alone.

Inwardly, I raged at Colton, at his barbaric cruelty and how easily he'd ripped Ellie to shreds. Sure, I knew she still grieved over his loss despite never wanting him back in her life. But to drive the knife so deeply into her heart with such a callous indifference...I swore I didn't know my son at all. Did I *ever* know him? Truly? That kid dressed for the boardroom yesterday wasn't my son. That kid was a stranger, a mask that looked, talked, and moved like Colton. Still, a stranger, nonetheless.

"Hey, man." Steve skated into the penalty box to sit beside me.

I watched Coach race up and down the ice, swearing, ordering, cajoling a better effort from the Vipers, and barely took in anything I saw. Only when Steve nudged me with his shoulder did I look at him.

"You okay?" he asked.

"Yeah. Just sore."

"When do you think the doc will pass you?"

"I'm out for at least a week."

Steve hissed through his teeth. "You're lucky if that's all you're out. Ribs gotta mend."

"I'll treat 'em with kid gloves."

"Ratcliffe, you stupid shit, are you blind?" Coach's bark came, "You let that puck get by you like a goddamn amateur. Pay attention and stop your goddamn daydreaming." He skated past, still yelling at the hapless Ratcliffe.

I felt no amusement at Ratcliffe's bungling, nor did I feel much compassion for him. Still a rookie in many ways, he had much to learn about playing with the pros. He had raw talent, however, and a gift for reading the players' body language. He knew what an opposing skater would do before the guy even did.

"He's good," Steve commented. "He'll go far." Smirking, he nudged me again. "He'll be another Grey Aldine."

"Maybe."

"Hey, that cute chick with you at the hospital...wasn't she the one with you in Boston?"

"Yeah. Colton's ex."

Steve's silence echoed across the rink. I sent him an exasperated glance.

"He dumped her in the middle of nowhere," I went on. "She was walking in that awful cold and wind. Remember?"

"Yeah."

"I missed the plane and had no choice but to bring her along. We're friends. She saw the news and came to see how I was."

"Colton dumped *her*? Just like that?"

"He's an idiot."

"I'd say so. She's a real hottie. And seems very nice, too. We chatted a little at the hospital."

I said nothing else. What happened between Ellie and me wasn't Steve's business. Nor would I want him to know. Steve was a good guy, and gave hell on skates, but he sure loved his gossip. Had I told him I not just slept with Ellie, and was falling deeply in love with her, the entire team would know within hours.

That shit, on top of my worry over Ellie, I did *not* need.

Eventually, Steve clumped back onto the ice, and another Viper sat beside me to rest. More than ever, I needed the focus and concentration on my job, not just to allay my fears, but to work my sore muscles. Sitting like a damn spectator messed with all my sensibilities.

Rising, I strode to the locker room and donned my skates. Wearing no jersey, just my jeans and a sweatshirt, I got out onto the ice.

Naturally, Coach saw me and exploded. "Aldine! What the fuck do you think you're doing? You just got out of the goddamn hospital an hour ago."

"I'm just working my legs, Coach," I replied. "I won't practice, just skate around the perimeter to stay in what shape I can."

My logic worked on him. He sent me a sharp nod, then returned to swearing at a fresh victim. Staying out of the way, I skated leisurely around the outer rim of the rink, half watching the practice while thinking of Ellie. I needed to see her. To hold her. But of course, without a vehicle, and doomed to stay at the rink until practice was over, I couldn't.

She won't answer her door. I already know that. She told me to leave her alone, so that's what I need to do. For a while.

My ribs screeched their annoyance for a short time, then my rushing blood soothed their irritation. As I loosened up, I worked on moves I'd seen figure skaters perform. Like the spin that landed the puck in the net, I dug the tip of my right blade into the ice and swirled cautiously.

Shit! It worked! I tried it again before my blade collapsed under me. Though I had few desires to become a figure skater, swift turns and spins might baffle my opponents, if even for a split second. That instant might be enough to slam the puck into their net.

Shunting Ellie and my worries to the back of my head, I practiced spinning turns as best I could despite the pain, swooping in such a tight circle I grew dizzy, then breaking from the turn to skate faster than a bird flew. I'm nothing if not determined.

Floating backward on only a single skate, I suddenly realized the entire practice had ceased.

Vipers, Coach, assistant coaches, employees, had all paused to stare.

At me.

I drew slowly to a halt. "What?"

"Come on, Twinkle Toes," Coach snapped with disgust. "We're done for today."

***

What do I do about Ellie?

At the moment, there was nothing I could do.

With the dusk came yet another slashing snowstorm. As Coach drove me through the blowing ice, plows with their flashing lights heading the other way, I wondered if we were in for another blizzard.

One-on-one, Coach Hunt dropped his hard ass attitude.

"You did good today," he said. "You impressed even me."

"Thanks. I thought that sharp spins might throw the opposition for a loop."

"It worked against Toronto." He shot me a wide grin, his teeth gleaming green in the dash lights. "The higher ups are going to offer you a new contract at the end of the season."

As I half expected the team owners to drop me, given my age, I felt no little shock at this announcement. "You don't think I'm getting too old for this?"

"Not me. For an old man, you skate rings around the kids. They think they can do what you do." He made a disgusted sound through his teeth. "They'll get hurt. Or worse, kill themselves."

"They'll learn."

"Yeah, right. Look, when you do retire, one day, I hope you'll stay on. Coach the next generation of Vipers."

"Teach them how to skate like a ballerina?"

He snorted laughter. "Yeah. You're gonna set a trend, Grey. Soon, all pro hockey players will learn figure skating just so they can outskate the opposition."

"Some teams demand figure skating exercises."

"Don't tempt me, I might insist on that, too."

"I think the Vipers should start, Coach," I said slowly. "It develops certain habits, muscles we may not use in hockey, enables us to make the ice our own."

He sighed. "I'm old school, you know that. But if you turn the contract down, maybe you'll work for us, and teach those skills."

I gazed out the window at the sheeting snow and ice, thinking of Ellie. If I no longer skated in the limelight, I might be able to court her openly. To let myself fall headlong into love. To have kids again, to maybe marry her. Of course, all that depends on whether Ellie wanted me to love her, wanted to love me back.

Right now, that's not looking too good.

"Jerry is behind us with your car," Coach said as he drove to my house and parked. "Don't drive unless you're off pain meds and clear headed. Got it?"

"Yes, sir." I sent him a quirky grin, then let myself out.

The freezing wind nearly knocked me off my feet as I shut the door and walked toward my car as Jerry pulled into my driveway. I accepted the keys and got in behind the wheel to park it inside my garage. Coach honked briefly as he took Jerry and himself into the screeching storm.

Shivering made my ribs ache with a fierce intensity. I let myself into my house, and belatedly thought of Colton. He hadn't returned to the hospital, nor did he call or text. And it didn't look like he'd come home after work. The kitchen, illuminated only by the light over the stove, showed me only darkness beyond.

Switching lights on, I made a brief search downstairs for him, and decided he hadn't returned to my house. Shrugging, I went back to the kitchen and poured a tumbler of whiskey. The mix of narcotics and alcohol didn't bother me at all. I'd taken both for too many years to let the combo stop me now.

I shed my coat, hung it in the closet, then picked up the TV's remote. I sank with a wince to the sofa, and channel surfed for a time. Selecting an action movie, I relaxed and sipped my drink, my thoughts always on Ellie. How she was. Did I dare try to call her again. Did she truly not want to see me again?

We did agree to walk away from each other.

"I fucked up, didn't I?" a voice said.

I didn't bother to turn around.

"I'll say." I sipped my whiskey.

Still garbed in his day job suit, his blond hair tousled, his eyes bloodshot, Colton ambled into my line of sight. He'd shoved his hands into his trouser pockets, but I noticed the bulge of his clenched fists.

"She won't return my calls. Or my texts," he said.

"You expect her to?"

"How else can I apologize?"

I clicked the mute button on the remote and eyed him. "You don't. You walk away from her; walk away from the damage you've done." My anger at his blatant and icy cruelty rose. "You're an asshole. I saw it for myself. Fuck, I can't believe you said what you did. What were you thinking?"

He shrugged, his eyes on the silent TV. "I wasn't. I got jealous. She's so comfortable around you, but she hates my guts. I guess I wanted to make her hurt for rejecting me, and for not letting me make everything up to her."

I snorted in disbelief. "You're an absolutely stupid and evil little boy. Ellie was in love with you, and all you do is stab her in the heart. The rampant cruelty in which you treat her, I sometimes wonder if you're really my son."

"Oh, I am." A faint smile flicked over his lips, but he still stared at the TV. "I'm just like you. You taught me by example. How to be cruel...how to hate."

"That's bullshit. You got that from your mother."

Colton slowly turned his head to meet my gaze. His expression didn't change, yet his blue eyes hardened like chips of ice. "Don't you dare slander her. Don't you dare.

I loved her and you didn't. She left. You never tried to stop her."

"God," I exploded, standing, ignoring the flash of pain that jabbed me in my ribs. "You'll blame *anyone* except yourself, Colton. You're so quick to point your finger, make accusations without evidence, and never *once* look inside yourself. You're purely innocent, aren't you? The angel. Ever the goddamn victim. You make me sick to just look at you."

His smile, having faded as I yelled, returned with a malicious edge to it. "I do? That's just fine, old man. Just perfect. I'm disowning you. You're no longer my father."

ELLIE

I had to get out.

After two days of sitting in my apartment, working until late, then sitting in the darkness until I grew tired enough to sleep. I tried to not think of either Grey or Colton and ordered myself to get over the hurt. Colton said what he did for the express purpose of hurting me.

Well, he succeeded.

Now I realized I let him have power over me by letting the hurt carry on. No longer. I took my power back by reminding myself that he can only hurt me if I let him.

Sick of my own walls, I donned my coat, a wool scarf, and walked out of my apartment. There was a café with free Wi-Fi only a few blocks down from my building. As the storm a few days ago had more snarl than bite, the sidewalks were mostly clear. What remained reflected back the sunlight and hurt my eyes.

At that time of day, late morning, the café had only a few patrons. The warmth and the scent of coffee greeted me as I stepped in, wiping my boots on the mat inside the door. The barista took my order of a plain coffee and a cherry Danish with a smile. As I waited for my second breakfast, I glanced around the place.

Unwittingly, I met the gaze of a middle-aged, good look-ing guy with gray in his hair, bright blue eyes, and a short-cropped goatee. He offered a quick dip of his chin and a small smile.

I looked away.

Seated at a table where I could watch traffic, I sipped my hot coffee. Not quite hungry, I nibbled on the Danish and wondered why I'd ordered it in the first place. Still, the carbs might help my desolate mood. Or give me a mental boost for my afternoon's work.

"May I join you?" someone asked.

I glanced up to find the cute dude standing near my table. "I'm not looking to get picked up."

He smiled, and sat opposite me, blocking my view of the street. "I'm not looking to pick you up. Name's Frank."

I looked at his outstretched hand, thinking of telling him to fuck off. But there was something in his kind gaze, his sweet smile, that lifted my hand without my permission and took it. "Ellie."

"Nice to meet you, Ellie. How are you this fine morning?"

"Okay."

He tsked. "I don't think so. If you don't mind me saying, you appear mighty down. That's why I came over."

"Do you always approach depressed strangers?"

"Nope. You're a special case, Ellie. I don't know why. I felt the sudden urge to help."

I shrugged. "I don't think you can."

"I'm a good listener."

"I don't want to talk about it."

"Okay, then you listen, and I'll talk." Frank grinned. "I've had my share of heartbreaks. Love bites, doesn't it? One day, you're on top of the world, happy with that special someone, and then——*bam!* Done and gone. You're alone, crying on your friend's shoulder."

"I don't have any friends."

Frank's brows rose. "C'mon. A beautiful gal like you without friends? How can that be?"

"Friends suck. They're almost as bad as boyfriends."

"Talk to me, Ellie. What happened?"

I needed to talk. I guessed a stranger might be as good as anyone to unload to. Frank seemed genuinely kind, interested, compassionate. While it felt strange to share my story with him, there was something about him that made me feel comfortable, even only knowing him for five minutes.

I sipped my coffee and began. "You're right. Love bites. My boyfriend of nearly two years cheated on me with my friend. We were camping when it finally came out, I left in the middle of the night. Started walking."

"In this cold? You could have died."

"I know. I got picked up by my boyfriend's dad. We, um, got together."

Frank whistled, smiling. "You go, girl."

I snorted. "He's old enough to be my father. But I may be falling in love with him. Is that a bad thing?"

"Don't be silly. Take real love where you can get it. So, what happened to him?"

I shrugged, drinking my coffee, and ignoring my Danish. "He landed in the hospital after getting hurt playing against Toronto."

"Playing against Toronto?" Frank's eyes narrowed. "Just who is this dude?"

"Grey Aldine. He plays for the Vermont Vipers."

All but choking, Frank laughed, his eyes dancing. "Now that is one hunk of man. I'd do him in a heartbeat."

I blinked.

Frank laughed again. "I'm gay, sweetie."

His humor and openness brought a smile to my face.

"You're one lucky girl. So what happened? Because if you don't grab him, I'll certainly try."

"Well, I went to see him, but we sort of agreed to part ways. Our age difference, you know. Then my ex showed up." I shut my teeth, looking at my coffee. "He said some things that really hurt. I'm not over him, not all the way. I walked out, away from them both. Now I'm depressed and angry and hurt and have no idea what I should do."

"First things first," Frank said, "are you going to eat that?"

"No." I pushed my Danish toward him.

He munched and spoke with his mouth full. "Okay, girl, first you must look out for yourself. *You* are most important. Get yourself together, do what you need to do. Don't hold these negative emotions inside. Let them out. Scream, exercise, talk to someone."

"I don't have anyone to talk to."

"You do now." He took another bite, crumbs coating his lips. "Negativity drags you down. Do things that make you happy. Stay in touch with your inner self. Don't be afraid to look at yourself in the mirror."

"How do you know all this?"

He smiled. "You see this gray hair? It came from living. In living, you learn, you gain insights. You're young, Ellie, far too young to become a cynical, jaded woman. And I can see that you're too sweet and kind to not find a good dude to love you."

I looked away. "You don't know me. I might be a terrible, awful human being who sets kittens on fire."

"Please." Frank snorted. "I'm a better judge of character than that."

"Maybe I'm a chameleon, like Ted Bundy."

"Nah. He had dead eyes. Yours are bright, filled with life."

Frank's kindness and humor took its toll on me. I couldn't help it.

I smiled, then chuckled. "They do, huh?"

"Yes, they do. Take my advice: Go see your hunky hockey man. Follow the trail that leads you to happiness."

"Maybe."

I drained my coffee. "Your turn. Tell me about you."

Frank and I drank two more cups of coffee, talking as easily as though we'd known one another for years. Perhaps his being gay helped with that. One: I had no worry he had nefarious purposes behind approaching me. Two: I suspected the stories of gay men being more sensitive were true.

"I've been alone for about a year now," he told me. "My boyfriend fell in love with someone else, too. I quit trying to find anyone else after that. At the moment, I'm happy living alone, doing as I please."

"What do you do for work?"

"Oh, I'm retired. I'd built up quite the portfolio of investments, now I live off the interest. I don't travel much. I do a bit of skiing, fishing in the summer, help out at the soup kitchens. I volunteer at nursing homes, read to hospitalized kids."

"No wonder you recognized my depression," I remarked.

"It was really easy to see."

"Your boyfriend must be an idiot to have let you go," I said.

"Same as yours." Frank grinned. "Their loss, right?"

"Exactly."

Taking a pen from his jacket, Frank wrote on a napkin. "This is my number. Call me anytime you need to talk. Okay?"

I accepted the napkin with reluctance. "I don't want to be a pain."

"You're not. I should run. Now, stand up and give me a hug."

Hugging Frank was like the last straw. I melted, my tears streaming down my cheeks. Finding such kindness after floating on a sea of grief and hurt dropped my defenses in an instant. His arms felt as strong and comforting as Grey's, and that made my tears fall faster.

Frank tilted my chin up to meet his gaze. "Call me, Ellie. Anytime."

"I will. Thank you."

***

My newfound friendship with Frank was what helped me get through the next painful and difficult weeks. We talked on the phone. We met at the café. We confided in one another. When the weather cleared enough, we met in parks and walked, holding hands, and we mostly talked. Other times, we held hands, and said nothing at all.

"You're like the big brother I never had," I told him once.

"You're like my baby sister." Frank chuckled. "I do have one. She's married with kids and lives in Maine."

"Why don't you find another guy to love?" I asked him during another walk in the park.

"I'm in no hurry," Frank replied. "I need to find myself, I guess. Just as I suggested you do."

"Seems like you have yourself together."

"Not enough to have a relationship."

Over those weeks, I healed to some extent. Any thoughts of Colton brought anger, hate, grief. Those emotions weren't there because I was over him. Frank helped me to realize they were there because I *wasn't* over him. Only when I could think of Colton with indifference could I say I had moved on.

Grey was yet another matter.

Thoughts of him brought a longing, a yearning to see him again, to just talk to him the way I talked with Frank. To cuddle against his strong chest, to listen to his breathing as he slept. To make sweet, sweet love to him, and hear his voice in the darkness.

"Do you talk to him?" Frank asked me after a month of our friendship.

"A couple of texts," I replied. "Just to say hi, how are you."

"You both still believe the age difference matters?"

"He could lose his career, Frank. Dating, or sleeping with, a twenty-two-year-old could cause a scandal that might end him. I don't want that. I can't be responsible."

"I think society today can handle it," Frank said. "There are worse things Grey can do to irritate people. Falling in love with a young woman isn't one of them."

"His son's ex?" I inquired dryly. "That's a stretch."

"Only if the fans *know* you're the son's ex." Frank eyed me sidelong.

"Too many of his teammates already do."

***

Feeling happy for the first time in quite a while, I hummed as I worked. My clients were pleased with me, and their payments came in as regularly as, well, my periods were. I gained another account, referred to me by a previous client, and had more work than I knew what to do with. My bank account grew slowly, and I paid my rent on time.

Need to start paying Grey back.

When I texted him for his address so I might start sending him monthly checks, he offered it.

Then he added I didn't have to start yet. *Take your time. It's good.*

Thinking fond thoughts of him, I headed for my kitchen to refresh my coffee cup. As I poured, I wondered how he was doing, if he had healed from that fight during the Toronto game. The news spoke highly of him, the Vipers being in the upcoming playoffs, speculation as to whether he'd soon retire.

If he retires, maybe we can see one another again, I thought.

My cup in hand, I started toward my computer with the plan to resume work. I passed the calendar I hung on the wall and gave it a cursory glance. After passing it, I halted, shock and dread sweeping through my veins.

I went back, my mouth suddenly so dry my coffee failed to wet it.

I'd marked my periods over the next several months. The red checkmarks informed me of when my flow would start. I'd always been regular.

Always.

"Oh, God."

I paged back through the calendar, realization dawning. "Oh, God."

In my grief and rage, I hadn't noticed my period hadn't come for the last two months.

Grey

I missed Ellie the way I'd miss my right arm and both legs.

After a particularly brutal practice that left me extremely sore and uncommonly tired, I didn't drive straight home from the rink. Instead, I stopped to down a few drinks at a pub I sometimes frequented.

Okay. More than a few.

In catching the eyes of both bartenders, I suspected the inevitable. Sure enough, the bigger of the two, a young dude with a bald head covered in tats ambled toward me. His bared biceps also held multiple tats. Arms with enough muscle to take me down should I offer a fight.

In my current condition, that was.

"Okay, gramps," he said, his tone genial. "Keys."

I blinked owlishly, pretending I had no idea what he was talking about. "Why?"

"Don't make me the bad guy here. Keys."

"How'm I 's'pose to get home?"

"Taxi, Uber, Lyft, take your pick. I'll even get one here when you're ready to leave."

I sighed, put out, and dug in my pocket for my car keys. "Leave me m'house key."

"Which one is it?"

I pointed out the correct one, and he took it off the ring before slapping it down on the bar.

"Need another round?"

"Sure, as long as y'asked politely."

As he had my credit card number, I'd no need to think about paying my tab while inebriated. He returned with another tumbler of whiskey, set it on the tiny paper napkin. He ignored the sour glance I sent him and left me to serve another patron further down the bar. The place wasn't full, yet it contained enough folks to keep both bartenders fairly busy.

I lifted my tumbler to sip from it when a sharp slap on my back nearly spilled the contents over my chin, my shirt, and the polished bar.

"Grey, you old prick," Devon Chambers exclaimed cheerfully. "How's it hanging?"

Devon, who played defense for the Vipers, sat on the barstool to my right. Nearly as big as I was, he was about eight years younger than me with an odd mix of blond and gray hair. His pale gray eyes took in my bleary state, and his welcoming smile faded.

"You okay, man?"

"Yeah. Just havin' a few."

The big bartender wandered back to take Devon's order. Devon nodded his greeting, and asked for a Bud. The tatted dude left to draw a bottle from the cooler, and returned, setting it in front of him.

"Plan to start a tab?" he asked.

"No." Devon pulled out a few bucks and pushed it across to him. "Keep the change."

Devon turned his attention to me then.

He eyed me again with growing concern. "Dude, you were a monster at practice tonight. What happened since?"

I shrugged and sipped my whiskey. "Dunno. Got too much on m'mind, I guess."

"Drowning your sorrows?"

"Can't. Lil fuckers swim better'n I do."

Devon laughed. "Come on. Tell me what's up."

I hesitated. Devon was no Steve. Steve adored his gossip and spread it faster than an old women's sewing circle. Devon, though, was steady, sharply intelligent, and if any rumors passed his mouth, I never heard of them. Among all the Vipers, coaches, and employees, I'd always liked Devon the best.

"I think I'm in love, man," I finally admitted.

"No shit?" Devon leaned his elbows on the bar, then took a pull from the bottle. "Is this a celebration, then?"

"She's twenty-two."

"Okaaay…" Devon drew the word out. "Big age differ-ence, but no biggie. It's not like you're sweet on a fif-teen-year-old."

I grimaced. "Gross, man. I ain't no ped."

"So what's the problem? She don't love you back?"

"She's Colton's ex."

Devon hissed through his teeth. "Ouch."

"Yeah."

He took a long thoughtful pull on his beer, then said, "If they're broken up, I still say there's no problem. She's free to do what she wants, yeah? Does she love you in return?"

"Dunno. We sorta agreed I'm too old for her."

"So instead of talking to her, you're sitting here drinking yourself under the table."

"I love 'er, man."

"Then talk to her, you dumb shit. Explore the possibilities. See how she feels. Lay it on the line. Grow a spine."

"And if the papers find out?" I eyed him sidelong through my blurry eyes. "I'm toast."

Devon shook his head. "How many more years do you have, bro? I mean, I don't want to shortchange you, but you're a year or two away from retirement. You won't be able to compete with the kids for much longer."

I nodded. "Owners plan to offer a new contract."

"Will you accept?"

"Dunno."

"No doubt about it," he went on, "you'd have a second career as a coach. Write your own ticket, go anywhere you want."

"'Cept Toronto."

Devon laughed. "They'd take you in a heartbeat, bro. You're too good for them to hold a grudge."

I half shrugged, half nodded, too drunk at the moment to consider a new career. My mind wandered to Ellie. I thought blearily about what she was doing at that very moment. Sleeping, most likely. I pictured her perfect face as she dreamed, her dark hair with the goofy streak of purple tangled as it spread over her pillow.

I gulped my whiskey, coughed as it burned its way down my throat and into my belly. "Christ."

"You're gonna have one helluva hangover tomorrow," Devon observed. "Good thing it's Sunday. No practice."

I nodded, not really caring if we had practice tomorrow or not. All I wanted was Ellie, to see her again, to kiss her, to hold her in my arms. I didn't even need her naked in my bed. Her lovely cheek pressed against my chest, her arms around my waist, was good enough.

"You obviously can't drive," Devon commented.

I stared at my housekey still sitting on the bar where the big dude left it. "Nope. Took my fucking keys."

"As they should. Look, I'll drive you home. If you're ready to go."

"S'pose."

As though he'd heard our conversation, the bartender wandered over to say, "We don't open till two tomorrow. If you swear an oath you'll drive him, you can have his keys now."

"Don't worry," Devon assured him as I shakily stood with his hand under my arm, "he won't be driving tonight."

The bartender handed Devon my keys. "I'm watching you, man. If I see him getting behind the wheel, I'll sic cops on him faster than a possum eats a tick. Got it?"

"Yep."

Unable to control my legs, since they wanted to amble in opposite directions, I staggered against Devon. He held me upright, his effortless good nature halting him from making any snide comments. Past the pub's doors, the sharp Vermont winter wind cut into my exposed flesh as quickly as a razor blade. The cold set my teeth to chattering like castanets.

"Over here," Devon said, guiding me toward his jet-black Toyota Tundra. "You'll warm up quick enough."

His truck failed in that regard. Even as the heat blasted from the vents, I slumped against the door, shivering. Devon shot me concerned glances as he drove through the nearly deserted streets.

"No hurling, bro," he warned me. "You think you're gonna, give me warning so I can pull over."

"Not gonna hurl."

"Better not. I'm not cleaning up your mess, or living with the stink."

"Not hurling," I murmured, drifting to sleep.

I woke with a jolt as Devon stopped the truck in front of my house. I stared blankly at the unlit windows, recalling that Colton had moved out weeks ago. He currently couch surfed with anyone who'd take him in, but a few rumors had reached me. Colton's immature behavior and bitter complaints left him with few friends to leech off.

"C'mon, bro." Devon slipped his strong hand under my armpit. "Where's your key?"

Hoping I put it in my pocket and not left it on the bar, I feebly searched my pockets.

Devon snorted in exasperation and stuck his hand into my front jeans pocket. "Don't get excited. I'm not feeling you up."

"Oh, baby."

Retrieving my key, he led me, staggering, up to my front door. After unlocking and swinging it open, he assisted me inside. He flicked on a light switch, then dragged me to my couch. Dumping me on it, he shoved me onto my back before picking up my legs.

"Sober up," he said, pulling my boots off. "I'll come by tomorrow and give you a lift to get your car."

"Thanks, man. 'Preciate it."

"You owe me."

"Yup."

Drifting to sleep again, I vaguely felt him cover me with a blanket. He said something else, but what it was I'd no idea. It may have been *Good night* or *see you tomorrow*. Either way, I never heard him leave my house.

***

I woke once in the darkness to make a staggering run to the kitchen. No way could I make it to the bathroom down the hall. Reaching the sink a fraction of a second before I barfed a volcanic mixture of whiskey and bile, I coughed and gagged, retching again and again until my belly surrendered all its contents.

Then I hurled a few more times for good measure.

Panting, I rinsed my mouth, and ran water through the sink to wash my puke away. Devon was far from wrong about the hangover. My head throbbed as though I'd received a second concussion. My stomach ached from vomiting, and all my muscles trembled with a violence I was helpless to stop.

Reaching the sofa, I laid back down, and tried to wrap sleep around me. No such luck though. Vertigo swept me into its embrace, making me think I'd hurl again. I heard a distant moan slip through my shut teeth. I felt sorry for myself.

Shit, what a loser you are.

"I'm never drinking again," I muttered.

I wondered if I lied.

I suppose it was a promise I didn't mean to keep. Would not keep. Like the promises to God under dire circumstances.

If you let me survive this, I swear I'll go to church twice a day, God.

I wouldn't go that far, but a long break from the whiskey bottle might certainly be in order.

I only dozed a bit through the rest of the night, coming fully awake at around eight. My sore muscles had stiffened, and I groaned as I sat up. Holding my head in my hands, I pondered a shower. Or the hair of the dog. Or both.

"Shower first." I stood, my stomach roiling in protest.

My head thudded as though a herd of wild horses galloped through it, but I discovered I could walk in a fairly straight line. I reached the hallway entrance when I heard a faint ding. Puzzled for a moment, I wondered what had made that sound.

Shit. It's my cell.

I found my phone still in my pocket. Pulling it out, I glanced at the screen, half thinking Devon had texted to tell me he was on his way to pick me up. No. It wasn't Devon who shot me a text.

Ellie had.

I read her brief and succinct message.

The strength went out of my knees.

I read it twice more, shocked disbelief forcing the wild horses in my head to halt. My hangover forgotten, I couldn't think of a single thing to text her in reply. What do I say? What *could* I say?

"Holy shit."

I read her message yet again.

I'm pregnant.

ELLIE

I didn't want to answer my door.

I knew Grey stood on the far side, banging his fist against the wood. Nausea churned my stomach with a dreadful mixture of terror and morning sickness. I couldn't face him. He'd sent no reply to my text. For a while, I thought he planned to ignore me and my delicate condition.

Would he take responsibility? Did he plan to yell at me for being careless and declare he wanted nothing to do with either of us?

I would if I were him. Hockey stars sure didn't need the scandal of impregnating a girl half his age. He'll throw money at me, then I'll never hear from him again.

The fist hit my door again.

"Open up, Ellie," Grey thundered. "We have to talk."

My legs shook as I walked slowly to the door. My mouth dry, my heart pounding, sweat running in swift rivulets down my ribs, I reached for the doorknob. In slow motion, I unlocked it, then turned the knob. At first, I stared at his coat, unzipped to reveal a plain gray sweatshirt under it, then gradually lifted my gaze to his face.

Grey looked horrible.

His bloodshot eyes, his lack of a decent shave and his slack cheeks spoke of either a desperate illness or a wicked hangover. I suspected the latter as Grey was too strong to get sick. Too *healthy*. He reminded me of the time Colton drank so much he missed the porcelain god when he hurled, and I had to clean the mess off the bathroom floor.

"Ellie," Grey exhaled.

I tried a wobbly smile. "Hello."

Instantly, he yanked me into his arms, holding me against his hard chest and flat stomach with enough strength to make my spine creak in protest. My breathing hitched as he squashed my lungs, but I reached around his waist to hold him just as tightly.

Spots danced behind my closed eyes reminding me I needed to breathe. I struggled from his grip and stepped back. I tried to smile again, but I knew it didn't work very well. Grey didn't smile back.

"Let's go inside," I mumbled.

He followed me into my apartment, then gently pushed me toward my couch with his hand at the small of my back. Obedient, I sat, my fears preparing me for the inevitable.

I'm already a dad, Ellie. I don't want more kids. I'll pay for the abortion...

"I'm not having an abortion," I said as he sat beside me and took my hand.

Grey's eyes widened even as he scowled. "Of course not, Ellie. That's not why I'm here."

"You want to know if you're the father."

"Yeah. I think I have the right to know, don't I?"

I sucked in a deep breath. "Grey...I don't know. It's either yours or Colton's. You won't insist on an abortion if the baby is his?"

"Don't be ridiculous." Grey slipped his arm around my shoulders.

I breathed in the faint odors of whiskey and something else, hoping the baby was indeed his. "I sure don't want Colton to be the father."

"He'd take care of you."

I snorted against his shirt. "Yeah, right. He can't take care of himself, much less a child."

Grey gently massaged my shoulder. "Look, Ellie, I can't tell you what to do. It's your life, all the way. If you change your mind about an abortion——"

"I won't."

"Then, I'm beside you all the way."

I met his startlingly green eyes. "Even if the baby is his?"

"Yeah." He smiled. "I've missed you too much, Ellie. I'm falling in love with you."

I settled my cheek against his chest. "I've missed you, too. I want this baby to be yours, Grey. But we agreed to not see each other."

"I know. And I don't care. Scandals, bullshit. I don't have to work anymore, not if I don't want to. I can get a job as a coach if I'm drummed off the team."

Caressing his chest, I murmured, "Even a coach isn't immune from disgrace. If this gets out, you may never work anywhere in the NHL again."

"I think you're over thinking this. This is the twenty-first century. Our ages be damned. I can fall in love and have a kid again. Even two kids. Or three."

"It's also the age of cancel culture," I replied. "Too many folks out there make attacks on celebrities for the smallest of alleged infractions. Behind the safety of their screens, they can make your life miserable."

"And there are just as many who think the opposite," he said, his breath warm on my cheek. "People who'll stand by me, the team, you. Right now, all I'm concerned with is you." He stroked his hand down my still flat stomach. "And the little one in here."

Comforted by not just his words, but his sheer strength, his fearlessness in the face of potential dire retribution, I sighed deeply. "I was afraid you'd run in the other direction."

"I'm hurt. How can you think so little of me?"

"Sorry. I've been so scared since I found out. Being afraid doesn't help me to think straight."

"How long have you known?"

"I peed on the stick yesterday," I replied. "It's positive."

"We should get you to a doctor," Grey murmured. "Start you on a plan of eating right. No booze, no caffeine, all that shit."

"Jeez, you're no fun."

"Sucks to be you. Maybe you should move in with me."

I sat up and jerked out of his arms. "Slow down, tiger. I'm not ready for that. I've missed you, and I think I'm in love with you, too, but there's a line I'm not ready to cross. Besides, Colton lives with you."

"Not anymore. He moved out weeks ago." Grey frowned. "I still plan to take care of your bills. I know you don't have insurance."

Standing, I paced, restless, not happy with that proposition, either.

"I can pay some of it," I said slowly, "I can work harder, earn extra. If we go to places like Planned Parenthood, get a midwife instead of a hospital, give birth at home, we may not have to pay that much."

"You've been thinking about this a lot, haven't you?"

"Nothing else to do when I didn't sleep all night."

Grey nodded thoughtfully, looking down at the worn carpet I paced. "I'm pretty well off, you know. You don't have to pay a penny."

"Do you know how much it costs to have a kid these days?" I demanded. "I do. I looked it up. A hundred grand, if not more."

"I guess we have time to argue about it," he said slowly. "I want you to move in with me. I want to look after you."

"That's not happening," I said stiffly. "Colton is still an issue, our relationship is an even bigger one. And I don't need looking after. I can take care of myself."

"Colton isn't a part of this."

"He is if I'm carrying his child."

Abruptly, Grey stood, pacing to the picture window just as Colton had all those weeks ago, standing with his back to me. "I know I'm the father."

"I hope you are."

"If I'm not, what then?"

I sank to the sofa and put my face in my hands.

Through my muffling, I said, "He'll have to be a part of the kid's life. I'll accept child support from him. I will *not* marry him, however."

"He says he still loves you."

Throwing my hair behind my shoulders, I snapped, "I don't care. He can take that love and shove it. Had he not done what he did, we wouldn't be having this discussion. The baby would be his, you a soon to be proud grandpa."

Grey turned, his eyes hollowed and his hands stuffed into his jeans pockets. "When was the last time you...and he..."

I wanted to smack him so badly my palms itched. "None of your business."

"It is actually. If you and Colton last had sex long before you and I——"

"Let's just say the fastest little sperm won," I growled. "Yours or his, I don't know. We may not know until after the kid is born."

"Why are you angry with me?"

"Because I can be," I snapped. "I'm scared, dammit. I have no one in the world to turn to, I'm pregnant and I don't know who the father is, and I certainly can't trust one potential father."

"I hope you mean Colton." Grey's eyes flashed with his own irritation.

"Yeah, I do." I turned to stride angrily toward my kitchen. "But that doesn't mean I'm entirely trusting you, either. Don't they say like father like son?"

Grey stalked toward me, his expression dark. "That's not fair. I'm here aren't I?"

"For how long? You talk pretty words, but can you walk the walk? What if you decide the kid is Colton's, then discover you don't owe me shit? You had your fun, now it's time to move on? Truth be told, I don't know you all that well. Not really."

"You know enough," he said, looming over me. "I'm not turning my back on you, or that baby."

"And what happens to your career?" I scowled; my arms folded under my breasts. "If you're tanked because of me and the baby, how long before you blame us for your ruined life?"

"That won't happen. I take responsibility for my actions. You know that."

"I don't. Not really."

Grey scrubbed his face with his hands, his bristles making a raspy sound from under them.

"My job has risks," he said, his tone low. "I could be benched for an injury at any time. Keeping that notion in mind, I saved money, put it into rock solid investments. I didn't blow my wad on high powered cars, beach houses, hookers. You see? You *can't* ruin my career, Ellie.

"Once my contract ends after this season, I can walk away. Just stop playing. Retire. What the internet says about me, us, won't matter then, will it? The fans will get over it, find another hero to worship. In a couple of years, I'll be a distant memory."

My anger drifted away like blown dandelion fluff on a stiff breeze.

"I suppose that's all true," I murmured, looking at the stained tiles on the floor. "That doesn't resolve what's between you and me."

"Time will do that. Just give me a chance to prove myself."

"And Colton?"

Grey sighed heavily. "The baby is of my blood, Colton's or mine. I'll raise the baby as I would my own. If Colton wants a part of the baby's life, we can work that out." He paused.

I looked up in time to see his faint smile.

"So what if the kid has two dads? These days, lots of kids do," he said. "Or two moms. He, or she, won't lack for love and attention."

I shook my head, unable to deny that Colton might grow up enough to become a decent dad and share parental responsibilities with Grey. If the baby was his after all, that was. Of course, if Grey and I love one another enough to marry, live together, plan a future...

"I need time," I said.

"For what?"

I met his puzzled gaze. "To know if this is real. To know if what I'm feeling, and what you're feeling is the real deal."

"I think it is," he said quietly. "On my part."

"You're ready to marry me, to spend the rest of your life with me?" When he hesitated, I laughed. "See? No. You're not. Nor am I. You know we both need time."

"I need to see you," he muttered. "You can't shut me out."

No. I can't. I need to see you too.

"Yeah," I said slowly. "I suppose we do need one another. At least for now."

Grey eyed me with suspicion. "For now?"

"Until we fall in love, or we don't." I smiled sardonically. "If we don't, then it's *sayonara*...have a good life."

Grey

"**S**he said she wouldn't shut me out."

Angry, inpatient, even scared, I paced the locker room after practice, trying to get Ellie to answer her cell. She ignored my voicemails and texts, not replying to either one. While I agreed to give her time, *she* agreed we needed to see one another.

So where did this agreement go wrong?

My fear growing, I shoved my phone into my coat pocket, and stalked naked into the showers. As I lathered my body to wash the stink of my sweat off, I considered going over to Ellie's apartment and banging on her door. The hour was late, but I knew she worked her freelance job until eleven or midnight.

She'll be pissed if I do that right now. I'll see her in the morning.

"Dude," someone snickered.

I glanced over at the occupant of the next shower to find Devon grinning at me.

"How's things with the 'lil lady?" he asked.

I growled under my breath, looking around for anyone close enough to overhear. "Use a bullhorn next time."

"Oh. Sorry."

"You know how these assholes gossip."

Devon grimaced. "Yeah. Is everything okay? You look up-tight."

After another glance around for eavesdroppers, I said, fast and low, "She's pregnant."

Busy washing his face, Devon sputtered soap from his lips and blinked. By his sharp yelp of pain, he got some in both eyes.

He rinsed quickly, then squinted at me. "Holy God. Are you okay with that?"

"Yeah, if it's mine."

"Jesus."

He continued to scrub while I shut my spray off and began to towel dry. Leaving the showers, I wrapped the towel around my waist, then fetched my street clothes from my locker.

As I dressed, Devon joined me, as his locker was opposite mine, and murmured, "Want to have a quick drink?"

I nodded without turning. "Yeah. I could use an ear."

"Fortunately, I've got two."

At the same pub, served by the same bartender, we both ordered beer. Over the bottles, I told him about Ellie, Colton, and which of us might be the baby's dad.

Devon listened with incredulity and a whole lot of sympathy. "I guess Colton doesn't know?"

"No, unless Ellie told him. I doubt it since she can't stand him."

"And you both, er, had sex around the same time?"

I moodily drank from my bottle. "Sounds like it."

"Sorry, bro, but this is a fucked-up mess. You have to figure out who the dad is."

"How do I do that? I'm shooting a full load, and I'm sure Colton is too.

Devon drank, then put his bottle down to signal the bartender for another round. Neither of us spoke until the big, tatted guy dropped fresh bottles on little napkins, took our money and departed.

At last, Devon shrugged. "Keep it simple then, bro."

"By doing what?"

"Claim the baby's yours no matter what. Be its dad. Don't let Colton even *think* there's a possibility he might have skin in this game."

I swallowed my fresh beer, thinking. "That isn't a bad idea. If Ellie is willing to go along with it that is."

"If the baby has dark hair, he's yours for sure. Blond, maybe Colton's." Devon grinned. "Genetics are funny things, ain't they?"

"Ellie doesn't know her parents," I said. "One may have been blond."

"How interesting is that?"

"Handy excuse for a blond kid." I grinned.

"I can see it now." Devon waved his hand gracefully in the air. "You invite me to the wedding, you and Miss Ellie tie the knot, have more babies, name one after me."

I laughed. "It takes two to tango, son. First, I have to get Ellie to agree to marry me. Right now, she won't even move into my house."

"Independent 'lil thang, ain't she?"

"You have no idea."

"I can't wait to meet her." He eyed me over his bottle. "I will meet her, yeah?"

"You know it, brother. Right now, I can't even get her on the phone."

"Women are more mysterious than God," he observed. "Let her have some space. She probably with girlfriends oohing and ahhing over the pregnancy."

"She doesn't have any girlfriends."

"No? That's weird. All girls have girlfriends."

"She ended hers when Colton slept with her friend."

"Yikes. That had to hurt."

"It did."

I told him of finding Ellie walking along the road in mid-winter with a blizzard headed in our direction, the cold well past zero. Devon gaped, choked on his beer, then coughed into his fist. His eyes wide, he stared hard into mine.

"Ellie isn't that hot chica with the purple streak that was outside our locker rooms in Boston? Is she?"

"The very same."

"She's hotter than a habanero, bro. What was Colton thinking?"

"He wasn't." I drank my beer in a long swallow. "At least not with his brain. Maybe he was thinking with his mini me."

"I talked with her at the hospital, too," Devon went on. "All I knew was she's Colton's lady. She seemed very nice, intelligent, articulate, sweet. I saw what you must see in her."

"Yeah." I set my bottle down. "She's all that and more. Funny, brave, and scared at the same time, kind, smart as a whip." I sighed. "And as independent as fuck."

Devon chuckled and clapped his heavy hand on my shoulder. "Tough gals are the best, bro. Don't let her get away. I know you'll regret it for the rest of your life if you do."

"If she doesn't love me, I won't have much choice. I'll have to let her go."

"Don't give up, man. You love her. Ellie will see that, give it back tenfold. Have faith."

"An expert, are you?"

He snorted. "Hardly. Girls scare me, man. If a gal said she loved me, I'd head for Canada."

***

"What's this fucking ass bullshit?" I growled.

Under gray and dreary clouds, light snow swirling in delicate, ghostly tendrils, I stopped my car in Ellie's building's parking lot. Determined to talk to her, I drove to her apartment. It was late morning, I thought I would take her to an early lunch...

Only to find her smiling cheerfully at a tall good-looking dude who appeared close to my age, then she hugged him. They shared a quick kiss on the cheek, a laugh, then proceeded across the lot to his car. He opened the door for her and walked around the hood to get in behind the wheel.

A myriad of horrible thoughts raced through my mind. Ellie already had herself another guy. She'd been two-timing both Colton and me. Did she lie about the pregnancy? Was the baby this dude's after all?

Confused, hurt, jealous, and growing angrier with every passing second, I jerked the shifter into drive, and followed them from the lot. It's easy to say I saw red. Truth is, I barely saw anything at all. Not the road, the traffic, pedestrians in danger of me hitting them. Amidst the phantom snowflakes that melted the instant they hit my windshield; I saw only his car.

He drove to a small diner about six blocks from Ellie's apartment. Had he driven further, I suspected I'd have never made it. I'd certainly have smashed my car into another, or worse, hit a kid crossing the street. The old cliché of being blinded by rage had a powerful element of truth to it.

I saw little except Ellie and the man she was with.

I parked in the diner's lot, and saw them enter while holding hands. A low, animal-like growl rose in my throat and slid through my clenched teeth.

How dare she fuck around. How could she say she could fall in love with me while seeing this asshole on the side? I thought I knew you, Ellie.

I guess I don't know her at all.

Locking my car, I followed them into the diner. Sucking in deep breaths helped me to control my fury, to not plunge my fist through the entrance's glass, or the dude's face. I stepped inside the restaurant, scenting the odors of frying bacon, coffee and maple syrup. I unzipped my coat, glancing around at the diners, the waitresses.

Still fighting to maintain a level of cool, I found them at a booth across the diner. The dude still stood, busy removing his coat before sitting opposite Ellie. My fists clenched, not knowing what I planned to say or do, I stalked across the diner.

Mid-smile, Ellie glanced up as I loomed over the booth. "Grey? What are you doing here?"

I observed the sharp lack of guilt in her open expression. Her utter lack of guile, her beautiful blue eyes wide with warmth, sincerity and...innocence. Taken aback for a split second, I glanced at the dude.

He smiled up at me, then scooted from the booth to stand. "Hi, it's a pleasure to meet you, Grey. I'm Frank."

I stared at his extended hand as though he held a venomous snake in it. "Is it, asshole?"

Frank blinked. "What?"

The low growl returned to my voice. "You heard me."

"Grey!" Ellie said sharply. "That's rude. Frank's being nice."

I turned my head slowly to look down at her, my fists shoved into my coat pockets. Making certain I didn't lash out or do something I'd really regret later.

"You cheating on me, Ellie?" I snapped. "You fucking this guy?"

My question slash accusation startled her into a slight recoil. "What are you talking about? Frank's my friend."

"Friends with benefits, *right?*"

Frank slid back into the booth, laughing under his breath. "I like this guy, Ellie. So he-man."

I controlled my fists with a powerful effort as Ellie's lips thinned in anger, her face blushing a furious red. She stared up at me in defiance, and still no guilt. Having been caught red-handed with the dude she fucked behind my back, I thought I'd see *some* kind of remorse, or even defensiveness.

Ellie displayed none of that.

"Sit down," she hissed. "You're making a scene."

"Sit with the girl who's two-timing me? Join you and your squeeze like nothing is going on? Are you shitting me, Ellie?"

Frank laughed again. "You're really making a mistake, man. I'm not sleeping with Ellie."

"We're friends, dammit," Ellie snapped. "We met about a month ago, he's someone I can talk to. And I really needed a friend, Grey."

"Why haven't you been returning my calls then?"

She swiped her hair back in irritation. "I told you I needed some space. Time to think. And a chance to talk to Frank about things I can't talk to you about."

"Oh?" I eyed Frank and his amusement with a hostility I knew would soon slip from my control. "Like what, Ellie? Are you comparing our bedroom techniques?"

"For God's sake, sit down." Ellie seized my sleeve to pull until I must either lose my coat or sit beside her.

As a waitress hovered nearby with a full coffee pot, watching, I opted to sit down. She advanced on us, pouring coffee into cups while watching my face carefully. Maybe she was a fan. Or she recognized the rage I barely kept in check.

All the while, Frank looked at me with a combination of amusement and resignation. "You really are making a mistake, big guy."

"I don't think so."

The waitress departed after leaving menus, leaving me to face my rival. Ellie snorted behind her folded hands, her fingers hiding her eyes. I glanced from her to Frank then back.

"Look, man," Frank said, his tone low. "Ellie isn't my type. You are."

ELLIE

T he rage leached from Grey's face like water seeping from a hole in a cup.

"What?" he croaked.

Frank grinned. "I'm gay. I find you far more attractive than I do Ellie. Sorry to disappoint, but she and I are not screwing each other."

Grey's Adam's apple bobbed as he swallowed hard. "Oh...I see." His eyes flicked to me briefly. "I, er..."

"Owe us both a sincere apology," I snapped. "I hope you're feeling really stupid right now."

"You really are gay?" he asked Frank.

Frank rolled his eyes. "Take me to bed and find out. Look, I get the jealousy part, I do. If I saw my boyfriend hanging with another dude, I might react the same way."

"You better not be homophobic," I warned Grey, catching his gaze. "If you are, you can get the hell out of here right now."

For the first time, Grey smiled, looking both ashamed and amused. "I'm not. I don't get all pissed and defensive if a dude makes a pass at me. You two just caught me out, that's all."

"I *am* tempted to make a pass at you," Frank commented. "But I do not want to make Ellie mad."

"Are you gonna apologize or not?" I demanded, not mollified enough.

Grey held his hand out to Frank, who shook it. "I'm sorry I busted in here hot. Not being able to get a hold of Ellie, then seeing you together, I thought...bad things."

"Sure," I grumbled. "Victim blame."

Grey leaned toward me to plant a kiss to my mouth. "You're so cute when you're mad."

I shoved him away, unable to stay mad at him any longer. "You're buying breakfast, you toad."

"I sure am. So, what's the big secret you can't talk to me about?" I met Frank's kind blue eyes.

"Go on," he said. "Just tell him."

I sighed. "I hadn't had a chance to tell Frank I'm pregnant until a short while ago. I wanted to talk to him so I could sort through my feelings." I looked into Grey's green gaze. "I'm...falling in love with you."

Frank slapped his palm on the table. "See? Now that wasn't so hard. Let's talk about the baby. How far along are you?"

Grey chuckled. "So, why couldn't you talk to me? I thought I was a good listener."

"You are." I scraped my hair back. "I'm still scared, Grey. Not knowing who the baby's father is, what I'm going to do, what happens when Colton finds out."

"He's bound to, you know," Frank added.

"Yeah." Grey took my hand under the table. "I suppose he is. Has he called you?"

"All the damn time." I snorted. "I don't answer him. I bet it's pissing him off."

"Probably," Grey agreed. "You need to be checked out by a doctor, Ellie."

"I know."

"After breakfast?"

"I guess so," I replied with another sigh. "If I can get in without an appointment."

The waitress returned to take our orders. We each quickly scanned the menus, made rapid decisions, and handed the menus back. After she departed, none of us said anything for what seemed like a long time. I caught Grey and Frank looking at one another as though seizing each other up before the fistfight.

My alarm grew.

Then, without warning, Frank winked at Grey.

Grey laughed.

"You know," Frank commented, "you should try me, sweet buns. You might find out you like it."

"That's what I'm afraid of," Grey replied. He eyed me sidelong. "Then I might not go back to Ellie's delectable body."

Blushing, my face hot, I looked around for anyone close enough to hear.

"Knock it off," I hissed. "We're in public."

"We could have a threesome," Frank said, much too loud for my comfort. "You satisfy Ellie while I satisfy you."

"Don't tempt me," Grey chuckled.

I covered my face with my hands. "Stoppit!"

Both idiots laughed like hyenas.

I scowled at each of them in turn. "Don't I have a say in this? No threesome. That's it, end of discussion."

I did my best to ignore them as they started talking hockey and speculations regarding the baby. Outside the big window that faced the street, the snowfall had thickened, coming down in sheets rather than swirling eddies. I briefly worried about another blizzard, the power going out, and this time no Grey to hold me through my fears.

He'll be there if I need him.

As he talked of the upcoming playoffs, the hope the Vipers get a chance at the Stanley Cup, I watched Grey's profile. I loved the play of his skin over his cheekbones and jawline, his animated grin, the way his shaggy hair tumbled to his shoulders like black silk. If we hadn't been in public, I would have dragged my fingers through that hair, kissed his sensual lips, and hauled him off to bed.

I am falling in love. His anger, his jealousy, tells me more about his feelings than any words. Can we have a future together? I caressed my stomach under my sweater. *I'll never be free of Colton if he's the father. Please, God, if you're there, let this baby be Grey's.*

***

"You're approximately eight weeks along," Janet, the nurse practitioner informed us. "Congratulations."

I held Grey's hand as she wiped the ultrasound lubricant from my bared belly. "Can you tell the baby's gender?"

"Sorry, no, not for a while yet. Do you want pictures?"

Grey grinned. "Yes, please."

Janet tore off the printed version of the baby inside me, not much more than gray and black blots. She traced a light circle around the fetus, which didn't look much like a baby to me. Grey folded it carefully and put the paper in his wallet.

"I'm going to give you a folder, Ellie," Janet continued as I sat up. "All the dos and don'ts you need to follow. You don't smoke, do you?"

"No."

"Good. Stay away from secondhand smoke as much as possible. Watch your alcohol and caffeine intake, no recreational drugs. You don't do meth, coke, or heroin, right?"

"Never."

"Most excellent. Eat plenty, don't worry about weight gain, you're young and slender, you'll drop the baby weight in no time. Do you have any questions?"

"When should I come back?"

"Once a month, honey, make an appointment with the receptionist. If you have any concerns, call right away. Agreed?"

"Yes, ma'am."

Janet smiled and patted my arm. "Your baby is healthy, Ellie. But don't hesitate to call if you feel there's a problem."

I liked Janet, liked her kind way of making me feel comfortable. If she recognized Grey, she made no comment. Nor did she appear to judge our difference in ages. I suspected that here at Planned Parenthood, she'd seen it all. She shook my hand, then Grey's while smiling warmly.

"The snow's really coming down," she commented, leading the way from the clinic's exam room. "You be careful out there."

Nor was she kidding. In the time since we'd arrived and now departed, the storm had dropped at least two inches. With threatening skies above, I expected more snow to follow.

I gripped Grey's hand as we crossed the parking lot to his car. "I guess you'll drop me off at my place then go to practice?"

Grey opened the car door for me, snow sliding from the window to plop onto his boots. "Didn't you hear? Hell froze over."

I sent him a quizzical glance and observed his grin.

"Practice is cancelled due to the storm," he explained. "City authorities are insisting people stay off the streets."

"This is Vermont," I commented as he shut the door to walk around the car to his side. I finished as he climbed in. "Snow is like the best thing ever around here."

"Not when the plows can't keep up. What we're having here is a fairly hard winter."

And Grey wasn't wrong. Traffic had become nearly nonexistent as he maneuvered the car through the rapidly falling snow. Despite the all-wheel drive, snow tires, and Grey's knowledgeable driving, we nearly got stuck twice. I held my breath, fearing the car would slide into a telephone pole and crush me.

We made it back to my apartment, thankfully. Grey walked me up to my place, and as I was searching my mind for the words to invite him to stay without sounding scared and needy, he said, "I think I should stay over. I'll sleep on the couch, though."

Seizing his coat's collar, I pulled him inside with me and slammed the door closed. "No. You won't."

Bending, Grey settled his mouth over mine in a long, promising and passionate kiss. "I was hoping I'd sleep in the bed with you."

Fixing us a quick dinner of pork chops, baked potatoes, and green beans wasn't easy. Grey hooked his arms around my waist, nibbled on my neck while I tried to bake the chops. Of course, his antics aroused me, my crotch warming as my imagination roamed to bed sports.

"We need to eat," I insisted, "in case the lights go out."

"I am eating," he murmured while nipping my neck.

"I meant food, dummy."

"You are delicious, my love."

Laughing, I shoved him away. "Set the table, Romeo."

We ate dinner without saying much, smiling at one another across the table. Outside, the wind whipped up the snow in an ominous howl, blowing past my windows. Yet, inside, we were warm, fed, and safe. We washed the dishes together in domestic harmony, then sat on the couch with our arms around each other.

I lit a candle and shut the lights off.

"Is this romantic or what?" I murmured, happy and content.

"Sure is," he replied. "What flavor are you hoping for? Boy or girl?"

"I don't know. I haven't really thought about that."

"Me, I'd like another son. I know I'd spoil a daughter," Grey chuckled.

"You'll make a great dad either way."

"Maybe. I didn't do such a great job with Colton."

I peered into his face in the faint light. "How much of it was you, and how much was his mom running off?"

"I wish I knew. I guess that's something we'll never find out."

"He'll grow up one day, right? Become a responsible adult?"

"I hope so."

I grinned. "What's that old joke? What's the difference between men and government bonds?"

Grey laughed. "Bonds mature."

"Ain't that the truth."

The wind rose to a shriek, rocking the building on its foundations. I clutched Grey harder, watching the snow whip past the window we faced. I hadn't closed the curtains so we witnessed the storm intensify. Screeching like a woman in agony, the wind grated on both my hearing and my nerves.

An irrational fear and paranoia swept over me. *What if the building collapses on us?*

"You really don't like storms, do you?"

"They scare me."

Grey kissed my head. "We're safe, baby. I'll never let anything happen to you."

"Some things are out of your control." I shivered.

"Will you let me distract you?"

As his right hand rested on my shoulder, I plucked it up, and placed it on my breast. "Yes."

"Oh, baby."

Grey's tongue slipped between my lips even as his hand slid under my sweater to tease my nipples with his thumb. I opened my mouth under his slight pressure, his talented tongue licking my teeth, invading my throat. He pushed his chest against mine, urging me to lie back on the sofa.

"I'm gonna make you forget all about this storm," he muttered thickly.

"Yes, please."

I barely heard the screaming wind as Grey helped me out of my clothes. Standing, silhouetted against the candle, he stripped his own from his muscular body. A mere shadow in the faint illumination, his thick, massive cock stuck straight from his crotch, and pointed directly at me.

Grey

Under my hands, Ellie's body shivered with fear, cold, or delight, I wasn't sure which. Even so, she lay on her back, her legs spread wide, her dark muff an enticing shadow in the candle's dim light. I controlled my lust filled urge to thrust my throbbing cock deep into her slick love tunnel, cautioning myself to pleasure her first.

I settled over Ellie's lower half and licked her clit, thrusting two fingers into her pussy. She thrashed, bucking her hips into my mouth, moaning and hissing between her clenched teeth. Her fingers tangled into my hair hard enough to hurt, pulling in her throes of pleasure.

"Oh, God," Ellie groaned, "stop-stop! I can't take it; I can't take any more."

I lifted my face, my chin dripping with her cum. "You want me to stop?"

"Stop, and I'll kill you."

Chuckling under my breath, I dove back in, eating her out, teasing her, holding her hips still, bringing her to her first orgasm. Her pussy gushed her arousal onto my tongue, both sweet and salty, Ellie's own tasty flavor. I breathed in the musky scents of sex and sweat, felt my dick harden further as it sought to climax far too soon.

Desperately thinking of anything nonsexual, I rose to my hands and knees. Ellie lifted her head to watch as I stood up, then took her hands. She made no protest while I urged her to kneel on the couch, her slender body bent over its back. I caressed her silken skin over her back and butt, anticipating my first thrust into her hot, wet pussy.

"C'mon," Ellie groaned. "Do me."

I pulled her backward while spreading her thighs. She glanced at me over her shoulder, her hair falling in thick waves over her shoulders. I gripped her hips in both hands and plunged my cock deep into her honey pot. I groaned through my teeth as her hot pussy seized my shaft, clamping down upon it like a vise.

Riding her slick juices, I thrust hard and fast. I grabbed a handful of her hair, pulled her head back and kissed her bared throat. Ellie's second orgasm shook her entire body, her sharp gasps and cries rising over the screaming wind outside her apartment.

I wanted it to last. I fought against my own rising explosion, seeking to hold it back, knowing far too well I couldn't. I hissed through my teeth, a long groan locked in my throat. My cock spurted into Ellie's pussy, my climax ripping through me with waves upon waves of sweet sensations. The exquisite and sharp pleasure, almost an agony, spun my head with vertigo.

I pumped into her in long slow strokes, wringing as much sweet sensuality as I could. Prolonging our union for as long as I could.

Ellie's quivering body all but fell out from under me. I dismounted and sat, breathing hard, on the couch. I pulled her onto my naked lap, her hair spilling over my chest and shoulders as she huddled in my arms. Despite the warmth of her apartment, the outside chill seeped through the windows under the wind's terrific force.

"I'm cold," Ellie murmured.

"Me, too. Let's go to bed."

Under her thick blankets and comforter, I spooned Ellie, my arm around her still flat belly. She hadn't begun to show a baby bump yet. Within a few weeks, though, she would. I caressed her soft skin, fervently hoping the child within her was mine.

"I love you," I whispered against her hair.

"I love you, too."

I tightened my arm around her. "We'll raise this baby together, right? Whether I'm the father or not?"

Ellie twisted in my arms to meet my gaze in the darkness. "Colton will believe the baby is his, Grey. As soon as he finds out I'm pregnant."

"Yeah. He will."

"He doesn't know about us. How can we make sure he doesn't ever know?"

"Ellie," I said softly, "he'll know soon enough. I won't hide from him. Nor can you."

"What will he do?"

"What can he do? He lost you because of his arrogance and stupidity. He can hardly blame you for moving on."

She shifted in my arms to face away from me. "You're right. He'll just have to accept us being together."

"And that he has a sibling growing inside you."

"Yeah," she chuckled. "I can hardly wait to see his face when he learns I'm carrying his little brother or sister."

"He'll take it hard at first," I murmured. "He's as bull-headed as I am. Still, this might help him to grow up. Be a man for our sake."

"I think that's like asking the snow to not be cold."

"He's not that bad, is he?"

"He's worse."

***

By morning, the storm had passed on. Lying awake with Ellie still asleep in my arms, I listened to the faint roar of snowplows clearing the streets. Unwilling to get up, warm and content to lie in bed with her, I pondered our dilemma.

Colton.

My son and her ex.

What would he do when he found out about Ellie and I?

When my thoughts grew too troubled to permit me to lie still, I rose from the bed without waking Ellie. Walking naked to her bathroom, I showered, and tried to push my thoughts of Colton's possible reaction from my mind.

He'll just have to accept it. He doesn't have a choice.

Ellie was still asleep when I ambled, damp and cold, to the living room in search of my clothes. I dressed quickly and dug my cell from my pocket.

Sure enough, I'd received a brief text. *Practice at three.*

That meant arriving at the rink by no later than one-thirty. And with the roads still under heavy piles of snow, I'd need to add an extra hour of travel time.

"Do you hafta leave?" a sleepy voice murmured.

Garbed in a fluffy robe, her hair deliciously disheveled, Ellie ambled, yawning, into the room. Fresh from bed, still smelling of musky sex, she hugged me. I stroked down her tangled hair, thinking she'd never be so beautiful than when she first wakes up.

"Yeah," I said, unfortunately. "Duty calls."

Ellie stifled her yawn against my chest. "I'd have to kick you out anyway. Gotta work."

"Can I at least have a cup of coffee before you toss me through the door?"

"Sure." She shuffled toward the bathroom. "You make it while I shower."

I was on my second cup when Ellie emerged from her bedroom, dressed in jeans and a wooly sweater, her hair wet and falling down her back in a dark river. She poured herself a mug, then sat with me at her small linoleum table. We sat in comfortable silence for a while, drinking the brew that enabled us to begin the day.

"Call me later?" she asked after a while.

I nodded. "Sure. Want me to come back tonight?"

Ellie drank from her mug. "You'd better not." She stifled a laugh. "You know what'll happen, and I won't get a damn thing done."

Too content to start an argument over Ellie moving in with me and quitting her freelance job, I stood to set my cup in the sink. Ellie tilted her head back for a kiss. Of course, I obliged her.

"Don't work too hard."

"You either. Stay safe out there."

"Will do."

I grabbed my coat and pulled it on, fetching my gloves from my pockets. "I'll brush the snow off your car, in case you need to go anywhere."

Ellie smiled. "You're so sweet."

"I do try."

My breath frosted in the deep cold as I crossed the parking lot. Snow and ice created a heavy crust on the windows of both cars. Other apartment dwellers, in suits and dresses, also cleared their vehicles, engines blowing cloudy vapors into the frigid air.

I was glad I took the extra time to drive to the rink. The roads, despite the plows, were icy enough to skate on. My fellow commuters crept the streets at a crawl, careful not to hit the brakes too hard and skid into one another. More fortunate than the idiots who thought four-wheel drive meant no sliding on ice, I made it to the arena with my car intact.

"All right, ladies," Coach bawled in the locker room. "I hope you enjoyed your day off because now it's time to skate."

And skate we did. For four hours, we chased the puck, slammed into one another, and swore like sailors. All the while, Coach bellowed and cussed, demanding more effort, more speed. With the upcoming playoffs in mind, we worked as a team, practiced the plays over and over until we could skate them in our sleep.

Worn out and in pain from overworked muscles and stiff bruises, I drooped in the shower, and daydreamed about retirement. All around me, Vipers laughed, told one another obscene jokes, made fun of one another's dicks. I let the crudity wash around and over me like the hot water that sluiced over my body.

"You been putting that thing to good use?"

Steve smirked, glancing down at my pecker before meeting my gaze again.

"Why would I tell you if I was?" I snapped.

"Aren't you banging that cutie you brought to Boston?" he asked, still grinning slyly.

A momentary murderous thought of Devon spilling his guts came to my mind, then departed just as quickly. Steve was on a fishing expedition. Devon hadn't told him, or anyone else, about Ellie and me.

At least I hope he hasn't.

"No. I'm not," I said.

"Too bad," Steve went on, soaping himself up. "She's a hottie."

"If you got laid once in a while," I commented dryly, "you wouldn't have to live vicariously through someone else's sex life."

"He can't get laid," Eddie called, laughing. "No chick wants a pencil dick in her. She won't be able to feel it."

Steve flushed a dark red. "Shut your piehole, asswipe, because you can't even get it up."

Eddie cupped his cock and shook it at Steve. "Come here and suck it. Then you'll see it up and strong."

Amid the laughter and snide comments, I shut the spray off and toweled the excess water from my hair and skin. "You should really learn to keep your mouth shut."

Steve scowled. "Eat my dingus."

"Sorry, I prefer a real man's dick in my mouth."

That brought another round of hooting laughter and even a smattering of applause. Under Steve's savage expression, I caught Devon's quick wink and grin. My towel tied around my hips; I dragged my fingers through my hair to loosen the tangles.

"Cheer up, Steve," I said lightly. "Someday your balls will drop."

"I'm gonna kill you, Aldine."

I tsked. "Wassa matta? Can't take a joke? Maybe you should grow up."

"Fuck you."

Turning my back on him, I strode amid the still laughing Vipers toward my locker. I'd scarcely left the shower area when an assistant coach yelled my name over the raucous laughter.

"Aldine! You're wanted."

I paused, glancing at him, puzzled. "By whom?"

"The big kahuna," the assistant replied. "He's upstairs, waiting on you. Get dressed, I don't think he wants to see you naked."

"All right."

The laughter and jests died away as I walked to my locker. Being summoned to the brass's office wasn't necessarily a good thing. As the team's owner, Mr. Owen Teasdale, only called a player to his office to give him the shaft, I slowly dressed with trepidation churning in my gut.

Did I do something wrong? What could I have done to piss him off?

Striding past me to his own locker, Steve glared balefully. "Now you're dead, Aldine. You fucked around and found out."

"Kiss my ass," I threw back.

Under the concerned stares of my teammates, I shut my locker. Accepting a few slaps to my back as I walked toward the assistant coach, I joined him at the door that led to the offices upstairs.

And climbed them to my fate.

ELLIE

Humming as I worked, feeling a contentment I hadn't truly felt since before Colton started sleeping with Lindy, my thoughts wandered to Grey. He hadn't called me, but I knew he would. Unlike his son, he kept his promises.

The day waned toward afternoon, the hours flying by as I researched and wrote articles for my client to post on his website and blog. Dusk darkened my windows, forcing me to turn lights on. As I did, I quickly regretted not asking Grey to come back after his practice ended.

I got more done than I thought I would. I can take an evening off to sit with him and watch TV.

Thinking I'd call him soon and ask him to come over, I sent the article to my client. I leaned back in my office chair, stroking my stomach under my sweater. In a few months, I'll have swelled like a beached whale. In seven, I'll deliver a baby. A mini-Grey.

I smiled to myself as I pondered my future with Grey. A mother, maybe a wife by then. I imagined both of us ecstatically happy, Grey retired from the team, maybe taking a job as a hockey coach. Or maybe becoming a stay-at-home dad.

A quick knock came at my door.

"You came back," I said as I bounced up from my chair. "You read my mind."

Smiling happily, I crossed my apartment to the front door. I didn't bother peeking through the fish-eye lens to view my visitor, for of course Grey had returned after his practice.

I unlocked the door and swung it wide. "I'm so glad you came back——"

Colton stared down his nose at me. "You were expecting someone?"

My happiness instantly morphed into annoyance. "What do you want?"

"To talk to you."

He pushed his way past me, striding in as though he still lived there. The sharp cold sweeping in after him forced me to close the door behind him, though I wanted to leave it open until I kicked him out.

"Get out," I snapped. "You aren't welcome here."

He gazed around as though he had every right to invade my home. "Who are you seeing?"

"None of your business."

"I'm making it my business." Colton swung toward me, his coat opening to reveal his workday business suit and loose tie. "You're my girl."

"Oh, please."

"I mean it, Ellie. I still love you. If you weren't so stubborn, you'd see it. But you won't return my calls."

"Because I don't want to talk to you, stupid. Now get out of my house."

"No." He paced toward me, his blue eyes snapping. "I want to know who you're fucking."

Defiant, I stared up and into his fury. "Do I need to call the cops?"

"You won't."

"And why wouldn't I?"

He set his teeth, baring them in a nasty grimace. "Because I won't let you."

A tremor of fear wormed its way into my belly. "Just try to stop me."

As I'd left my phone next to my computer, I whirled and stomped toward it. Colton's hand gripped my upper arm, yanking me around and back to him. His nails dragged through my sweater and into my flesh as I yanked my arm loose.

"Don't touch me!" I cried.

"Don't call the police." Colton's fierce expression collapsed. "Please, Ellie, give me a break. I really do want to talk. I need to know why you can't love me again."

"I thought that was obvious."

I folded my arms over my breasts to hide my shaking hands. Colton had never been violent with me. Ever. But something had changed. I sensed a mean streak in him that hadn't been there before. As though his previous good nature had vanished under a specter that looked and spoke like Colton.

"I know I did wrong," he admitted. "I'm truly, truly sorry I hurt you. It'll never happen again, I swear it."

"Why are you so obsessed with me?" I asked, nervous, but honestly curious. "I can't be the only girl you'd be interested in. Or who might love you the way you want."

He ran his hands through his blond hair. "You're the only girl I want, Ellie. Sure, I've dated a few since we split. None of those girls compared to you. Not in the way I feel."

"I'm sorry about that," I said. "Colton, we can't go back to what we were. You have to move on."

"Meaning you have? Moved on, that is?"

"That's exactly what I mean."

"Who is it?" Colton asked, his voice tightening. "Who are you cheating on me with?"

I laughed. "Now that's funny. You accuse me of cheating when you fucked Lindy behind my back."

"That's different."

"Oh yeah? How?"

For a moment, he looked mulish, as though he had zero intentions of answering me. "It's natural for dudes to play around. Especially before marriage."

"Really? Why is that? Why is it okay for a guy to cheat, but it's not okay for a girl to move on?"

"Look," he went on, impatient, "it won't happen again. I've learned my lesson. I promise."

"Good. Then maybe you'll make the next chick a happy camper."

"Come on, Ellie," he snapped. "I'm begging here."

"You're not on your knees," I observed.

"You want me to kneel? Here. I'm kneeling, begging you to come back. To marry me."

He did it. He actually lowered himself to his knees, looking up at me with a weird expression, one I couldn't quite read. It appeared to be a mixture of sullen anger, humiliation, and defiance. Not exactly a recipe to make me enfold my arms around him and swear to adore him.

"Nope," I said. "Not working. Time for you to leave now. Goodbye."

Colton stood, his sullen anger exploding into rage. "You bitch."

"And you're a prick," I replied. "A stupid asshole who thinks he can get away with anything. All he has to do is smile and look pretty and I'll fall at his feet."

"I'll make you regret this."

I rolled my eyes. "I already regret ever meeting you."

"I should beat you to a pulp."

Fear entwined its way around my heart, crushing my chest until drawing in a full breath became difficult. Still, I hid my feelings as best I could, gazing at Colton with a neutrality I certainly didn't possess. While I didn't believe the old Colton would ever succumb to the impulse to hurt me, I'd no idea what this new Colton might do.

"And you'll be in jail before you know what hit you," I said.

Colton paced forward; his fists bunched. "Really? The cops won't know a thing if you're not around to call them."

Panic sped up my spine. *He wouldn't. Would he?*

"Touch me, and I'll fight back. You won't come through it unscathed, dipshit."

Frantic, I thought about a potential weapon, once again thinking I was stupid to not have a baseball bat handy. As Colton continued to advance, his expression stiff, unyielding, I knew he meant what he said. If he couldn't have me, no one could.

Colton planned to kill me.

I grabbed the only thing I could——my set of keys on the nearby table.

I slipped the keys between my fingers as a long-ago self-defense course taught me even as Colton reached out to seize my shoulders. He loomed over me, his eyes bright with hate and murder. I didn't recognize the man I once loved, whom I'd slept with, and hoped to spend the rest of my life with.

That's coming true. He'll be the last one I'm with in this lifetime.

"Not today, asshole," I snarled, and slashed his face with the keys.

Colton stumbled backward, crying out, his hand rising to the bleeding cuts across his left cheek and nose. I gave him no time to recover. Raking the keys across his forehead, forcing him back another step, then I leaned my weight away from him.

I kicked him solidly in his balls.

Choking, his face turning purple, Colton dropped to his knees. His hands clutched at his crotch, cradling his jewels, his mouth working but the only sounds that emerged were "*Urk urk urk*". While I had the impulse to strike him again, punish him further, the fresh panic overwhelmed it. If Colton got up again....

Whirling, I slammed the door open and fled.

I clattered down the stairs, running headlong, my terror nipping at my ass. Without a coat, the cold instantly bit through my sweater and jeans, yet I knew that returning to my apartment for winter gear might cost me my life.

"Ellie!"

Colton's wavering, pain-and-rage wracked voice followed me to the parking lot. The snow packed asphalt, shining and treacherous, slowed me considerably. I'd never escape him if I slipped and fell.

Under the lot's light post, my car almost gleamed as a potential refuge. Its windshield held a thin veneer of ice, perhaps not enough to make it legal to drive. Hoping for a cop to pull me over, I lunged into my car and jabbed the key into the ignition. It started with a sweet roar, and I blessed its ability to turn over in the coldest of temperatures.

Colton staggered into view, screaming something I didn't hear over the engine. I yanked the transmission into drive, popped the headlights on and floored the accelerator just as Colton reached his truck. No doubt now——he planned to chase me. My tires spun, my car sliding sideways before traction finally caught. I drove from my slot, turning the wheel sharply to exit and charged into the street.

I barely saw anything beyond the ice coating my windshield.

Peering through a small chink, I saw headlights coming in the opposite direction, and kept my car in what I hoped was the right lane.

Behind me, Colton flashed his lights, honked his horn. He wanted me to pull over.

No way, José. Grim, scared out of my mind, I fought to accelerate on the icy road. My speedometer read thirty miles an hour. A proper and legal speed limit under normal conditions, a dangerous pace on ice when I barely saw anything through the glaze covering my windshield. The heater wasn't melting it fast enough.

"Oh, shit, this is bad, this is really, really bad."

Colton's truck hung onto my rear like a bad dream. If I stopped, he'd surely yank me from my car and do what, God only knew. There weren't enough people around to help me if Colton really meant to hurt me. I wished I could believe he only meant to scare me——and really wouldn't lift a hand against me.

"If you want to scare me, dude," I hissed, "you're managing just fine."

A pity the honking and light flashing didn't attract the wrong attention. No red and blue flashing strobes ordered him to pull over. No helpful cop lay in wait to catch me speeding faster than the conditions allowed.

"Go away!" I shrieked at my rearview mirror. "Stop chasing me, go away!"

Colton rode my ass so hard, I wondered why he wasn't yanking on my hair.

If I lose control, he'll slam right into me. That was another fear I certainly didn't need. My car tried to slide into vehicles parked on my right. I corrected the skid, fiercely hanging onto the wheel, and gently pushed the accelerator.

Thirty-five miles an hour.

Still Colton chased me, but he'd given up on the honking and flashing.

Less than half a block ahead, the green light turned yellow.

Fresh panic seized me.

I hit the brakes hard instead of pumping them, terrified of Colton's truck smashing into my car.

The light flashed red.

Skidding out of control, I slid sideways into the intersection. I screamed as my car spun a full one-hundred-eighty degrees. Colton's headlights now burned through my windshield, not my mirror.

His truck crashed into my car's front end in a wild tangle of twisted metal and shattering glass.

Grey

Owen Teasdale beckoned to me from behind his teak desk, offering his hand to shake. "Come in, come in. Have a seat."

I shook his proffered hand, unsure of what sat behind his genial smile and pleasant expression. Sitting where he indicated, I glanced around the office I'd never been in before. Enlarged photos of Vipers from varying years, including one of me sinking the puck into the opposing team's net, hung on the dark wood walls.

"Thank you for coming, Grey," he said, walking to a sideboard that held tumblers, carafes of alcohol. "Can I get you a drink?"

"No, sir. I'd better not," I politely declined. "I have to drive, and the streets are a mess."

He poured what looked like whiskey for himself. "They certainly are. I have a driver, so I'm safe in that regard."

He returned to his massive leather chair and pulled a large envelope from under a pile of others.

My walking papers. Maybe a check for my severance.

I breathed deeply in resignation as he slid the packet across his desk toward me. His mildly pleasant expression didn't change.

"So, am I sacked?" I asked, wanting to get this over with.

He looked startled. "What? Heavens, no. This is a new contract, should you wish to stay with the team for another season."

"Oh." I swallowed hard. "My contracts usually come through team attorneys. Not you yourself, sir."

"Yes, well, this time around I'm handling it personally. Take a look. Please."

He leaned back in his chair, his drink in his hand. "I'd be a proper idiot if I sacked you right before the playoffs." He took a sip. "You, my dear Grey, will take us to the Cup." He smiled widely. "I have faith in you."

"Well, thank you, sir."

"Open it, open it."

I obeyed him, sliding the thick bundle of pages from the envelope. I scanned past the legal jargon, all familiar as the same words were in every contract I'd signed with the Vipers. I felt Mr. Teasdale's eyes on me as I leafed through the contract.

My gaze fell on the offered salary nearly halfway through. Stunned, I felt my breath leave my lungs and not return. I heard his faint chuckle as I stared, transfixed, at the ridiculously large number with the multitude of zeros after it.

I swallowed hard. "Sir..."

"That's a true value I place on you, Grey," he murmured over the rim of his tumbler. "You're worth every penny."

Nearly strangling, I lowered the contract. "But——"

"No. If you need time to think it over, that's fine. I understand you may be getting close to retirement. That offer is to keep you one more season, if you will. I don't want to lose you. Not yet."

I grinned. "May I borrow a pen?"

Even as he passed one to me, he said, "You should consult with your attorney before you sign."

"Is there anything different in it I should know about?"

Smiling, Mr. Teasdale shook his head. "No. It's a duplicate of all the other contracts you've signed. Except for the remuneration, of course."

We made small talk as I went through the contract initialing where required, then signed my name at the end. I noticed he'd already signed his name to it, making me believe he had no doubt at all I'd stay on for another season.

"Please, let's have a drink," he said as he gathered the contract together. "As a celebration."

"All right."

He poured whiskey into a tumbler for me, and another for himself. Still standing, he lifted his. "To the Stanley Cup."

I stood to clink my glass to his, grinning. "To the Cup."

The whiskey burned like molten gold down my throat. We both sat, talking not as employer to employee, but as near to being friends as I'd ever come to a team's owner. I'd played for the Vipers for ten years, and until that evening, had only met him on formal occasions.

"What do you think of the new kid?" he asked. "Ratcliffe?"

"He has a ton of skill," I replied. "He's a natural on ice. In my opinion, he needs tempering. Experience. And he'll go far one day."

Mr. Teasdale smiled slyly. "Folks in the know say he'll one day replace you."

I grinned with a shrug. "Let's hope it's after next season."

My cell buzzed in my coat pocket. Embarrassed, I planned to ignore it. Mr. Teasdale gestured toward me with his glass.

"Go ahead, answer it."

"Sorry."

I pulled it from my coat and looked at the screen with a frown. "It's my son."

Why would Colton call me? He hated my guts, disowned me. Was he calling to apologize? My nerves grated like a steel edge on porcelain. He'd never apologize, not in a million years.

Still, he was my son. I clicked the answer icon.

"Colton?"

His voice choked. "Dad."

Instantly alarmed, I forgot where I was, and who I was with. "Did something happen? Are you okay?"

"Dad."

I rose, meeting Mr. Teasdale's concerned gaze briefly. "Tell me what happened."

"It's Ellie, Dad. She was in an accident. She's in the hospital."

***

I charged through the ER's doors like an enraged bull. My dry mouth barely formed words. The questions. I directed at the receptionist behind the glass. I felt the curious stares from waiting room patients and family, half listened to their whispers.

The receptionist put her phone down. "Ms. March is still in the trauma bay. If you'll just take a seat——"

Spinning, I jogged through the rows of chairs and curious eyes, seeking not just Ellie, but also Colton. Perhaps recognizing me, or simply recognizing the panic I was sure was clear on my face, two uniformed cops intercepted me.

"Mr. Aldine?" one spoke up.

"Yeah, is she okay? Is Ellie okay? How badly was she hurt? When can I see her? Where's Colton, where's my son?"

"Slow down," one of them said quietly. "Please stay calm. Okay? You gonna be calm now?"

Under both sets of watchful police eyes, I sucked in a deep breath. "Yeah. I'm calm. Will you tell me what happened?"

The cop, his name tag reading J. Stanforth, jerked his head at someone behind him. "You really should ask your kid."

Colton sat miserably on a waiting room chair, his back to me. I glanced askance at J. Stanforth, then at his partner, T. Robertson. Both nodded, and J. Stanforth put his hand on my shoulder.

"Don't blow up," he said, his tone a warning. "Don't make us arrest you too."

"Arrest? What?"

Colton looked up as I stepped around the row of chairs.

First, I saw the deep lines, gashes really, that crossed his face and forehead.

What the hell did that? Was he in the accident too? His blue eyes glimmered with unshed tears, his skin pale where it wasn't lined with scarlet.

In addition to the weird cuts, he had scrapes across his cheeks, similar to a road rash. Shards of broken glass glittered in his hair. Dried blood trailed down his right cheek from a hidden cut like a small black river.

I glanced down.

A pair of handcuffs encircled his wrists.

I gulped back the urge to swear. "Colton. What happened?"

My son looked away, swallowing convulsively. The cop, T. Robertson, knocked him lightly on his shoulder.

"Go on," he said. "Tell your old man you chased the girl into the intersection where she skidded out of control.

Then you slammed your truck into her car because you couldn't stop either."

Colton chasing Ellie? Ellie fleeing? Was she in fear for her life? Colton has never been violent in his life.

My knees buckled. My blood ran so cold that if my temperature was taken right then, it would have a negative reading. I sat down hard, unable to think, to comprehend what I'd just been told. Colton chased Ellie, in their cars, until Ellie lost control. Colton put her in the hospital.

"Oh, my God."

I rested my face into my hands. "He's under arrest for assault, attempted kidnapping, and reckless driving," J. Stanforth said dryly. "He told us everything."

I looked at Colton's face, recognized his misery, his guilt. "What happened to your face?"

Colton turned away without answering.

"Ms. March, in defending herself, slashed him with her keys," T. Robertson replied. "She also kicked him in the family jewels before fleeing. The rest is from the crash."

My rage swelled, pulsing in my temples, igniting a fire so terrible my entire body shook. I dared not look at him. If I met his unhappy gaze, his feeling sorry for himself attitude, I knew I'd lose all possible control. Clenching my fists helped to keep that fire, that fury, under some semblance of my own power.

I nearly lashed out when T. Robertson pulled me to my feet and urged me to stand away from Colton.

"You said you'd be calm now," he said. "I mean it. Chill, man. Stay cool."

I turned my back, sucking air into my lungs, shoving my fists into my coat pockets. At length, I managed a tight nod of acquiescence. Both cops relaxed, and only then did I realize how close I'd come to being taken down and handcuffed alongside my son.

"Will she be okay?" I asked, my voice hoarse.

"We haven't heard much about her condition," J. Stanforth replied. "We got most of what happened from her before the EMTs loaded her into the ambulance. The rest from him."

I suddenly spun on both cops, forcing them to recoil and reach for their Tasers.

"Where's her doctor?" I demanded, terrified again. "I need to talk to them. It's urgent."

"You can't go into the trauma room," T. Robertson explained. "But, maybe I can get a nurse's attention. Stay here, all right?"

I nodded, rubbing my mouth with fingers that still shook uncontrollably.

J. Stanforth watched me closely. "What's your relation to the lady?"

I sank back to a chair, but away from Colton. "We're friends. She... she...Colton dumped her. Bad scene. I helped her out."

I caught Colton staring at me as though he'd begun to suspect Ellie and I were more than friends. My rage surged.

He saw it, and quickly turned away again.

I dared not speak. I knew that if I did, I'd reveal my love for Ellie. *We have to keep it a secret for a long while yet. I just signed a huge contract that will enable me——us——to retire in luxury after next year.*

At last, a nurse in scrubs, her stethoscope looped around her neck, came toward us. T. Robertson followed just behind.

"Mr. Aldine, what can I do for you?" she asked as I met her halfway between the trauma rooms and where Colton sat.

I lowered my voice, conscious of T. Robertson's closeness. "Ms. March is pregnant."

The nurse nodded. "Yes, we know. Ms. March informed us. Are you the father?"

"No, I..." I half-turned, involuntarily, and looked at Colton.

He watched us closely, surely understanding that something important was going on, and that it involved him. Unfortunately, the nurse didn't bother to keep her voice down as I had.

"The baby's fine," she said briskly. "There's no problem there. Now if you'll excuse me——"

Just as she turned to go back the way she'd come, Colton burst from his chair. His handcuffs, linked to his belt, kept his hands from rising as he lunged at me. Taken off guard, J. Stanforth reacted quickly and seized his shoulders.

"Ellie's *pregnant*?" he screeched. "She's gonna have my kid? Why would she tell you and not me? Why, Dad? *Why?*"

"Maybe because you're an asshole," T. Robertson muttered, pushing Colton back to his chair. "If I was her, I wouldn't tell you, either."

The cop's response enabled me to keep my mouth shut. Turning my back on him again, I paced as close to the trauma rooms as I dared. Staring down the short hallway, I stood, setting myself to wait. All night if I had to.

T. Robertson stood in front of me. "You gonna be cool?"

I nodded. "Yeah. No worries."

"Okay, we're gonna take the kid to jail. He'll be booked. You can get him a lawyer tomorrow."

Cold again, I half turned to stare as J. Stanforth lifted Colton by his arm. "Do me a favor. Lock him up and lose the fucking key."

ELLIE

*B*right lights. Blinding. Colton's truck brilliantly illuminated. Colton's expression over the steering wheel suddenly tight with horror.

The crash. Red and blue strobes. Voices. Gentle hands helping me from my car. Laying me down. Lights in my eyes. Voices, asking my name. Putting something hard around my neck.

My baby!

"I'm pregnant," I whispered into the faces looming over me. "I'm pregnant."

"Okay, Ellie, you're gonna be okay. Don't worry. Ellie, we're gonna put you in the ambulance now."

Sirens. Red and blue strobes. A mask over my face. No pain, not yet. I must be hurt though. Injured. How bad?

Is my baby all right? I lifted my hands to cover my belly, but they wouldn't move. Warm tears trickled from my eyes, down my temples to run into my ears.

My head cleared.

I blinked the tears away, unable to turn my head. I rolled my eyes as much as I could to observe the bright ER lights outside the ambulance window.

The EMTs, their voices low, spoke in soothing tones. *We're at the hospital, Ellie. They're gonna take good care of you.*

Bright fluorescent lights burned my eyes as I was wheeled from the ambulance and into the trauma ward. Nurses took my blood pressure, peered into my eyes, asked me where I hurt. I didn't know. I just knew I was hurt.

Is my baby all right?

"My baby," I whispered to a nurse looming over me.

"You're pregnant?"

I managed a tiny nod.

"Okay, we're gonna check you out, honey. Just stay calm."

Doctors in scrubs. Nurses in scrubs. Needles in my arms. The pain finally emerged from hiding. My head. My neck. My shoulders. My legs.

"Am I broken?"

The doctor patted my shoulder with a gloved hand. "That's what we're going to find out. Ellie, the techs are going to take you to X-Ray."

Panic surged. "My baby! You can't! No."

"Easy, Ellie, it'll be all right, we're looking out for the baby, too. I promise, your baby will be fine."

I wept. At the pain, the fear. I needed Grey. Where was Grey? Did he know what happened? The techs wheeled me down a hallway, into an elevator, then up two floors. Then down another hallway where other techs took control of my body.

I lost track of time.

Maybe I blacked out. Or perhaps my brain simply faded out.

I woke next in the same trauma room, the same doctor leaning over me to snap a light in my eyes.

"You have a broken collar bone and a minor concussion, Ellie," he said. "Your baby is fine, alive, and doing well. Now I'm going to prescribe a pain medication that's safe to take while pregnant. You'll stay here at least for tonight. Is there anyone you want us to call? Your relatives, or the father?"

I shook my head a fraction.

"Okay, I'll get a nurse to contact someone."

A nurse spoke from behind him. "Dr. Williams? There's a guy in the waiting room. He's been waiting to see her."

"Do me a favor and tell him he can see her when she gets to her room," the doctor answered.

The nurse left, and the doctor patted my hand, smiling. "I'm going to give you a mild anesthetic to set your clavicle, Ellie."

"'Kay," I mumbled.

He injected me with a needle, asking me to count backwards from one hundred.

I made it to ninety-seven.

***

My head cloudy, as though someone had stuffed it with cotton wool, I blearily watched the television that hung on the wall. A news channel, I thought, talking about the weather. My pain drifted on those very same clouds, coming and going like the tide. A brisk nurse brought me a glass of ice water a while ago, which I sipped occasionally.

"Ellie?" Grey stood in the doorway; his face haggard, almost old. His coat hung from his hand, dragging across the tiles as he paced a few steps into my room. "They said I can finally see you."

I tried to smile, but something failed to work. Still, Grey must have gotten the message, for he crossed the room to my bed. Bending, he kissed my cheek with the lightness of a feather's brush. He smiled, but it looked strained, as though he didn't know how to smile either.

"The doc says you're still sedated," Grey went on. "So I can't stay very long."

My fingers twitched. Grey saw that and took my hand in his.

"Baby," I rasped.

Grey nodded, his face relaxing slightly. "The baby's fine. You're both fine, Ellie."

This time, I felt my facial muscles stretch as I managed to smile. "Love you."

"I know. I love you, too, honey."

A nurse in pink entered the room behind him and stepped around the bed. Ignoring Grey, she inspected my eyes with the bright light, checked my blood pressure and took my pulse.

At length, she asked, "You can have something a little stronger than water. Would you like a ginger ale?"

I nodded. "Thanks."

"Sir, I'm sorry, but I have to ask you to leave. Ellie needs to rest."

"I know." Grey bent to kiss me again, this time a light, sweet kiss to my lips. Rising, he winked. "I'll be back in the morning."

"'Kay."

I drifted to sleep before the nurse came back with my ginger ale.

***

"He's out on his own recognizance." Grim, Grey stuck his phone in his pocket. "He pleaded guilty. The DA cut him some slack because of his clean record."

I watched him step closer to where I laid on his comfortable and roomy sofa, aching from my head to my ankles. I'd looked in the mirror the day after the accident, just before Grey came to fetch me. My face was swollen, bruised and scraped from its impact with the airbag. Though I had no other busted bones than my left collarbone, the terrible wrenching of my body had created massive bruising all over.

Grey sat on his coffee table; his hands clasped together in his lap.

"The judge issued a restraining order," he went on. "He can't come near you, or he gets his bail revoked."

My throat sore from the whiplash, I couldn't speak much above a whisper. "Will he try?"

"I doubt it. The attorney told me he's remorseful and grieving, saying that he's responsible for this. Claims he never wanted to hurt you, only that he lost his temper."

"Bullshit."

"I know." Grey sighed, dragged his fingers through his hair. "I can't believe he'd even *threaten* to hurt you. Colton isn't violent."

"He's changed," I murmured. "He wasn't himself."

"Great," he muttered thickly, "my son is possessed by a demon."

That remark struck me as hilarious, yet all I mustered was a harsh and brief barking laugh.

"Don't," I gasped. "Hurts."

"Sorry. That's the image that popped into my head."

"He might grow up," I whispered. "Knows I'm pregnant."

"Yeah. He says the baby's his." Grey met me gaze with a mixture of frustration and amusement. "Maybe the added responsibility of potentially being a dad might force him into behaving himself."

"Maybe."

"He's not allowed to contact you in any way, shape, or form," he continued. "Until the restraining order is lifted, and after he's sentenced next month."

"Will he go to prison?"

Grey shrugged. "Can't say. First offense, he may only get probation."

I couldn't decide if I wanted to see Colton sentenced to prison. He threatened to kill me. He wanted to hurt me, he said he should beat me to a pulp. As it was, I was nearly killed by his behavior. Could I forgive him? If he's my baby's father, could I allow him to be part of our kid's life?

"What are you thinking?" Grey asked.

"Can I forgive him?" I met his green gaze. "Should I?"

Shaking his head slowly Grey replied, his voice soft, "I can't answer that, Ellie. I'm not sure I can, or will, forgive him. He almost killed the lady I love, and my child with her. Whether Colton is the biological dad, I'll be the father."

"Yeah."

He suddenly shunted his eyes from mine, looking at his hands. "I guess I'm assuming you want me. In your life, that is. Am I being an ass for thinking that?"

"No."

I can't have this conversation right now. I can't talk, I'm hurting far too much to deal with this. Nor could I put those thoughts into words.

Instead, I offered him a tiny smile. "Not now."

He nodded. "Sorry. You're right, this isn't a good time for making assumptions, right or wrong."

"Grey."

He stood up. "I'll get ice for your shoulder."

I shut my eyes. Obviously, my non-answer hurt him. *He thinks I don't want a future with him, more kids, marriage. Somehow, he'll have to understand.*

Listening to him rummaging in the kitchen, I wondered if I did indeed want to spend the rest of my life with him.

Do I?

Before Colton arrived to "talk", I would have answered the question as a yes. I loved Grey with all my heart. But was this what I had to look forward to? Constant strife with Colton, keeping him around because he was my baby's daddy? Risking not just my life but that of my child, too, should Colton "lose his temper"?

All this was too much to think about. Not when my shoulder burned as though a hot coal had been planted inside it. Not when even my hair hurt. Above all things, I craved the sanctuary of sleep, the peace and healing of deep slumber.

Grey sat once again on the coffee table, a rubber ice pack in his hand. "Here."

He gently settled it where the coal burned, over the nylon strappings that kept my bone together. The pressure from its weight hurt far worse, at least until the ice numbed it. Tucking the thick quilt that covered me more tightly around my body, Grey kissed my forehead.

"I have to go to work now," he murmured, his tone regretful. "I'll be back as soon as I can."

"S'okay."

"I want you to take a pill." He cupped my cheek. "I know you don't want them, but if the doc says it's safe, then it's safe."

I dipped my chin in a tiny nod. In too much pain to argue, I suspected I'd never sleep unless I accepted the medication. I didn't like taking them, yes. I worried they'd hurt the baby. Still, me and the kid both needed the rest.

Grey slipped the pill between my lips, then helped me to drink from the glass of water he held. Thirsty, I drained the glass, then relaxed. He adjusted the ice pack and kissed me again.

"Sleep, baby," he said, stroking my hair from my face. "I'll be back soon."

I listened to him put on his coat, then leave the house via the garage. His headlights splashed across the front windows.

Then he was gone.

Listening to the wind crash around the eaves, I shivered. I was alone for the first time since Colton entered my apartment. What if he kept a key? What if he's out there right now, waiting, watching, for Grey to leave for his practice?

I was helpless if he came in, decided to finish what he'd started.

Terror hummed through my veins like live wires. I listened for any sound, stared around the room, as much of it as I saw in the near darkness, waiting for Colton's shadow to loom over me.

I laid there, waiting, listening, for I don't know how long.

Grey

"I've lost her, man." I took a large swig from my beer, nearly choking on the thickness that suddenly swelled in my throat.

It finally slid downward into my belly, burning along the way. I suspected I'd be in no shape for driving if I kept up the drinking pace I'd already set. I didn't need to lose my keys again and the tatted bartender already eyed me sidelong several times.

"How do you know that?" Devon asked. "Did she say so?"

"Not in so many words."

"You're gonna break something by jumping to those conclusions."

I snorted, then wiped the beer that invaded my nostrils. "Look, as soon as she could, she moved back to her apartment."

"She's independent."

"She's been keeping me at a distance," I went on. "Her barriers are back up."

Devon drank from his own bottle, gazing up at the television over the bar. I, too, watched the weather station predict warmer weather arriving for the week. Moody, depressed, I found no joy in the break from the bitter and horrible cold and snow. Without Ellie, I found little joy in anything.

"Look," Devon said, "give her space. I think she needs it. After what Colton did, she may need time to figure things out."

"Like what?"

Shrugging, he replied, "If I was a pregnant chick whose potential baby daddy is a vindictive son of a bitch, I'd need time to think about my future. And my kid's future."

"She has one with me," I nearly moaned.

"Yeah, but think about it, bro: You might be the baby daddy's daddy. You three are in a very bizarre situation."

"Tell me about it."

"The playoffs are in two weeks." Devon turned his face to meet my eyes. "We need you, bro. I mean, need you at a hundred percent, ready to rock and roll. Toronto will be after your ass, big time."

I nodded. "I'll be ready."

"You sure about that?"

"I have to be."

Devon nodded, thumped me on my shoulder. "How's Colton?"

"He goes back to court the week after the playoffs," I said, my eyes on the TV. "I haven't spoken to him, nor do I want to."

"Think he'll do jailtime?"

"No," I admitted. "He's had a clean record till now, a good paying job, he admitted his guilt. I believe he'll get probation."

"That might not be all bad."

Staring at the TV without seeing it, I wondered how I felt about my son. Any and all thoughts of Colton brought little more than confusion, despair, anger, and grief. My love for him, once unquestioned and absolute, had morphed into a fearful sort of hatred. I didn't want to hate my one and only son. But I feared I did so now.

"Talk to Ellie," Devon advised. "Clear things up with her. If you don't, I worry your head won't be where it's supposed to be come game time."

I nodded, taking another swig of my beer. "It'll be where it's supposed to be."

***

Ellie opened her door a crack, peering around the edge as though fearing what, or who, was on the other side. "Grey, it's late."

"Can I come in?"

After a slight hesitation, she opened it further. "Okay. I wasn't sleeping anyway."

I stepped inside, not liking the furtive glance she shot up and down the hallway outside before closing and locking us inside her apartment.

"He won't violate the restraining order," I assured her.

"He might."

As Ellie wore a thick sweater, I couldn't see the baby bump I knew lay under it. Nor could I slide my hand under there to feel it. Her body language, crossed arms, rounded shoulders and suspicious gaze informed me such a move might get me kicked in my balls.

"How are you?" I asked.

"I'm okay. You?"

I followed her into her front room where she'd been watching television.

Ellie clicked it off and beckoned me to sit. "Want a beer? I still have some since I'm not drinking anymore."

"No, I think I've had enough for the night."

She perched gingerly on the edge of her armchair. "I thought you'd been drinking."

"Yeah."

"So, why'd you come?" Ellie, her posture still defensive, met my eyes easily enough.

She had healed quickly in the last few weeks, her bruising and scrapes gone. The sling containing her left arm, wrapped tightly to her torso, indicated her collarbone needed more time to heal.

"Will you come to the big game?" I asked.

Her wide smile replaced the suspicion and warmed my soul through and through. "Of course. I can't wait."

"I'll send you a VIP ticket," I said, a thrill of hope gushing into my blood like a waterfall. "I'll even send a limo to pick you up."

"Just a cab," she said, blushing. "Or a Lyft."

I shook my head, smiling. "Nothing except a limo for you, baby. Don't worry about the expense. I'm so hot right now, I bet the team's owner will pop for it."

Ellie laughed, a sweet, uncomplicated sound. "I'm not a limo kind of girl."

We shared a warm smile; a deep connection I'd thought I'd lost. My love for her surged until I knew I'd never conceal it and it forced me to blurt what I'd hoped to simply ask.

"What's happened to us, Ellie? Do you not love me anymore?"

She looked away. "I think I still do."

"You think?"

Rising, she stood to walk to the window, her barriers back up full force.

"Grey," she began slowly, her back to me, "you have to understand…If Colton is my baby's father, what's to stop him from becoming violent again?"

"Me."

Ellie turned at the deadly note in my tone. "Maybe. Maybe not, I have to protect my child. If I let Colton see the baby, have visitations, I'm opening up both of us to his temper. I'm also standing between you and your son. That's not a place I like being."

"So you'd rather walk away from us both?" I demanded. "What about my rights as a father? What if the baby's mine?"

"Then I'd trust you to do what's right."

"Of course I will," I snapped. "How can you even doubt it?"

"I don't. I also don't want to force you to choose between me and Colton."

Lowering my head, I rubbed my eyes with the heels of my hands. A headache loomed behind them, the excessive beer I'd drunk had created a weird sensation of not quite vertigo, and not exactly dizziness. My anger pulsed in my temples like a drum, a dull throbbing that threatened to spill into my stomach and cause me to barf.

"You are not standing between me and Colton," I said, my voice low. "He put himself on the wrong side."

"He did. But that doesn't change how I feel. If I'm not with either of you, then you might have a relationship with him. A good one."

"Only if he's the baby's father," I replied, weary, looking up at her. "If I am, he'll view my sleeping with you as a betrayal. There may not be any going back after that."

Ellie nodded. "Yeah, I see your point."

"I love you, Ellie. I don't want to lose you."

"Will you turn your back on Colton to keep me?"

"If I have to."

Swinging back to the window, Ellie stared out, her reflection clear in the glass. "I need time, Grey. I have to sort things out for myself. Do what's best for both me and the baby."

"I know."

"I'll come watch you play. We have time to figure things out before the baby's born."

"And if you decide you don't love me?"

My heart beat faster as Ellie turned, her arms hovering protectively over her stomach. "That's not the question. I *do* love you. The question is whether or not I can spend my life with you."

***

"Five for fighting!"

The ref's whistle screeched in my ear at the same time Toronto's forward cracked his fist across my cheek followed by a second blow to my nose. Hot blood coursed over my lips, the pain unfelt, easily ignored due to the hot fighting blood in my system.

As players from both sides yanked us apart, I delivered a heavy kick to the bitch's left knee.

His right skate slid his weight forward while his left skidded backward, making him look like a ballerina attempting a split. His sharp grimace of pain, while his mates dragged him away from me, told me, with much satisfaction, that he was now out of the game.

"In the penalty box," yelled the ref, pointing.

"Good job," Devon cried in my ear, his tight grip on my arm hauling me with him.

The screaming of the fans in the bleachers, their feet thundering, made nearly any sound that needed to be heard impossible. I skated, wiping blood from my chin to the penalty box. The instant I sat down, the team's doc applied a compress to my freshly busted nose.

I shut my eyes, tilting my head back, barely hearing over the thunderous noise the announcer informing the crowd that the Toronto forward was not coming back. Outraged screams from the Canadian fans yelled for my blood.

Coach landed beside me. "You finish this, Aldine, you got it? We're up by one. You sink that bitch into their ice."

Unable to nod under the doc's pressure, I managed a tight grin. "You got it, boss."

He slapped my thigh, then departed, barking orders as the game carried on. It had been an intense, bloody game to this point. Toronto knew the only way to win was to hurt me. And badly. I had slid out from under, out-skated, danced out of the reach of thrown punches, and dodged a body slam that took the intended body slammer from the game.

"You're almost done bleeding," the doc commented.

I sat up, against his protests, to watch as the Toronto team scored. Both teams were now tied. Our fans booed while the opposition's fans screamed in delight. The triumphant player raised his stick high, skating in a circle, under their adulation.

Now it's time to blow them out of the water.

I waited, tense, watching the clock until my penalty was up.

The buzzer sounded.

Blood leaked, unheeded, from my nose as I lunged across the ice. With Devon at my side, I intercepted the Maple Leaf who possessed the puck, dashing toward our net. A Canadian guard slammed into Devon, knocking him away from me. Barely aware of the pair banging into one another as both chased after me, I focused on the puck.

Stealing that puck.

Our net closed in.

Eddie readied himself to block the slice.

The Vipers had less than a minute to score.

If we failed, both teams would play on, heading into over-time.

Sudden-death.

I snatched the puck from between the Canadian's skates.

Spinning, I swung wide, dashing past the murderous Maple Leafs, feeling their fear, their hatred, like a caul on my skin. Under the screaming fans, I heard the hissing of skates, the cursing as the sweating Canadians fought to catch me.

Up ahead, the goalie waited, tense, expectant.

Ready to move in any direction, to catch, to block, to stop the puck from getting past him.

Seconds passed.

I feinted low.

The goalie dropped, his legs spread.

Swinging my stick, I slapped the puck high, sending it flashing, a dark comet, over his head and into the net.

The buzzer shrieked.

I skated past the net, slowing, sweat and blood cooling on my face as the Vermont Vipers fans roared their approval and triumph.

"You did it, you old bastard!" Devon slammed into me, hugging, screeching, kissing me just as the rest of my team wrapped their arms around us both. I laughed out loud, happy that Ellie sat in the VIP box, and saw it all.

ELLIE

I stood off to one side of the locker room door, trying to remain unobtrusive, unnoticed. A crowd of lucky, noisy fans mixed with the sports reporters waiting to get a photo and a quote from the hero——Grey Aldine. I, too, waited for him, but suspected he'd be celebrating with his team tonight. Not with me.

That's okay, it's part of his job.

At length, freshly showered, garbed in street clothes, a bandage over his nose, Grey stepped from the locker room. A few others emerged behind him for the impromptu press conference, one holding his hands over his head for quiet.

"We'll make a few comments now," the Coach announced, "but we'll be hosting a more formal news conference in an hour."

I absently wondered if I might sneak in to watch and listen. Then I saw press badges hanging from lanyards, and instantly quashed that idea. Grey glanced around and saw me.

While I smiled and offered a tiny wave, he kept his expression neutral. Still, I caught his swift nod and swifter wink. Pleased, I only half listened to the shouted questions, the camera flashes going off, Grey's answers as to his plans for the Stanley Cup.

"There's only one plan for the Cup," he said. "Win it."

Ragged cheers rose from the fans. Security surged forward when they sought to charge into the small circle that included Grey. The Coach, Grey and the other Vipers retreated into the locker room.

The disappointed fans relented, fell back, and dispersed under the orders of the big security dudes. The press reporters headed for the elevators, preparing their questions for the more formal press conference.

My cell buzzed.

Grey.

Smiling, I clicked his icon, his grinning face. "Congrats. You did it."

"*We* did it, babe. The entire team. Look, I don't have much time. I just wanted to say I'm sorry I can't see you tonight."

"I didn't expect to see you. You have a job to do."

"Yeah." His sigh came through loud and clear. "I have this press conference, then a team celebration. Will you go to dinner with me tomorrow night?"

"A private celebration?"

"At the finest steakhouse in the city." I heard his grin in his voice. "And we'll be taking the limo."

I laughed. "Big spender."

"You know it. I'll be spending it on you."

"Maybe I'll let you."

"Maybe my ass. Look, I gotta go. I love you."

"Love you, too. Stay safe."

"The driver will take you home."

"I know. Bye."

"Bye."

I hung up, feeling giddy and stupid and over my head in love. Vermont's own hero, the man who carried the entire playoffs on his broad shoulders, loved *moi*. Me. He'll carry the team to victory in the Stanley Cup, I *knew* he would. All my fears and worries over who fathered my baby fell apart to crash on the cement floor. The question of whether I wanted Grey in my life seemed far away and unimportant.

His triumph was mine.

I tucked my phone in my pocket, and, under the interested gazes of the security guys, I walked in the fans' and reporters' wake. Up the elevator to the main floor, I worked my way through the feverish crowds to the main doors trying to avoid being bumped in my left shoulder.

The limo driver caught sight of me as I huddled in my jacket under the brilliant lights and bitter cold. He drove to the curb where I stood, parked, and got out. Though embarrassed by his solicitude, I waited until he rounded the big car and opened the rear door for me.

"Thank you," I said, sliding into leather comfort and blessed heat.

"Did he win, Miss?"

I grinned. "He sure did."

Chuckling, the chauffeur stepped back to his place behind the wheel. "Home, Miss?"

"Yes, please. And you'll be needed tomorrow night. Private celebration, you know."

In the rearview mirror, he tipped his cap. "I'm looking forward to it."

***

For the occasion, I bought a slinky black dress with slender spaghetti straps, black do-me heels and discarded my sling. My collarbone protested when I flexed my arm. Still, I had no intention of ruining the fine dress that clung to my figure by wearing a damn sling. Talk about an eyesore.

In the bathroom mirror, I studied my injury. My collarbone was still swollen, slightly shaded in old, yellowish bruising. A distinct knot showed the break, and, I guessed, always would. I hoped that this fancy place Grey planned to take me to had low lighting.

Freshly washed and brushed, my hair hung past my shoulders and chest. A touch of mascara and blush teased my face, accenting my cheekbones. I rarely wore makeup, but I guessed a playoff win was worth a bit of excess. Pursing my lips at my reflection, I added a faint pink lipstick to them.

I'd no sooner donned a long black wool coat, rarely worn, when Grey's sharp knock came at my door. Seizing my keys and purse, I unlocked it and jerked it open. In a swift flashback, I imagined Colton just beyond, grinning with malevolent intent.

My heart froze.

"Hi." Grey eyed me up and down, obviously pleased with what he saw. "You're stunning."

I'd never seen him in a black tie and dinner jacket before. He'd removed the bandage, but his broken nose looked raw and swollen. Still, he grinned widely, and his green eyes danced with pleasure. His fingers caressed the tiny bulge my dress could never hide.

"The three of us are going to have a wonderful dinner." Grey held his arm out to me. "Shall we?"

"After I lock up."

I locked my door, slid my keys into my purse, and slipped my arm through his. "Aren't you cold without a coat?"

"The sight of your beauty, my love, brings a fire to my heart."

I stared up. "Where's Grey Aldine? And who are you?"

He laughed. "I tend to wax poetic when I help win a playoff game."

"And how often does that happen?"

"This is the first."

Our chauffeur tipped his cap, smiling, as Grey escorted me to the limo. "Good evening, Miss."

"Good evening, Landry."

Grey assisted me into the limo's rear seat, then sat opposite me.

"There are drinks and wine, sir," Landry said before he shut the door. "Help yourself."

"I think I will."

Grey found a chilled bottle of champagne in an ice bucket. "Ah, nineteen-nineteen, what a great year that was."

As the chauffeur drove from my apartment's parking lot, Grey popped the cork. Champagne fizzled over his hand and dripped onto the leather seat. With a grin, he poured himself a glass without spilling a drop, and handed me a bottle of sparkling water.

"Here's to the Stanley Cup."

"To the Cup."

We both sipped our respective drinks, gazing into one another's eyes. Perhaps he saw the love I couldn't hide from him. I certainly noticed the love he felt for me gleaming in the lights of passing streetlamps.

Is tonight more than a celebration of a game win? Is this the night we fall in love all over again?

"Did Colton attend the game?" I asked, sipping again.

"Nuh-uh. We don't talk about him tonight." Grey smiled, but his eyes were hard. Glinting. "He's a taboo subject. Off limits. Tonight, there's only you and I."

"And Billy the Kid."

Grey laughed. "I like that. Billy the Kid."

"Until we know the sex and come up with a name, we'll call him Billy."

He nearly killed the bottle of champagne by the time Landry drove to a smooth halt in front of the priciest restaurant in all of Montpellier. It appeared with utmost regularity as the top social spot in the city's gossip columns. People went to this place to be seen, and hopefully be recognized.

My mouth dropped upon realizing where we were, the liveried valet opening the door for us with what almost appeared to be a bow.

"No way," I muttered, climbing out.

"Way. I told you this is a celebration."

"I hope you can afford it because I sure can't."

Grey took my hand, then kissed my palm. "I can afford it."

The maître'd actually *did* bow as we approached him. As though Grey was a royal prince and he a servant. He accepted my coat with a smile and handed it to the person I assumed was the coat clerk.

"Welcome, Mr. Aldine. We've been expecting you. Please come this way."

My cheeks flushed hot as wealthy and bejeweled people stopped what they were doing——eating, drinking, talking——and stared as Grey and I passed among the candle-lit tables. Silence fell. Not even a fork clicked against a plate as we strode through the cream of the elite like royalty.

I tried to look nowhere save straight ahead as Grey marched on, his hand in mine, his aura that of the very prince I imagined him to be.

"Oh, my God," I muttered, my face a bright red, I was sure. "They're *staring*."

"Ignore them," Grey murmured, smiling down at me.

"I can't."

"Sure you can. You're as good as they are."

Right. I'm a poverty-stricken freelancer who lives in a cheap apartment and counts every penny. They live in mansions and count millions. Sure. I'm as good as they are. Shit, I forgot my diamond necklace at home.

After seating us in a quiet corner, well away from the eyes, the maître'd snapped his fingers to a waiter. With another bow, he left us to gaze at one another over the candle. Talk and clinks of forks resumed, yet I continued to feel eyes gazing our way, peering through the dim ambiance toward the once-again Vipers MVP.

"Relax," Grey murmured. "You're beautiful."

"Yeah. I'm also poor, pregnant, and not married. I think they saw all that." I ran my hand nervously, self-consciously, through the purple steak in my hair.

"They saw me with a gorgeous lady with the grace and poise of a supermodel."

"I wish."

Grey took my hand over the table. "Tonight, you're my lady. We're going to celebrate the win. We're also going to celebrate us. And celebrate Billy the Kid."

Chuckling, I squeezed his fingers. "All right. I'll do my best rich, supermodel impersonation. For you."

***

After we'd dined on expensive food, and Grey enjoyed plenty of expensive wine, Landry delivered us, the win, and each other, to Grey's house. I shivered under the biting wind while Grey tipped the chauffeur. I tripped up the steps to his front door, Grey's arm around me, and stumbled, laughing, into his house.

He didn't turn on any lights.

Picking me up in his strong, powerful arms, he carried me up the stairs to his bedroom. In my exhausted state, I did my best to undress, anticipating a session of long, sweet, lovemaking. Giggling, I slipped under the covers as Grey, swearing a blue streak, fought to get his shoes off.

"Come to bed, lover," I intoned, my voice husky.

"I'm trying."

At last, he crawled into bed beside me, deliciously naked, his cock hard against my hand. Grey nuzzled my throat, kissing me, his hand on my breasts. My head swam with love, with lust, with a hunger that didn't require food to satisfy me.

Grey's body relaxed. His cheek on my shoulder, he snored through his broken nose.

I snuggled against him, drowsing, finding a comfortable and secure place for my left arm.

Then drifted to sleep.

***

Bright sunlight and a sharp voice roused me from my deep and luxurious slumber.

"What the fuck is this?" someone shouted.

Bleary, I lifted my head to blink at Colton's shocked and furious face.

Grey

G roggy, I lifted my head from my pillow. And blinked. "What?"

Colton stood in my bedroom doorway; his skin drained of all color. His mouth opened and closed, his eyes flicked between Ellie and me, lying together, naked, in my bed. Groaning, I shut my eyes.

"Who invited you?" I grumbled. "How'd you get in here anyway?"

"I kept a key," Colton snapped. "It's a damn good thing I did."

"The restraining order is still in place," I commented dryly. "You can't be near her."

Ellie sat up. "You wanted to know who I was sleeping with. Now you know."

"You *bitch*."

At the title, the venom in his tone, I opened my eyes and leaned my weight on my elbow, staring hard at Colton. "That's uncalled for. You cheated on her, harassed her, assaulted her into a vehicular collision. And you still blame her for your stupidity."

"How long has this been going on?" Colton demanded.

Ellie, her right hand holding the bedsheet over her bosom, grated, "None of your business."

"I'm making it my business."

Sitting up fully, I rubbed my eyes, the bed clothes pooled in my lap. Colton wore his go-to business suit, his overcoat, his hair neatly brushed for the office. The man standing in my doorway was my son...and yet, he wasn't. Just as Ellie told me, Colton had changed and not for the better.

Colton's upper lip curled. "She isn't supposed to be at my father's house. How was I to know?"

"You know now," Ellie retorted, then flapped her fingers. "Scoot."

"No."

"Want your bail revoked? One call and you're in the slammer," Ellie said.

Colton's expression scared me. I'd seen less malicious intent on the faces of hockey players than I did on Colton's right then. Ellie's fears were justified. What I hadn't wanted to believe, what I'd hoped was a mistake on Ellie's part, proved to be true.

Not caring that I was naked, I got out of bed and donned my jeans. "Let's go downstairs."

Colton followed me willingly enough. I led the way into the kitchen, switched on the lights. He sat at the island as I made coffee, took mugs out of the cabinet. He refused to meet my gaze as I sat across from him, waiting for the coffee to brew.

"I came by to congratulate you," he said at last. "On the game."

"Okay."

"When did it start? Between you and Ellie?"

"Not long after you left her to wander down the road in the middle of the night in the dead of winter."

He grimaced and looked down. "That was stupid of me."

"Yep."

"I still love her."

I wanted to say that Ellie loved me now, that I wanted to spend my life with her, have more kids with her. But something told me to keep my mouth shut, to wait on him.

Colton finally looked up with an expression of grief, of pain, written across his face. "Is the baby mine?"

"We don't know."

"So...it could be yours."

I let the silence speak for itself.

"Shit," he muttered. "What a fucking mess."

Rising, I crossed the kitchen to the coffee maker, and poured us both full mugs. As I set his in front of him, Colton wrapped both hands around it as though craving its warmth. Or strength.

"I want kids," he said at last, and took a sip.

"So do I."

He barked a sharp laugh. "You have one...Christ, that could be my little brother or sister."

"Yep."

"Or your grandchild."

"Yep."

Silent again, not looking at me, he drank his coffee. I sipped mine, feeling thankful Ellie had chosen to remain upstairs. For some reason, Ellie's presence brought out the worst in him. He was reasonable and calm with me, yet turned into a vicious, jealous monster while around her.

"What are we going to do?" he asked.

I shrugged. "I plan to take care of her."

"No." He swallowed hard. "If the baby's yours. Or mine."

"If the kid is mine, it's obvious," I answered slowly. "I'll ask her to marry me, maybe have more kids."

"And if the kid's mine?"

For a long moment, Colton revealed a naked vulnerability, a tearing grief that broke my heart to witness. I wanted, craved, to take him in my arms and hold him as I once had when he was little. To comfort him, tell him everything would be okay, Daddy will take care of everything.

"She wants you in the child's life," I said quietly. "To be a part of it. To be the baby's father."

"She said that?"

"Yeah."

Something in him seemed to unwind, to relax, and a tiny smile quirked his mouth. "That's something."

"You hurt her too badly for her to go back to you, son," I went on. "You have to realize that. For the sake of the baby."

He ran his fingers through his blond hair, mussing it. "Jesus, I can't believe Ellie and my own dad, fucking each other. You're old enough to be her father."

"Why is that a problem? She's consenting adult."

"It just is." He stood up abruptly, the vulnerability and grief gone from his face, leaving behind a dull rage. "I have to go to work."

I walked behind him as he crossed my house to the front door. "I'll protect her, Colton," I said as he opened it. "So help me, I'll see you in jail if you so much as look crosswise at her."

He half turned with a bitter smile. "Fuck you."

***

"What will he do?" Ellie sat at the kitchen island, huddled in my bathrobe, hardly touching the breakfast I cooked for her. Her makeup from the previous evening had smeared, creating dark shadows around her eyes. Her dark hair fell in tangles around her shoulders, and she'd finally put her sling back on.

"There's nothing he can do," I replied. "He comes near you again, he goes to jail."

Ellie shook her head. "I didn't want him to find out. Not so soon."

"It'll blow over."

"Why is he so obsessed with me?" she cried. "*He* cheated on *me*. He forced me into running, almost into your arms. But he keeps blaming me for everything."

"I don't know."

I took a bite of my eggs, unable to say more. Where Ellie was concerned, Colton's normal sense of reason and fairness had failed. During our conversation, he'd waffled between acceptance of the situation and utter rage. Perhaps there was a psychological reason for this. If there was, I had no idea what it could be.

"There's no way this can have a good ending," Ellie complained.

"It will."

"How can it? I'm pregnant by either the son or the father. Colton is as pissy as a spoiled toddler whose dad took his favorite toy from him." Ellie pushed her plate away.

"You need to eat."

"I'm not hungry."

"You still should eat," I went on gently. "Billy needs his breakfast, too."

Ellie sent me a glower that might have split my head had it been a little sharper. "Dammit. This is a clusterfuck."

"It is what it is," I answered. "Colton will see reason. Eventually."

"And if he doesn't?"

"He won't have a choice. Now eat before that gets cold."

Clearly reluctant, Ellie scooped eggs and fried potatoes into her mouth, chewing hard and fast. The image made me chuckle, garnering for myself another hard glare. I obeyed my own order and ate my breakfast.

"We should consider a paternity test," I suggested, then sipped my coffee.

Ellie nodded without looking up. "I know. If Colton knows the baby isn't his, he might chill."

"Or chill *because* the baby is his."

"No, I don't think so. If he's the father, he'll become more obsessed with me. He'll get worse, not better."

"Either way, he has to understand we're together. Right? He's a part of the family no matter what, but he's not the one for you. I am."

When Ellie refused to look at me, nor did she answer, a chill crept into my soul. "I am...yes?"

"I want you to be," she answered quietly. "But here I am, stuck between a rock and a hockey player. I told you I don't like being between you and Colton. I can't help but feel things are getting out of control, like really fast. Now that he knows about us, I'm uneasy. Scared even."

I nodded, seeing her point. "I'm a bit nervous now, too. I hate feeling that he's trouble, because he shouldn't be. I'd never in a million years have believed he'd threaten to harm you or chase you the way he did."

Ellie glanced up. "Until he did it."

"Right. Until he did."

***

We spent much of the day on the sofa watching movies, eating popcorn. As Ellie's only set of clothes was the slinky dress from last night, she wore a pair of my sweatpants and a shirt, both of which were far too big for her. We cuddled in ways that ensured none of our broken or injured bits hurt.

Ellie yawned lazily. "I should really go home."

"Please don't." I tightened my arm around her. "I want you to stay with me."

"I have deadlines, Mister MVP. You know? Work?"

I kissed her cheek. "I'll pay you double to stay here and watch another Clint Eastwood flick."

"My client is expecting my article."

I smirked. "Tell him to come see me. I'll give him an article to post."

Ellie wiggled out of my arms. "You need to take me home."

I sighed as she mounted the stairs to change, wishing I could convince her to live with me, let me take care of her. Ellie's independence glowed on her like the full moon, and I couldn't ask her to give it up. Not yet anyway.

Back in her black cocktail dress, her fuck-me shoes, she tossed her coat over her shoulders. I stood to help her left arm slide through the arm, then bent to kiss her sweet, luscious lips.

"Move in with me and I'll set you up with an office," I said, holding her lightly around her tiny waist. "You can keep your freelance job."

"Sure. And you'll be talking nonstop, kissing me, distracting me and I'll never get a thing done."

I grinned. "Yep."

The doorbell rang, breaking us apart with the precision of a surgeon's scalpel.

"That can't be Colton again," I muttered, turning toward it.

"Hope not."

I stepped to the door and swung it open...

I blinked in shock.

A reporter and a cameraman from the local news station, their van parked at the curb, stood on my steps. More news vans pulled in as the reporter thrust a microphone in my face.

"I already gave a news conference," I began.

"Mr. Aldine," the reporter said, not withdrawing the microphone as the camera zoomed in on me. "We're here to get your comment on your relationship with your son's girlfriend. What can you tell us?"

"What?" I stammered. "What did you say?"

"We're told you got a young girl pregnant, sir," she continued, merciless. "Is she of age? She's your son's fiancée, yes?"

As I floundered in the face of the world's end, I caught more cameras, more microphones, more questions barked at me. I craved to turn, run into the house, and slam the door shut. My feet seemed rooted to my front step.

Is the young woman pregnant, Mr. Aldine?

Is she of the age of consent?

Why would you make a pass at your son's fiancée?

Can we get an interview from her, sir?

ELLIE

I blew my nose into Frank's hankie, still crying. Since my pregnancy, I couldn't seem to keep my emotions under control. Or maybe Frank's kind eyes, his genuine caring, allowed me to lower my inhibitions, so to speak, and cry over our coffee.

"Look at the headlines," I sobbed, tapping that morning's edition on the table. "Accusing Grey of being a pedophile. They believed Colton without giving Grey a chance to defend himself."

Frank nodded. "That's the way the world of news turns."

"It's not fair." I blew my nose again.

"How'd you get home and away from the reporters?"

I wiped my wet face and started to offer him his hankie back. Realizing I'd filled it with snot and tears, I hastily took it back. "We waited until they got cold enough to disperse," I replied, my voice hoarse from weeping. "The wind picked up and none of them wanted to camp on his lawn."

"Bunch of weenies."

I smiled weakly at Frank's attempt at humor. "Right."

"Did Colton give them your address?"

"We don't think so," I said slowly, clutching my coffee mug. "Grey took me home, and no one was waiting to interview me."

I recalled the terrible expression Grey wore after the shock of finding reporters on his doorstep, not asking about the playoff win or the Stanley Cup. It scared me.

But asking about how and why he stole his son's "fiancée".

"Grey... he's furious," I went on. "He's ready to do who knows what to Colton. The shit squealed to every news station in this city. It's gone beyond that now. Cable news shows are talking about it."

Frank nodded behind his lifted cup. "I saw the talking heads on CNN chatting about you and Grey."

"It's no one's fucking business," I yelled, then instantly regretted my explosion.

Heads within the café swung toward us. I shifted my gaze and lowered my face. "What he did, it's unforgiveable, Frank. He hinted to them that I'm underage. You know what'll happen to Grey's career? His contract for next season will be revoked. There's talk of the league suspending him. He won't get a chance at the Cup."

My fragile self-control broke, and I began to sob again. "This is my fault. I knew it would happen. I *knew* it. I've ended his career. Because of me, he'll end it in disgrace. Shunned. Called a f-fucking *pedophile*."

Frank reached across the table and placed a fresh hankie in my hand. "I always carry an extra."

When I managed to quit crying, blow my nose, and wiped my face again, I caught Frank's gentle smile. "What?"

"You can prove you're not underage, my sweet girl. Go public. Show your birth certificate. Grant an interview where it's passed around. Tell the public the truth."

I gaped in horror. "I *can't*."

He sipped his coffee. "You don't want to end Grey's career, do you?"

"Of course not."

"Then have your fifteen minutes of fame and enjoy the fuck out of it."

My coffee had grown tepid as I cried. I sipped anyway, pondering what Frank said.

Call a news conference. Tell the truth. Show the truth of your age. Denounce Colton as the liar he is.

"I'd have to tell them how he dumped me, humiliated me." I swallowed. "I'm not sure I can do that."

"You told me, didn't you?"

"Yeah, but you're my friend."

"I was a stranger when you told me, sweetie. Remember?"

"Yeah, no...maybe." I drank again, grimaced, and set my cup down. "It's been so long."

Frank leaned forward, his gaze intent. "I'll help you. So will that hunk you adore. You write, don't you? Write an editorial for the local paper. Explain what happened. Post it on the net. Put it on any and all chat boards, Instagram, Facebook, tweet it, blog it. Grey is the next best thing to a national hero. Turn yourself into the wronged heroine, the lady the evil ex exploited out of jealousy."

"Are you kidding?"

"I am deadly serious, girl. Use what you know, the blogging, the article writing. Make the netizens fall in love with you. Make them support Grey Aldine as not just a hockey hero, but the father to the ungrateful son. Turn their hearts to you and your hunk. Word will spread, I promise."

I nodded slowly. "Yeah, it will. And the crazies will crawl out of their holes in the ground and make it all bad again. They'll say I'm lying about my age, and that Grey is a pedophile. You know they will."

"Sure." Frank smirked. "And their crazy voices will be drowned out by the chorus of adulation from those you touch."

"You're nuts, Frankie."

"*You're* nuts if you don't follow my advice. Step up to the plate, swing at the ball. I know you'll knock it out of the park."

I covered my face with my right hand, my left arm still strapped to my torso. "I'm not sure I can."

Frank dragged my hand from my face. "You can. I said I'd help, and I will. Where's Grey now?"

I drew in a ragged breath. "He got called to the Vipers' owner's office. A five o'clock meeting, but first he's meeting with his coach and NHL officials. Frank, what if the owner revokes his contract?" I gazed into blank space, horrified. "It's my fault."

"First, you don't know what'll happen. Second, Grey can sue for every penny in that contract, and he'll win. Third, I'm willing to bet the dude stands by Grey through it all."

"Why do you think that?"

Frank smiled. "Because Grey is his ticket to the Stanley Cup."

***

"You're writing a press release," Frank advised, standing behind me. "Use formal language, don't jazz anything up. Just tell the truth in simple terms. Don't get emotional, don't accuse, or point your finger. Let the editors read between the lines that Colton lied."

I sucked in a deep breath. "Okay. Here goes nothing."

With Frank's help and encouragement, I spent the rest of the afternoon writing my version of events. Also with his help, I found the email addresses of the editors of every major paper and cable news network we could think of. After writing my press release, I copied and pasted it into my email program.

I then hit "Send".

"Holy shit," I breathed. "Will they read it, you think?"

"They see your name in their list, they'll click your link." He kissed my cheek. "I promise. Now the letter to the editor of the city's major newspaper."

That letter proved easier to write as I could and did point the accusing finger at Colton. I touched upon my humiliation at being dumped, my feelings when I walked away from the camp that night, meeting Grey before I died, our mutual and instant attraction.

Grey Aldine is no pedophile. I am twenty-two years of age. True, Grey Aldine is much older than I am. True, Colton Aldine was once someone I loved deeply. My love for Grey is complete and total. That Colton has chosen to reveal our relationship to the press in a negative light was his choice, and his alone. I am writing this of my own free will, and have little desire for anything save to set the record straight.

"Yay," Frank yelled. "Now send it. Demand it be published in tomorrow's daily edition."

I added that into the subject line of the e-mail and sent it. My confidence in telling my story grew and then doubled. I no longer felt helpless against Colton's shitty jealousy and petty revenge. Hope grew within me that Grey's sterling reputation would be reestablished in the minds and hearts of all fans of not just the Vipers, but of hockey in general.

"Now what?"

I turned to Frank, grinning in delight, happy that I'd done something positive for a change. All my life, I'd been swept along with events out of my control. Now *I* was in control. I could and would make a difference by changing the terrible effects of Colton's accusations.

And turn folks who read the news against *him*.

"Blogging," he answered, drinking the coffee I'd brewed. "Write a short but concise blog, no more than five hundred or so words in length. Readers lose interest if a blog goes on too long."

"You know this how?"

"Never mind. I know. Now write."

My shoulder throbbing from the activity I forced my left hand into, I grit my teeth and wrote. After a few changes, suggested by Frank to make it more emotional and heart wrenching, I posted it on every blog site we thought of. Copy- paste soon grew repetitive, and very boring.

I sat back, rubbing my sore collarbone, and craved a strong drink. "What now?"

"The phone." Frank smiled. "You're going to arrange a news conference to begin at six o'clock tonight. The sooner you get your story out, the better."

Horrified, I glanced at my computer. "It's four now. It'll never happen in time."

"Then you'd better get started, girlfriend."

***

Garbed in a conservative dress, wearing sensible flat shoes, sweating buckets I hoped didn't show in my armpits, I waited at the podium as reporters, camera folks, and newspaper editors filed into the conference room I'd reserved at the best hotel in Montpellier. Only with Frank's help did my impromptu news conference come together as smoothly as it did.

I glanced toward Frank, who sat in a chair in the front row, but to the far left of me. He offered a confident smile and nod, granting me the assurance I needed to sip at the glass of water and lift my chin.

The conference room, minus its table, was huge. Reporters and their teams packed it completely. Lights shone into my eyes, making me blink, and I felt the need to step back, protect myself.

Only a steel resolve that Colton would never win this round kept my feet planted, the words I'd planned to say welded firmly within my mind, my chin raised high.

I've got you, you shit. I won't let you ruin Grey's career. That's what you want, isn't it? His career in flames, his name in the muck while you gloat over him in triumph, revenge complete. And with Grey in ashes, I will be too. But that's not gonna happen, sonny. Not while I can still fight back.

"Ready whenever you are, Ms. March," the organizer said.

I nodded and faced the press. "I'd like to make a short speech," I began, "then I'll take questions. I apologize in advance if I appear nervous, I'm truly not. I'm scared stiff."

A patter of laughter greeted this comment, granting me more confidence. A swift glance at Frank boosted my morale even further. Smiling into the brilliant lights, I said, my tone clear and strong, "First, I must tell you who I am. My name is Elenore Jean March. I work as a freelance social media manager, and I am twenty-two-years-old."

Reporters jotted notes. The cameras focused on my face, on my dress, on the stupid purple streak in my hair.

Lifting my chin, I went on. "What I plan to tell you is both personal and humiliating, and I ask your indulgence in bearing with me. It's true I was, and I must emphasize *was*, Colton Aldine's girlfriend. Here we get to the difficult part of my story."

I swallowed hard. "Three months ago, on a camping trip with friends, I discovered Colton Aldine had not just been cheating on me with my friend, he had informed me he no longer wanted me around. He had, in his words, fallen out of love with me."

I paused, letting my words sink in.

"Hurt, betrayed, alone as never before, I left the camp and started to walk. In the darkness, the winter's cold, I walked away. From Colton, from the friends who weren't...and I expected to die that night."

I smiled slightly. "Until Grey Aldine saved my life."

Grey

"Mr. Aldine, you must listen to me," the NHL official begged. "The league is calling for a full investigation. They may suspend you until it's complete, which may not be for months."

I glowered at him, a man named Todd Billings. "I haven't done anything wrong."

"That's what we need to find out," he went on, slightly breathless. "We must clear your name before the Stanley Cup. Therefore, we must talk with the young lady."

"Absolutely not. I don't want her dragged through the mud."

I met Coach's grim gaze and read his mind. Billings was right. In order for me to be cleared of this bullshit scandal, he must interview Ellie. Her age *must* be proven, and right now. We both needed to come clean so Colton's story of me sleeping with an underage girl could be diffused.

But what will that do to Ellie?

"Is Mr. Teasdale planning to cut me?" I asked Coach.

He shrugged, helpless. "I don't know, Grey. All he said was for us to meet with him."

We stood in his jumbled office at the rink, me, Billings, Coach, and his assistant. I walked to the window, my hands stuffed in my jean's pockets, scared to my bones. If Colton's allegations weren't proven false, I stared into the ashes of my career. Mr. Teasdale couldn't afford to have a scandal-ridden jock on his team. It brought bad press.

"You're not looking at jail," Coach said quietly. "Your lady's age can be proven easily."

I barked a hard laugh, not turning around. "I'll still be vilified. I cuckolded my own son, slept with his 'fiancée'."

"Were they planning to marry?" Billings asked.

"No. Colton carried on with Ellie's friend, dumped her flat. Even the friend decided she didn't need the risk of him cheating on her and kicked him to the curb."

"A soap opera," Coach muttered. "Christ."

I finally turned and leaned against the window's sill. "How can this be salvaged? Is my career toast?"

"It depends on Mr. Teasdale," Coach answered. "He'll probably jettison you in order to save the Vipers' name." He shook his head. "The internet has already burst into flames; ESPN can't talk about anything except you. Everyone and their brother wants an interview with Ellie. Where is she right now?"

"I took her home," I replied, "and hopefully no reporter knows her address."

"She is in fact pregnant?" Billings asked. "Yes? Are you the father?"

Angry at the question, knowing it was one that sat on the lips of everyone behind a computer screen, every talking head in the nation, I didn't want to answer. It was one that *had* to be answered, and to say I didn't know sounded lamer than a three-legged goat.

"She is pregnant," I said slowly. "We need a paternity test to know who the father is."

"This just gets better and better," Coach snapped. "Why couldn't you have kept it in your pants, Aldine? Or at least wrap it up! A girl young enough to be your daughter, are you for real? You couldn't find someone your own age to stick it into?"

I spun away, furious, mortified, and, unbelievably, hurt. Of all the people I worked with I thought would stand by me, Coach was the one I expected would do so. He knew me. He trusted me.

Or so I thought.

"This is not getting us anywhere," Billings said. "We need to focus on Ms. March's age, that she wasn't a minor when all this took place. Then we prove Colton Aldine's allegations are false."

"In other words, I need a great PR guy," I grumbled.

"We have to convince the league that you're not a pedophile, and that you're an asset. Not a liability."

"When Mr. Teasdale cuts me loose, that won't matter." I stared out at the frosty, gray day, feeling as cold and dismal inside me as it was outside. It wasn't an opposing player who ended my career. My own son took it from me through spite, jealousy, and a sheer streak of meanness I never knew he possessed.

"The league may fine you," Billings commented. "Even if they don't, your name will go into history for all the wrong reasons."

"Because I fell in love," I murmured.

"They can't and won't look at it that way," Billings snapped. "You're locked in a love triangle and brought embarrassment to the league. They won't forget that easily."

"And what if he's vindicated?" Coach demanded, his swings between support and vilification of me making me dizzy. "His name cleared?"

"Then this will be swept behind us, forgotten." Billings hesitated; I turned to find him gazing at me. "If the Vipers win next month, this will be forgotten within hours."

"Ah." I smiled bitterly. "My name hinges upon not just proving my son is a catastrophic liar, but also winning the Cup. Is that it?"

"In a nutshell, yes."

Coach eyed his watch and sighed heavily. "The big man is upstairs. Time to meet with him and find out if Grey's career ends right now."

Thanks a bunch for the confidence and support, old man.

He led the way from his office, followed by the assistant, then Billings. I trailed the pack, my heart a heavy lead ball in my chest. There's no way Teasdale can keep me on. The contract for next season——the tremendous salary——would be burned to ash in his trash can. All that remained was the formality of giving me the axe.

Teasdale's personal assistant, a youngish man in his late twenties, opened the door to his office for us. Was that a look of pity he sent my way? I ground my teeth. I didn't need pity. I needed what I wouldn't get——Colton admitting he lied.

Owen Teasdale stood up to shake hands, even mine, his face a neutral mask. Coach and Billings took the chairs in front of his massive desk while the assistant and I stood like soldiers at parade rest. When he finally sat, without having said a word, his eyes rested on my face.

"Well, Grey," he said at last. "Is the girl underage?"

"No, sir," I vowed. "She's twenty-two."

"Your son lied?"

"Yes, sir."

"They weren't engaged?"

"No."

My voice halting, I explained how I met Ellie on that winter night when I'd missed the plane to Boston. His face gave me no idea as to his thoughts as I spoke of the blizzard, our mutual attraction, Ellie's hurt that Colton had cheated on her.

"We fell in love," I said. "It's true we have a big age difference. I'm not sorry about that. I am, however, sorry that I've embarrassed the team, you, and the league."

"I see." Mr. Teasdale, still with no readable thoughts crossing his face, gazed into the distance.

None of us spoke. The clock on the wall ticked the minutes by, the only sound in the room. I glanced at the inscrutable expressions of both Coach and Billings, and my heart dropped even further into my boots.

As long as he doesn't humiliate me when he gives me the chop. I can go out with dignity, retire, live with Ellie and our kids in privacy. Or so I hope.

I read the headlines within my mind. *Star Viper, team's MVP, retires before Stanley Cup. Aldine's departure shrouded in scandal. Aldine's son exposes the truth…*

"Well, then," Mr. Teasdale said at last, rousing me from my imaginings, "there's only one thing I can do."

I stared down at my feet, my stomach in knots. "I won't make a fuss in the press, sir. Thank you for the years you've given me."

"Do you mind if I finish before you jump to conclusions?"

I glanced up, my thoughts wild, and found Teasdale smiling. "Uh, sure. Yes."

"I'm not stupid enough to cut you now, Grey," he went on. "I'm standing behind you a hundred percent."

"You're *what*?" Billings demanded. "The league will demand an investigation."

"Let them. What's going on between Grey and his lady is private. She's an adult, she can make her own decisions. Once it's known she's not underage, this will all blow over."

As Billings blustered, stammering his remarks on the face of the NHL, scandal, and how he cannot possibly see how

I should remain on the team, I felt my feet grow numb. I wasn't going to be axed. My career was still intact. I still had the chance to win the Stanley Cup, my name gold once again.

"Now look," Mr. Teasdale snapped, impatient. "We do have to prove Grey is on the right side of morality. That's a given. The sooner the better. If the press continues to gnaw on this like an old dog with a bone, it will get worse. Grey, would your lady be willing to step up and show the world she's not underage?"

"I- I don't know, sir," I replied, still taking in the fact that I haven't been sacked. "I can persuade her, I think."

"Good. Now we have to consider an offensive tactic," Mr. Teasdale went on. "That means suing your boy for slander, defamation of character, all that rot. I'll get the team's lawyers working on that. Now, Grey, it's time to work on your image in the public's eye. We need to turn you into a hero."

***

For the next hour, we talked over ideas on how to sway the public opinion away from Colton's lies. Suing him appeared at the top of the idea chain, and a quick investigation from the league came second.

"If the league finds you innocent," Mr. Teasdale explained, "then it's all over. We win the Cup, and this will be forgotten."

"There will still be naysayers," Billings argued. "People who will scream cover up."

"No matter the outcome, there will always be someone to scream cover up," Teasdale replied. "Those opinions won't sway anyone. Gentlemen, we can't let ourselves be intimidated by the uneducated few. I have enough faith in Grey to tell you that my contract with him for next season still stands. Cup or no Cup, Grey Aldine plays for my team for as long as he wants the job."

My gratitude for his faith in me, his confidence in my ability and in my innocence, reached my lips and got no farther. Mr. Teasdale's assistant entered the office before I spoke, gathering the attention of everyone in the office.

"I'm in a meeting," Mr. Teasdale said, annoyed.

"I know, sir. But there's something you have to see."

The young man reached for the flat panel television's remote and clicked the screen on. Excited, grinning, he glanced at me before scrolling through channels. Pausing on a local news station, he stepped aside, clearing the way for us to watch.

"What is this?" Mr. Teasdale asked.

"A news conference, sir," the assistant explained.

"Who the devil is that?"

I locked my knees to halt them from giving way and tumbling me to the floor. "That's my lady. That's Ellie."

"What?"

Teasdale stood, walked around his desk to stand beside me. "What is she doing?"

"She's clearing Mr. Aldine's name, sir," the assistant said. "She's telling everyone the truth."

In shock, in vapid disbelief, I watched as Ellie, smiling, confident, utterly beautiful, stood behind the podium and fielded questions from the press. The purple streak in her hair shone brilliantly under the lights and gave her the illusion she was much younger than she was.

"As you all see," she said, gesturing, "that's my birth certificate. Proof I'm not underage. Remember, after you pass that around, I need it back."

A general chuckle rose from the big room.

"Ms. March?" someone asked.

Ellie pointed at someone behind the camera. "Yes? What's your question?"

"Who is the father of your baby?"

My heart sank despite the sudden surge of hope and pride. What would she answer? That she didn't know? That could be as bad as naming either Colton or I as the baby's father.

Ellie's smile blossomed. "I'd really rather not say at this time."

I jolted as Mr. Teasdale's fist thumped my back. I glanced askance at him and witnessed his grin.

"Vindicated, son. You're gold."

ELLIE

"**M**s. March!" yet another reporter called.

My smile becoming stiff, no longer as natural as it once was, I pointed toward a lady reporter I recognized from a local news station. "Yes?"

"Were you formally engaged to Grey Aldine's son?"

"No, I was not. He never proposed marriage.

"So why, in your opinion, did he make up that story? Why would he want to cause his father problems by claiming you are underage?"

"That's a question you'll have to ask Colton Aldine," I replied. "I can't speak for him. As I did have a relationship with Colton, he should be very aware of my age."

"Ms. March!" another call went up.

The conference continued even as I grew wearier of question after question. It seemed that none of the reporters exhausted themselves from the sheer number of queries they possessed, and then threw at me. I wasn't sure how long we'd been at this, but it seemed hours had passed since I first stepped to the podium.

I shot a glance at Frank. He made a rapid slash across his throat, and I wanted to kiss him.

After taking a deep breath, I said, "Thank you all for coming. I'll take one more question, then this conference is at an end."

"Will you forgive Colton for what he's done?" someone asked.

I hesitated. "I can't answer that at this time. Thank you."

Under the barrage of shouted questions, I retreated from the conference room and ducked into a nearby office. Relieved that the ordeal was over with, I listened to the chatter as the news crews wrapped up their cameras and coiled their electric cables. I leaned against a desk and waited for Frank.

Thirty minutes passed before he slipped inside.

"You were awesome, Ellie," Frank gushed.

I hugged him tightly, grateful for his strength, his easy nature and most of all his love. His strong arms made me feel safe and secure just as Grey's did. I breathed in his cologne and loved him for his friendship.

"All good?" he asked.

"I want to go home."

"Okay. Most of the newsies have departed, but a few are lingering for an extra soundbite. I tell you what. Stay here for a few minutes until I can get the car parked out back. We'll play mob bosses and sneak away."

"Sounds good."

After he departed, I relaxed further, the remaining stress of my very first, and hopefully only, press conference slipping from me in small stages. I wondered where Grey was, and whether he'd gotten shafted from the team. Tension returned upon the image of him losing his job even as I bared my soul for all the world to see in order to save it.

"Let's go," Frank said when he returned.

I took his hand and let him lead me from the office. Inside the conference room, voices and laughter rose like a warning. If I'm seen, those news folks would be on me like white on rice. Not daring to look back, I hurried down the broad hallway with Frank——just another couple staying at the hotel.

He opened a rear door and hustled me through the darkness and cold to his car. Like a "mob boss", he ushered me into its interior, and shut the door, gazing around for any potential cameramen to pounce, yelling *There she is!*

"Do you know where Grey is?" Frank asked as he got in behind the wheel.

"No," I admitted. "Probably in meetings."

"Let's hope this whole thing worked and his career isn't flushed down the toilet."

As he drove from the hotel's lot and into downtown traffic, I pulled my cell from my pocket.

Clicking Grey's icon, I listened to his voice inviting me to leave a message. "His cell is off."

"Makes sense if he's in meetings."

I breathed deeply. "Thank you for what you did."

"What I did? I merely booted you into stepping up." Smiling, he took my hand. "You've got guts, girl. I hope Grey appreciates that."

***

Frank walked with me from his car to my apartment. As we stepped into the hallway that led to my home, I stopped abruptly, drawing in air in a sharp gust. A shadowy figure of a man leaned against the wall, one boot resting on it, the other keeping him upright. He'd bowed his head and didn't look around.

"How about that," Frank murmured, tugging me forward.

Grey finally looked up as we approached, his face expressionless.

He got sacked. The press conference was for nothing. His career is over and it's my fault.

He dropped his foot and took me into his arms. I hugged him, not daring to ask the dreaded question.

Frank, of course, did not share my doubts. "You're still on the team, aren't you?"

Grey lifted his face from my shoulder as though seeing him for the first time.

"Yeah." He smiled, caressing my hair. "The owner backed me up." Grey bent to kiss me. "But it was Ellie who salvaged my reputation."

"It worked?" I stared up into his green eyes. "The conference?"

"Made all the difference in the world. Now no one can doubt us, or why I'm still on the team. All thanks to you, Ellie."

I blushed, delighted. "But Frank did a lot. If he hadn't helped, I don't know that I'd have had the courage."

Grey held his hand out to Frank. "Thank you, my brother."

Frank joined us in our hug and kissed both of our cheeks. "Don't mention it. I'm just glad it all worked out."

After ruffling Grey's hair, Frank paced away from us. "I'll leave you kids alone. Take care of her, Grey. She's a real gutsy gal."

"You know I will."

I fumbled in my purse for my keys as Frank departed, Grey's arm around my waist. I let us into my dark apartment and switched on the lights. "I don't think I have anything to celebrate with."

"That's all right," he said. "Just being with you is celebration enough."

After we'd removed our coats, Grey took me to my sofa and sat me down. He pulled me against him, my cheek on his shoulder, and held me.

"What you did was incredible, Ellie," he hushed. "Just saying thank you is hardly enough, will *never* be enough."

"I also plastered the Internet with my story," I said, happy, contented. "Rather *our* story. I'm so glad you kept your job."

"Me, too. I really thought it was toast."

"It would have been my fault."

"No," he murmured against my hair. "I made my choice, too. Remember, it takes two to tango."

I chuckled. "I guess so."

"How'd I get so lucky to fall in love with you?"

"Everything happens for a reason. Or so they say."

He kissed my brow. "Look, there's nothing wrong with your apartment, but I changed my mind about celebrating. Let's go out. Then go to my house."

"What if we're recognized?"

"Everything happens for a reason."

***

After taking me out to dinner at an on off-the-main-drag restaurant, Grey drove us back to his house. Without turning on the lights, he locked the world out and carried me up the stairs to his bedroom. He laid me on his bed, and slowly undressed me, piece by piece, with love and a tender respect for my still injured bones.

Sliding under the blankets with me, wonderfully naked, Grey kissed me, his tongue tangling with mine, arousing me, teasing me, making me forget there was a world beyond the walls of his bedroom. Riding on the waves of intense pleasure, I existed in a microcosm of love, his cock sliding into me with the ease of coming home.

"I love you," he muttered thickly into my ear, thrusting easily into me. "I love you, I love you."

Unable to reply through my tight gasps amid the marvelous sensations, I dug my nails into his back, nipping his throat, my pussy convulsing around his driving shaft. I climaxed hard, crying out, clinging to his naked flesh, brilliant stars wheeling behind my closed eyelids.

He groaned, long and loud, as he thrust into me, his seed spilling inside me yet again.

Let this baby be his. Let Billy be his child. It must be.

In the languid aftermath, Grey curved his body around mine, protective, his hand caressing the small mound where Billy lay sleeping.

"Let's get a paternity test," he murmured against my neck. "Tomorrow."

"Yeah. We need to know."

"I don't know what I'll do if the baby is his."

I gripped his fingers. "You'll raise him as your own, love him unconsciously, teach him to play hockey."

Grey chuckled. "And if he's a her?"

"You'll love her unconditionally and teach her to skate. She'll grow up to be a champion figure skater...or hockey player."

"She'll be as beautiful as her mother."

"And be as hard-headed as both you and Colton."

Grey's silence stretched out. I felt his tension and twisted in his arms to face him despite the darkness.

"What?" he asked quietly.

"I don't know if I can forgive him."

"I don't know if I can either."

"I should. *We* should. Somehow." I caressed his bristled cheek. "As you'd always said, maybe he'll grow up. He might surprise us, and get over me, his obsession with me."

"That would be a surprise."

***

"We won't have the results for a few weeks," the nurse practitioner, Janet, told Grey and I. "But I'll call you the moment they come in."

She had swabbed Grey's inner cheek for his DNA, drew a sample of my blood, and smiled at us both. "I'll send this off to the lab right away."

"Thanks."

"Meanwhile, how have you been feeling, Ellie? Any problems?"

"No, none at all. I'm eating right, limiting caffeine and alcohol like you said."

"Great. I want to get another ultrasound when you come get the results."

"Okay."

Grey paid the receptionist for the visit and held my hand as we left the office. "Practice starts again tomorrow. Will you please stay at my house with me?"

I leaned against him. "All right. I want to work, though. I still have deadlines I need to meet."

Grey feigned a huge, defeated sigh. "Deadlines, shmedlines. Stick with me, baby, and you'll never have to work again."

"Yeah, yeah."

After swinging by my apartment for my computer, clothes and toiletries, Grey returned us to his house. He pushed the button to open the garage door and drove slowly up his driveway and inside. I stepped out of his car as the door rattled downward on its rollers. Grey paced around the car's front to the house entrance leading into the kitchen.

I caught a swift glimpse of a shadow ducking under the downward sliding door and started to turn toward it.

The knife glittered in the last of the sunlight before the garage door shut it out.

Colton grabbed me around my neck, pulling me hard against his chest. I barely had time to register what had happened, much less feel any fear. The blade rested against my throat.

"Miss me, baby?" he hissed into my ear.

Grey swung around, his eyes flat, his mouth tight, as he grasped the situation faster than I had. Colton's grip on my neck made movement almost impossible, but I struggled anyway. I yanked on his elbow, disregarding the danger of the knife he held.

"Stay back, Dad," Colton snapped. "I'll kill her, I swear I will."

"Let me go," I screeched, fighting like a cat trapped in a sack. "I'll kill you, you son of a bitch."

Colton laughed bitterly. "Right, sure you will. It's your fault, bitch. You and your fucking press conference. Because of you, I lost my job. I've lost everything. And now you'll pay."

Grey

"**Y**ou want to die, son?" I forced my tone to remain level and calm despite my rage, my terror.

Ellie's fierce attempts to free herself gave me some hope that I might take Colton down and save her life. The hate, the jealousy, I saw in my son's eyes kept me rooted to my garage floor.

"You can't do anything, old man," he sneered. "I've got your sweet little bitch."

"Let me go," Ellie screamed.

"Why should I?" Colton snapped. "I walked into work this morning. My boss flat-out fired me. Why? Because I told the truth about you and my illustrious dad." Colton laughed. "My name is plastered all over the internet. You know what they're saying? I'm a damned liar. Every message board in creation is talking about me."

"You lied about us both, asshole," Ellie shrieked.

"Did I, sweet cheeks? You spurned me for this old man. I got my revenge."

"You kill her, and you'll kill your own child."

Colton froze for a moment, his mouth loose, his eyes wide. "My——my baby? The baby's mine?"

"Yeah." I injected annoyance, derision, and irritation into my tone. "The kid's yours. But you don't deserve him."

The knife faltered, dropped a scant inch from Ellie's throat. "It's a boy? I'm going to have a son?"

"Billy the Kid," I replied, slowly pacing toward them. "You use that knife, Billy dies with Ellie."

Uncertain, Colton looked down at Ellie, and the knife he held. "I want kids."

"Then put that knife down and let's talk about it. This isn't smart, son. You'll go away for murder. You'll never have the chance to have kids if you hurt Ellie."

"Ellie..." He dropped the knife away from Ellie's throat and hovered it over her bosom. He still didn't let her go.

I shut my teeth tightly, and tried a kind smile, extending my hand to him. "Give me the knife, son."

His eyes swimming with tears, Colton stared at me. I saw him waver, caught between his jealous anger and the realization of what he'd done. There was no going back from this. He'd committed a serious felony and faced years in jail. No slap on the wrist this time around.

All I could hope for was that my *son*, not this imposter, took over.

Do the right thing, Colton, you know what that is.

"What have I done?" he rasped. "Dad. I'm so sorry."

Not waiting for Colton to surrender, Ellie took advantage of his lax arm, and wrenched herself free. Though I would have rather she had stepped away from him, in case he changed his mind, she grabbed his wrist, and plucked the knife from his hand.

With more compassion than I thought she possessed toward him, Ellie tossed the knife to the floor near me, and seized Colton's hands.

"Colton," she said softly, "why are you doing this? You're only hurting yourself. You're smart, talented, gifted. You'll get another job. Would cutting my throat have solved anything? Anything at all?"

His mouth quivered as his tears rolled down his cheeks. "No. It wouldn't. Ellie, I'm so sorry. About everything. I'm not smart." He made an attempt at a smile and cupped her cheek. "If I was as smart as you say, I should have just let you go." He met my gaze. "If I lost you to anyone, I'm glad I lost you to him."

"Colton," I exhaled, exhausted. Ellie stepped aside in time for me to take my son in my arms. Sobbing like a lost child, Colton clung to my shoulders.

I confess several tears ran down my face and were lost in his jacket. "I love you, son."

His voice muffled, he muttered, "I love you, too, Dad."

***

Gripping Ellie's hand as though I feared drowning, my stomach churning with a tension I couldn't release, I waited for Janet to call us into her office. The results had arrived. Billy the Kid's parentage would now come to light.

I hope you're the baby's father, Dad, Colton had said. *I don't deserve to be a father. Not yet anyway. I need some time to figure my life out, I guess I need to grow up. If Billy is mine, I'll do right by him and Ellie. And you. But I need to be far away from you both, take advantage of the second chance you both have given me. I need maturity, I guess, and perspective.*

Ellie squeezed my fingers, obviously far calmer than me. "It'll be all right, Grey."

"Will it?" I asked. "The judge gave Colton permission to leave the state for work. What if he never comes back?"

"He will."

I shook my head. "I don't know."

Before leaving, Colton offered a sample for testing his DNA.

I'm sure the kid is yours, Dad, he'd sworn. *If not, I'll send child support. And I'll be cheering you on at the Stanley Cup game.*

"Dammit," I muttered. "What's taking so long?"

"We still have ten minutes to our appointment."

"Shit."

"Calm down. You're acting like you've never had a kid before."

At her laughter, I scowled. "Very funny. My last kid didn't need a paternity test to prove he's mine."

"Chill out. You're making a spectacle of yourself."

At long last, a nurse ushered us into the practitioner's office. Janet, the lady Ellie trusted with her——our baby——smiled and shook our hands over her desk. I continued to clutch Ellie's hand as we sat in the guest chairs.

"The paternity test came back," she said, opening a folder. "I'm glad we had Colton's DNA to test, as such a close relationship may have muddied the waters a bit."

My tongue had frozen itself to the roof of my mouth. I couldn't say a word as Janet rifled through several pages, as though searching for the right one.

"Ah, here we are," she said.

Ellie squeezed my fingers, smiling in anticipation.

Of course she can smile. We all know who the mother is.

"Congratulations, Grey," Janet finally said, you're going to be a father."

All my air left my lungs as Ellie laughed, triumphant. She lunged from her chair to hug me, yanking my head against her chest. Her hair smothered me, her arms around my neck threatened my ability to breathe.

"I——I'm the father?"

I swept Ellie's hair from my face to gape. "Truly?"

"Truly. You were a ninety-nine point nine percent match. Colton didn't even come close."

"That's my kid." I turned to Ellie, grinning like a fool, laughing. "That's *my* kid!"

***

It was the championship game of the Stanley Cup Finals.

Cursing, I wiped sweat from my face with my jersey, drifting across the ice as the buzzer sounded for the end of the third quarter. The Vermont Vipers were tied with the

Buffalo Sabres with a score of two to two. Neither team had scored since halftime, and nerves had grown quite frazzled.

Though I'd forced all thoughts of her from my mind, Ellie sat in the VIP's box as a guest of Owen Teasdale. I felt her eyes on me as I stepped off the ice to meet in the locker room with my brothers and Coach.

"You okay, Aldine?" Coach bellowed.

I nodded, breathing hard as I sat on the bench. "You know it, boss."

"Good. I'm holding you back to rest up. Ratcliffe will take your place until the middle of the third period." Coach glowered around at us all. "You ladies have done me proud; I'll tell you. But it's not enough. You know the plays. Make 'em work. Chambers, you get the puck to Aldine. No one is faster on skates than he is. You all guard him with your lives. Take the punches, give back what you got. But make sure Aldine keeps that fucking puck."

It felt strange to watch Ratcliffe skate in my place, the Sabres' center making him scramble for every foot of ice. Still, the kid held his own, his raw talent and athletic speed, his youth, all challenged our opponent's greater experience. I knew the opposition was growing angry and perhaps scared when the Buffalo defenseman body slammed Ratcliffe into the barrier and slammed his elbow into the kid's face.

The buzzer screamed. The ref yelled, "Five for fighting!"

"Aldine, you're in," Coach roared.

Clearly, Ratcliffe had taken a hard hit. His face bloody, his eyes unfocused, he needed Devon's assistance to skate off the ice. My anger, simmering like a volcano no longer dormant, sent me toward the Buffalo guard as he headed for the penalty box.

"You fucker," I growled, "he's just a kid."

The guard sneered. "A kid shouldn't be playing in the big leagues."

"Do that again and I'll kill you."

He swung a punch at my face. I dodged it easily, laughing, and spat on his jersey as I skated past him. In a rage, he chased after me, but was caught by his teammates and shoved toward the box. Turning, I flipped him the bird, and joined my crew.

"This is it, gents," I said. "We have less than two minutes in the quarter. Keep those fuckers off me. Got it?"

Devon mock punched my jaw. "You do your job, shithead, and we'll do ours. You sink that motherfucker. Got it?"

I grinned. "You know it. Let's rock and roll."

Facing the Buffalo's center, the ref holding the puck, I stared into his eyes. He stared into mine. He well knew he was down a man. He also knew he had little chance of protecting his net from me should I get the puck.

I smiled.

The ref blew his whistle the instant he dropped the puck.

I fought for the puck, seized it, and spun. As treacherous as his guard, the forward stuck his stick between my ankles, and tripped me. I fell face first onto the ice, cracking my still healing nose. I half-heard the crowd roar as I got up, bleeding profusely, saw the bastard race toward our turf with my Vipers on his heels and his Sabres protecting him.

Eddie, our fearless goalie, waited. Ready.

I raced toward the group fighting for the puck down rink.

The Sabre slashed the puck toward our net.

The puck flew through the air.

And landed in Eddie's mitt with the ease of a catcher catching a baseball.

The crowd screamed.

The puck in play again, I seized control of it, and charged toward the Buffalo net. I passed it to Devon, who feinted a pass at Steve, then sent it back to me.

The Sabres lost sight of the puck for a crucial second. That instant was enough time for me to feint a pass back to Devon, and instead sent it to our guard. The guard kept it, racing, racing toward the net, the Sabres hot on his heels.

I swept wide, skating hard and fast, coming in from the right.

The goalie paid me no attention at all. All he saw was the guard and the puck coming for him straight on.

Our guard shot the puck to me.

I caught it.

And sent it hurtling into Buffalo's net.

I never heard the buzzer over the screams of the crowd. Smothered by my team, with more of my brothers skating onto the ice from the side, I laughed and yelled my triumph. We won! The Vermont Vipers won the Stanley Cup.

As a team, we skated slowly in front of the bleachers, each of us taking a turn to hold the Cup high overhead. No man was unimportant enough to not take his turn——we all won it.

All of us.

***

I stood on the ice, my team bunched behind me, my image high and huge on the big screen over the rink. The crowds had gradually quieted after the ceremonies of accepting the massive Cup. Though under normal circumstances, the game was over, and they should be headed for the exits.

Instead, the fans waited, knowing something else was occurring.

Owen Teasdale escorted Ellie onto the ice.

She minced rather than walked, carefully making her way toward me. My heart swelled with love and pride as she, while somewhat confused, kept her hand on his arm. I glanced away from her face to find the cameras had included her on the massive screen.

"Grey?" She eyed me with clear bafflement as she glanced from me to Owen and back.

I knelt on the ice before her.

Ellie slapped her hands over her mouth, instantly understanding what was happening. Her blue eyes huge in her lovely face held tears of what I hoped was joy and not mortification. A murmur rose among the bleachers as they, too, guessed what was about to happen.

"Ellie March," I said, my voice loud and clear ringing across the ice and the stadium. "Will you marry me?"

"Oh, my God," she cried as the crowds, and the Vipers, whooped. "Yes, yes! I'll marry you! I love you!"

Owen handed me the box I'd entrusted to him. Still on my knee, I opened it, revealing the diamond engagement ring I'd bought. Taking it out, I slid it onto the ring finger of her left hand. I stood to take my Ellie, the mother of my child, my future wife, into my arms and kissed her.

I don't recall ever receiving a standing ovation before. Ellie and I sure got one now. Every fan in the stadium stood, clapping, yelling, cheering, as I lifted Ellie's hand above her head, grinning.

"This is my Ellie," I bellowed. "My lady! The mother of my kid. Can you say hello?"

Under the thunderous noise, I scooped Ellie into my arms. I skated around the rink's edge with her, kissing her, observing her blush, heard her wild laughter. Above us, the big screen showed us both, up close and personal, my grin, her arms around my neck, our cherished kisses.

"I love you," I whispered, skating toward the ice's exit. "I'll always love you."

Ellie's laugh rang across the stadium. "And I love you, my champion."

EPILOGUE – One Year Later

Ellie

"It's time to quit," Grey announced.

He held Joey against his broad shoulder, rubbing the baby's back in an effort to get him to burp. Joey gurgled, waved his chubby arms, then spit a gob of milk on the towel.

Grey sat the baby on his lap, then wiped our son's tiny mouth. "Okay, champ, nighty night."

Though the late afternoon streamed brilliant sunlight through the living room's curtains, Joey often napped until early evening. I curled up on the sofa as Grey set

Joey in his cradle at the sofa's end. Joey offered a protesting squawk before snuggling into his blanket and falling asleep.

"Won't Owen offer you a job as a coach?" I asked as Grey returned to his place.

With more gray in his shaggy hair and the lines around his eyes and mouth growing deeper, Grey sighed and shrugged. His nose had never fully recovered over the last two seasons and carried a permanent bend to the right. His left cheek bore a scar from the jagged edge of a broken stick. With this season's end, his contract with the Vermont Vipers had now expired.

"He offered me a new contract," Grey murmured. "He hopes for a third Cup win."

"No," I said, immediately and emphatically. "You can't. I don't say this to put you down, but you are too old. This is a young kid's game, and that, my love, you are not."

He smiled. "I'm forty-two. It's time to quit."

"You sure don't need the money."

"True. Coaching makes decent money, though. I can demand a big paycheck to coach the Vipers to another Cup. The question is: Do I want to?"

I leaned my cheek against the sofa's back, watching his face. "It's just as physical."

"Yep. And it's a good reason to stay in shape so I can keep up with my very virile and energetic wife."

"You'll work out downstairs as you always have."

Part of me craved to have Grey home, sharing baby duties, keeping house, raising Joey and his siblings we hoped to have. The other part of me knew Grey would hate being home all the time. He may talk about fully retiring, toss the idea around like a ball, make plans to work on the house, add an addition onto the rear but I knew better than to think that would make him happy.

"You'll go crazy," I murmured. "Maybe you should take a coaching job."

"Yeah, I might," he admitted. "I want to stay here with you and Joey. Do stuff I've never been able to do."

"Like what?"

"Oh, I dunno. Write a book."

I laughed. "I'll write the book. You go to work. Look, I want you here, I really do. But you'll be like a caged tiger. You'll get under my feet. Then you'll piss me off."

"But you're so cute when you're pissed."

The doorbell chimed, jerking me out of the pretense I wasn't nervous, the vague hope he had changed his mind and decided not to come. Grey took my hand as he stood, bringing me up with him. He hugged me briefly as though offering his courage, winked, then walked to the door.

I wiped my sweaty palms down my jeans, my stomach filled with a riot of butterflies. True, we'd spent time talking on the phone. Yes, we'd communicated in text and email. We'd forgiven one another.

That's not quite the same as having him walk into my home.

Grey's voice rose in greeting, excitement, though I couldn't see past his big frame to view our visitor.

"It's so great to see you, it's about damned time, too." Grey swung the door wider.

Smiling, his arm over Grey's shoulders, Colton walked in.

It had been over a year since he held the knife to my throat. Like Grey, he'd aged a bit in that long year. He'd cut his hair, for instance. His face, handsome yet rounded and childish, had grown hard angles. His blue eyes snapped with a smile, and his welcoming grin disarmed me immediately.

"Ellie," he cried, crossing the room in long strides. "You're as beautiful as ever."

Crushed under his strong arms, I hugged him back, for once truly and happy to see him. "Colton, I'm so glad you're here. Meet your brother."

He stepped to the cradle and looked down, his face softening. "Hiya, bro. How's it hanging?" He glanced up. "Can I hold him?"

I looked to find Grey accompanied by a tall woman with rose-gold hair and blue eyes. Grey grinned as he shut the front door, obviously knowing who this woman was while I hadn't.

"Ellie," Colton said, taking the woman's hand, "meet Sylvia. My fiancée."

"Oh!" I cried. "How wonderful to meet you."

As though I'd known her forever, I embraced her, gushing over her beautiful fall of hair, pushing her close to the cradle.

"This is my son, Joey," I said, picking the baby up without waking him. "Here, hold your brother."

Grinning, Colton gently held Joey in one arm as Sylvia crooned and tickled Joey's tiny fingers. I held Grey's hand as Colton stared down into his sleeping brother's face, awed, transfixed. Sylvia couldn't seem to stop smiling, meeting my gaze.

"I want a baby so bad," she said. "We agreed after our wedding would probably be best."

"When is that?" Grey asked.

"Tentatively planning for this summer. Then a cruise to the Bahamas for our honeymoon."

"We need to save money for both," Colton added, glancing up. "My job pays well, but we're trying to buy a house, too. That's a lot of cash."

I caught Grey's eyes, and I knew what he was thinking. He wanted to help pay for some of their expenses. Nor could I object. I gave him a subtle nod and a wink. He slid his arm around my waist to squeeze me hard against him.

"Congrats on the game, by the way," Colton added, sitting down with Joey still asleep. "Are you retiring now?"

"Thinking about it."

"You are getting up there, Dad."

Grey rolled his eyes. "Thanks for the reminder."

"Welcome."

"May I?" Syvia asked.

"If you can get him away from Colton."

Colton passed Joey over to Sylvia, who had surely held babies before. She cooed and clucked, clearly in her element, smiling with utter delight.

She'll make a great mom, I thought. *Colton finally grew up. It's almost hard to believe.*

For the next few hours, we talked and laughed in perfect, family harmony. My gaze met Colton's frequently, the passionate love we once possessed had grown into a firm and powerful friendship. I might be his young stepmother, his father's wife, I was also his half-brother's mom. His easy way with both Joey and I told me exactly how much he'd matured, moved on from what we had.

Grey took Joey to his nursery for a diaper change, followed by Sylvia. Colton and I sat on the same couch and looked at one another.

"You've forgiven me?" he asked, his voice low. "Really?"

"I really have."

"I'm thankful, Ellie." He scooted across the couch to sit beside me. "Thankful you're in Dad's life, thankful for Joey, and because you wouldn't take me back, I found Sylvia."

"She's perfect for you."

He grinned. "Yeah. I'm over the moon in love. She's everything to me."

"I can see that."

"Sorry I missed the wedding."

Grey and I had a small wedding in the courthouse, with only a few special friends to witness it. "We didn't want anything formal. Anything more may have brought the reporters down on us."

"Wouldn't want that." Colton grimaced. "I've had to change my name. Being Grey Aldine's son isn't easy, especially after what I did."

"Give it time. People forget, move on, there's always another crisis to grip their attention."

"We don't want to move back here," he went on. "Sylvia likes New York and we're nicely anonymous. My boss likes my work and says he doesn't want me to ever leave the company."

"Just come back and see us now and then."

He kissed my cheek. "You know it."

Grey, Sylvia, and Joey returned. Freshly awake from his nap and with a clean diaper, he grinned up at me as I took him from Grey. Holding him in my lap, I fed him as we discussed where to go for dinner.

"As I haven't been forgiven by the people of Vermont," Colton said lamely, "let's go somewhere with little light."

"I have just the place," Grey commented. "Son, I'm really glad you came. We're a family again. I've missed that something terrible."

Colton and I smiled at once another.

"We're family," I murmured. "But you'd better not call me 'mom'."

Colton and Sylvia laughed, holding hands. "Never," Colton said. "Mom."

THE END.

Thank you so much for reading! I would love it if you could write a brief review on Amazon – as an indie author, your support means everything! I truly appreciate your time and I hope you enjoyed my book!

Visit the following link for a free book when you join my mailing list!

https://bit.ly/free_steamy

If you loved My Pucking Ex's Dad, you will love Pucking Around with the Coach!

(Available in the Amazon store)

A one-night stand turned coach? Oh, hockey practice just got complicated! This steamy one-night stand, fake relationship hockey romance will give you ALL the feels! Read chapter one on the next page!

sneek peek

Pucking Around with the Coach

A one-night stand turned coach? Oh, hockey practice just got complicated!

So, I had this unforgettable night with a charming stranger. Sizzling chemistry, promises of breakfast—then poof, he vanished.

And guess who's my son's new hockey coach? Yeah, that guy. Liam Wilkinson, superstar hockey player, walks into my life—annoyingly sexy and grumpy.

When the press shows up at that first practice and catches us privately talking, a meddling assistant tells them we are dating to avoid a scandalous story in the papers.

Now, I'm stuck in this mess. Balancing our snarky arguments with stolen moments isn't easy.

But Liam's hidden battles and my son's hero worship pull me deeper.

Just when our walls start to crumble, a misunderstanding shatters it all. Now, hearts are on the line, and I'm left wondering if, this time, it's a game I can't win.

(Available in the Amazon store)

Chapter One – Kate

"It's one night, Kate. Just one night out of the over twenty-five hundred he's been alive," Liza, my best friend said.

I paused my dishwashing and tried to do some mental math. My son was seven and since the day he was conceived, we'd never spent a night apart, so seven multiplied by the three hundred and sixty-five days in a year...was mental math I couldn't do, so I took her word for it.

"This is why you're an accountant and I'm a kindergarten teacher," I tell Liza. "My kids never ask me to do that kind of math in my head."

Liza laughed. "I didn't ask you to do any math. I'm just asking you to hang out with me. I will handle all your math needs." Liza jumped off my kitchen counter where she was watching me clean. "In fact, I'll buy all your drinks. Zero math for you."

I gave Liza a look. "I don't need your charity," I told her.

That wasn't exactly true.

Liza and I met in the sixth grade and have been friends ever since, but our lives took vastly different turns after high school. Liza went on to attend Rutgers and had the whole picture-perfect college experience with ivy-lined brick buildings, a terrible first-year roommate, and a massive crush on a hot young professor. On the other hand, I got pregnant three months before we graduated, turned down going to Rutgers with her in favor of a cheaper and easier-to-handle community college, and had my son, Liam, at eighteen.

I was a changed person the second I became a mother. All my carefully set plans to go to college and have all those life experiences I dreamed of during my senior year of high school were put behind me. Willingly. I was so excited to be a mom, it was something I also had always wanted, just after I graduated college with a degree in education and a teaching certification.

But, after years of hard work and support from my parents, I finally had my son and my degree.

"It's not charity," Liza said. "It's desperation on my part. I am *desperate* for you to come out with me. Have you ever even been to a bar?"

I rolled my eyes. "You're being dramatic. You know I've been to a bar."

Liza folded her arms over her small chest. She was so toned, and it seemed so effortless. She was not one to work out or even take the steps over the elevator. As far as I knew, the only working out Liza did was in the bedroom. In fact, people were shocked that I was the one who got pregnant in high school and not Liza. I was the quintessential good girl. Not that I was judging Liza, I was actually envious of her freedom, and she was the best friend anyone could ever ask for.

Her boobs were small but so perky she almost never wore a bra and often wore tiny shirts, like the one she had on tonight. Liza was wearing a scrap of fabric for a shirt. I knew it was a hot pink tube top, but it was so small I could've only worn it as a headband and paired it with a matching neon tube skirt. Of course, she looked amazing in it. Liza was all tall and lean with her red bob and green eyes.

I was petite myself, hardly over 5 feet tall, and before Liam, when I was still in high school, I was in pretty good shape as a former basketball player, but I felt like my breasts sagged too much now after breastfeeding and my stomach had no hope of being completely flat again. But still, I wasn't totally down on myself. My long brown hair held natural waves that I always got compliments on, and my eyes were a dark shade of green that I rarely ever saw on others.

Besides, it was hard to be down on myself when my son looked so much like me. I don't know what I did in life to be so lucky, but he looked nothing like his father. My genes completely took over and did all the work. And though I didn't have a brother, I guess if I did, he would've looked just like my Jack. His hair was the same wavy brown and he liked to wear it a little shaggy, which I loved, and we had the same eyes. He was so handsome it was hard to see me as anything other than the same.

"Okay, listen here, babe. You need to come out with me. Just for tonight. If you don't get out there and see the dating scene, you're going to be single forever. I know you don't want that." Liza took the dish from my hand and slid it into place on the counter while I dried my hands, so happy to be done with the dishes.

"How do you know I don't want that? I'm very happy with my life right now, maybe I do want to be single forever."

Liza sighed. "Now is the perfect time to start dating."

I walked through the galley kitchen, past my charming breakfast nook, and over to the couch where I promptly plopped down. It was floral and secondhand from my parent's basement, but a slipcover and some throw pillows made it like brand new. Liza plopped herself down right next to me. I could hear Jack in his bedroom, the door cracked open, still playing his hockey video game. Or maybe he was just watching hockey. It was hard to tell but if he wasn't playing hockey, he would be watching it.

"Now is a terrible time to start dating." I threw up my hands as if she just suggested the most Ludacris thing ever. "I just got the house and it's my first year teaching. You can't expect me to take care of Jack, run a house, and be a first-year teacher all while dating some man."

"Okay, well I wasn't really thinking about that." Liza brushed her bangs aside. "I was more thinking that since you finally moved out of your parent's house, it would be the perfect time to invite a boyfriend over for some—"

"Remember—" I said with a smile plastered on my face— "that Jack might be listening. So, choose your words carefully."

Liza laughed. "Right, right. All I was going to say was, you used to tell me between having a son and still living with your parents, you couldn't date. Now you have this nice new house."

She was right. I had used that as my excuse in the past, or maybe it wasn't really an excuse, it was true. But for three whole weeks now, I was a proud homeowner. Or more like the bank owned the house and I was making payments. I'd just landed a coveted position at the same school Jack attended teaching kindergarten. The pay was good, and the time was right so Jack and I left my parents' place to live on our own.

The house wasn't exactly new like Liza said, but it was nice if not tiny. There was one bathroom, two bedrooms, and a small kitchen and living room area, but damn I did love it. I decorated the place with bright colors, probably because my mom preferred muted tones, and thrifted almost all the furniture leaving it looking cool and eclectic. But best of all Jack loved it. He was very happy at my parents' and had his own room there as well, but I think just the two of us living together made him feel more normal. He'd already had a friend over and asked if he could again. Of course, the answer was yes.

"Maybe not having my own place wasn't what was holding me back," I said, grabbing a pillow and holding it on my lap. "Or at least not the *only* thing."

"Kate, not all men are like Dennis," Liza said, reaching out and taking my hand in hers. "In fact, most aren't anything like that scumbag ass—"

"Assistant," I said staring daggers at her. "I don't have an assistant, Liza." I tilted my head toward Jack's open door.

"Sorry," she said in a whisper.

I waved her off. An apology wasn't needed. Dennis *was* a scumbag asshole. We had been dating all four years of high school before I got pregnant and because of that, I wasn't all that worried when I took the pregnancy test and there were two pink lines. I figured if we made it through braces, acne, his parents' divorce, mono and all the drama that comes along with high school, we could make it through this. Fuck, was I wrong.

Very quickly, it became clear that I enjoyed being a parent while Dennis did not. He hardly took care of Liam, he stopped coming over, and then he wouldn't even respond to my texts. Finally, after a year of trying, I'd had enough. But we weren't done there. When Jack was four, and old enough to know what was going on, Dennis made his triumphant return to our lives. I was so eager to give Jack a happy family that I took Dennis back only for it to implode in my face and scare me away from men...maybe forever.

I just hoped that Jack wasn't going to have issues when he was older. I tried to shield him from as much of the trauma as I could, but I knew he wasn't clueless about what was going on.

"No, no. You're right. I've let Dennis control my feelings for far too long." I set the pillow I'd been holding aside, suddenly feeling inspired.

"Exactly. You need a new man." Liza's eyes lit up in delight.

"I do. And Jack needs a dad in his life." I pushed up from the couch like I was going to find him right that second.

Liza grabbed my wrist and tugged me back down on the couch. "Easy there, tiger." She laughed. "You need to start slow. Find a guy to go to dinner with first. Better yet, find a guy to have a drink with tonight."

I could feel the blush warming my cheeks and was thankful for the millionth and one time for Liza in my life. She was born with that gene that helped people be cool and know all the social rules while I was not.

"Yeah." I laughed. "That sounds more reasonable. Besides, the last thing I want is to have another man come in and then out of Jack's life."

"Exactly," Liza said. "Hey! Let's find you a guy to fuck tonight."

I laughed, Hard. "Yeah, right.

***

One hour later, Liza and I headed out to Downtown Chicago.

I was wearing a tight dress that hadn't seen the light of day in years but thanks to a pep talk from Liza, full-glam makeup, and a push-up bra, I was feeling good.

My mom was more than happy to have a sleepover with Jack for the night and with him taken care of, there was really nothing holding me back. We hopped in an Uber and headed to the trendiest bar in the trendiest part of town, The Whale in Logan Square. It was packed, but the whole glamorous, mid-century feel was really my vibe, so we made our way to the bar and secured ourselves some cocktails.

The crowd was decent, a nice mix of ages with everyone being chill, and Liza and I were able to secure two of the blue leather bar stools with tufted backs easily, as most people migrated to the patio because of the nice late September weather.

"I'm impressed, Kate," Liza said, sipping her vodka cranberry. "You're doing very well."

I laughed but her compliment meant a lot. —I wasn't sure if I was fitting in, doing the right thing. "Thank you, thank you."

We talked about my new job and her latest breakup. We laughed over drinks and shared an appetizer of fancy deviled eggs and for the first time in seven years, I felt my age. I wasn't worried about anything other than finding the bathroom. And when a very handsome, very nice man whom Liza introduced as Cal, her friend from work, joined us, I decided it was the perfect time to venture off and find that aforementioned bathroom.

As I made my way toward the sign pointing to the restrooms, I passed a rowdy group of four women and one man. They were all fawning over him, even taking pictures with him maybe, or possibly exchanging phone numbers. He looked vaguely familiar, but something happened in the moment I caught his gaze. He was wearing jeans and a black button-down shirt, nothing special but it looked good on him. His hair was blond and cropped close to his head with matching stubble dotting his jaw. He was hot, there was no denying it, but his eyes were the most piercing blue I'd ever seen. His gaze bore into me as I made my way past him and down the hall. He even swiveled to keep his eyes on me as long as possible.

Suddenly feeling heated, I hurried into the restroom, did my business, and freshened up in the mirror. I couldn't tell if I was being ridiculous or not, but I felt...something. Eager to get back out there and see if he was still standing there, I pushed out of the bathroom and right into a woman trying to get into the bathroom. I recognized her as one of the women talking to the hot guy in the hall.

"Uh, excuse you," she snapped.

"Sorry," I mumbled, even though it was just as much her fault as it was mine.

"I swear this place is going downhill," the blond said to no one in particular. "Lettin' anyone and everyone in here." She glared at me like I was personally offending her as I tried to inch away from the bathroom.

"I'm not sure what your problem is," I muttered as I turned my back to her.

"You can't talk to me like that," the blond shrieked. It was like she was an overgrown toddler, getting pissed off over nothing and then yelling about it and acting completely irrationally.

I continued walking, it wasn't worth my time. I just wanted to get back to Liza and my nice night.

"Hey, bitch," she yelled. "I'm talking to you."

I wanted to laugh, really, I did. The whole situation was absurd. Nothing happened and this prima donna was losing her mind. I whipped back around.

"What did you just call me?" I asked.

The blond folded her bony arms across her chest and glowered. "You heard me, bitch."

"What the fuck, Celin?" a deep, velvety voice said from behind me. "Now you're picking fights in line to the bathroom, what's wrong with you?"

I turned around and there he was, the hottie with the killer eyes.

"Liam, no. That's not...I was just—"

"Can I buy you a drink?" Liam asked, looking directly at me.

I was almost too stunned to speak. "Me? I—uh—sure."

"Perfect." He offered me his arm and I took it, but we didn't make our way back out to the bar. We continued down the hall, past the bathroom, and to a small, private patio in the back. It was just as nice as the one in the front but there were only a few other people out there. "Sorry about that," he said. "I'm Liam."

"Kate," I said, my head still spinning from everything that had just happened. "You look so familiar," I said. "I just can't place you."

"Trust me, I would remember you if we'd met before." Liam pulled out the wicker chair at the small table for me and I sat down.

"What are you drinking, Kate?" he asked as he took his seat.

I nibbled on my bottom lip. It wasn't that the run-in with that Celin woman was so bad, it was just...everything. I was out, trying to have a good time, and getting called a bitch was not a good time. If someone was going to yell at me and put me down, I should've just stayed home.

"Can I just get some water?"

Liam nodded and then motioned for the waiter. "Are you okay, Kate?"

His casual use of my name surprised me. I liked it.

"Yes, I just...I just don't go out much," I said. "Maybe I should've stayed home tonight."

Liam took my water glass from the quick waiter and handed it to me. "But then we wouldn't have met."
I gulp down half in one go. "True. But it is yet to be determined if that's a good thing."

Liam smiled and he looked so handsome it hurt. "Fair enough. Make me work for it. I like that."

"You're not drinking either?" I asked, pointing to his glass of coke.

"No."

"Then why come to a bar?"

Liam smirked. "To meet beautiful women."

I laughed. I couldn't help it. "That was so cheesy."

"Okay, yeah. It was." Liam laughed too.

"Listen, you're obviously really, really hot, and for some reason, you want to talk to me, but I'm not that girl." I gulped down the rest of my water.

"And what girl would that be?"

"The Celine. The kinda girl who is hot and goes to a bar and meets the hot guy and goes back to his place to fuck."

Liam raised his eyebrows. "Interesting. But did you notice how fucking awful that Celine woman is? I don't want to be with that girl."

I laughed. "Fair enough."

"I caught your eye. Don't lie. We both felt it when we saw each other. I'm attracted to you, and I know you're attracted to me."

I swallowed. Hard. He was right and I didn't want to lie. "Yeah. Yes. I...I'm attracted to you."

Liam leaned in all close, the small table suddenly feeling even smaller. "Then let's cut to the chase. You asked why I came out tonight, I came out to meet a woman. Now that I've seen you, you're the woman I want. Come back to my hotel with me."

"What?" I laughed. I was nervous...but also excited. "We don't even know each other."

"Kate." Liam took my hand. "That's the whole point. You said you're not the kind of woman to go to a hotel room with a guy, but I'm the kind of guy to take a beautiful woman back to my hotel room. I want you to be that woman. Come with me."

Liam smiled and rubbed his jaw. He was making it impossible to say no. I channeled my inner Liza and tried to think about what she'd do.

She'd say yes, you idiot, I thought to myself.

Once I thought about it, a one-night stand with a really hot guy was definitely one of the college experiences I was missing out on, and this guy was giving me that experience on a silver platter.

"I have a room at the Waldorf, just to sweeten the deal and let you know I'm not broke," Liam said.

I laughed." I want to say yes, it's just...I can't believe I'm going to tell you this but, it's been a long time for me. Since I had sex, I mean."

"Damn." Liam let out a low whistle. "Sounds like I found you just in time."

His response was surprisingly reassuring. "Okay, Liam. Let's get out of here."

(Available in the Amazon store)